George Eliot and Intoxication

George Eliot and Intoxication

Dangerous Drugs for the Condition of England

Kathleen McCormack

First published in Great Britain 2000 by
MACMILLAN PRESS LTD
Houndmills, Basingstoke, Hampshire RG21 6XS and London
Companies and representatives throughout the world

A catalogue record for this book is available from the British Library.

ISBN 0–333–73492–0

First published in the United States of America 2000 by
ST. MARTIN'S PRESS, INC.,
Scholarly and Reference Division,
175 Fifth Avenue, New York, N.Y. 10010

ISBN 0–312–22711–6

Library of Congress Cataloging-in-Publication Data
McCormack, Kathleen, 1944–
George Eliot and intoxication : dangerous drugs for the
condition of England / Kathleen McCormack.
  p. cm.
Includes bibliographical references and index.
ISBN 0–312–22711–6
1. Eliot, George, 1819–1880—Characters—Alcoholics. 2. Drinking
of alcoholic beverages in literature. 3. Eliot, George,
1819–1880—Characters—Narcotic addicts. 4. Literature and
society—England—History—19th century. 5. Eliot, George,
1819–1880—Political and social views. 6. Didactic fiction,
English—History and criticism. 7. Social problems in literature.
8. Narcotic habit in literature. 9. Alcoholism in literature.   10.
Alcoholics in literature.   I. Title.
PR4692.D78 M38   1999
823' .8—dc21   99–33013
                                                    CIP

This book is printed on paper suitable for recycling and made from fully managed and sustained
forest sources.

10   9   8   7   6   5   4   3   2   1
09 08 07 06 05 04 03 02 01 00

Printed and bound in Great Britain by
Antony Rowe Ltd, Chippenham, Wiltshire

for

Michael Clapson

with love

Contents

Preface

In a 1990 number of *Literature and Medicine*, scientist J. W. Bennett, discussing George Eliot's 'Janet's Repentance,' wondered why literary critics seldom write about alcoholism. He believes that the difficulty of the task arises from a habit of denial. Whether or not this is true in my case, I would add that writing on drugs creates problems of tone, for it often does not meet the challenge of simultaneously avoiding both sanctimoniousness and jocularity. During the years I have been writing this book, much jocularity, if little sanctimoniousness, has attended descriptions of my project, jocularity divided pretty equally between George Eliot's reputation as the ponderous (and excessively sober) dispenser of moral wisdom on the one hand and my own motives in choice of topic on the other.

One of my ambitions as I have prepared this work has been to avoid either jocular approval or sanctimonious condemnation of drinking and drugs while proving that George Eliot's drug metaphors begin with but extend far beyond the traditional interpretation of them as representations of her characters' dreams, hallucinations, and illusions. Indeed, George Eliot's fiction demonstrates how she distributes references to alcohol and opium plentifully to create an elaborate and comprehensive pattern of metaphorical figures and plot-level facts which draws often on the contents of a well-stocked pharmacy of substances related to the medical, recreational, linguistic, social, physical, political, and artistic causes and effects of nineteenth-century intoxication.

Kathleen McCormack

Acknowledgments

Although I owe thanks to many people and organizations who have supported my research and writing, the following have either sustained their widely varying kinds of support with unvarying steadiness over a long period or else entered the history of this particular book in spectacular, pivotal ways.

The Florida Education Fund (McKnight Programs in Higher Education) supported the project through a year-long Junior Faculty Fellowship. Two National Endowment for the Humanities Summer Seminars, each, in its way, kept it alive. A Fulbright-Hays Summer Seminar in Italian Civilization helped change writing on *Romola* from a chore to a joy. The editors of the *Victorians Institute Journal*, Mary Ellis Gibson and Beverly Taylor, have granted permission for the reappearance in different form of material which appeared in the 1986 volume, as has W. A. Kelly regarding some more recent work from *The Bibliotheck*. George Papas has created the pictures.

Among the individuals (in addition to my family) who have shown sustained encouragement and/or pivotal brilliance, I must thank Jeanne Ali, Bill Baker, Bonnie Boddicker, Robin and Linda Evans, Graham Handley, Ray Langley, Don Lawler, Mildred Newcomb, Meri-Jane Rochelson, Jeannette Shumaker, and Florence Yudin.

At the pharmacy of the monastery at Camaldoli, the *Padre Speziale* provided Lewes with a remedy for his sore throat.

1

George Eliot and Victorian Intoxication

The whole life of Society must now be carried on by drugs: doctor after doctor appears with his nostrum, of co-operative Societies, Universal Suffrage, Cottage-and-Cow systems, Repression of Population, Vote by Ballot. To such height has the dyspepsia of Society reached; as indeed the constant grinding internal pain, or from time to time the mad spasmodic throes, of all Society do otherwise too mournfully indicate.

Thomas Carlyle
Characteristics 1831

Among nineteenth-century authors, the Romantics, whether British or American, receive most credit or blame for demonstrating two connections between intoxicating substances and literature: their roles as stimuli to artistic creativity and their roles as metaphors for intense and dangerous love. Not only does much Romantic poetry and prose suggest a belief in a causal relationship between drugs and creativity, but it also often assigns a metaphorically poisonous potential to passionate love or lovers, in particular women lovers. *Confessions of an English Opium Eater*, 'Kubla Khan,' 'Lamia,' 'Ligea,' and 'Rappaccini's Daughter' provide some of the most obvious examples of these two drug-related aspects of Romanticism.

As Romanticism gives way to Victorianism, however, the later nineteenth-century British culture both discards and carries forth earlier attitudes toward intoxication. Temporally sandwiched according to the traditional periodicity of British literature studies between their Romantic predecessors on the one hand and the

Modernists (who also frequently associate intoxication and artistic creativity) on the other, Victorians seldom speak of drugs as a stimulus whether or not they maintained habits.[1] At the same time, many Victorian authors sustain the Romantic association between intoxication and love. Consequently (as with a number of aspects of Romanticism), attitudes toward drinking and drugs both change and remain the same as Victorians largely abandon expressing the notion that chemical escape can provide artistic inspiration but retain a tendency to figure dangerous, intense, possibly illicit passion and its objects, especially women, as poisonous.

Indeed, the common Victorian figure of society as a human body results in a dramatic increase in opportunities for literary references to intoxication in the writing of mid-nineteenth-century British authors. Traditionally viewed as didactic, community-oriented, and earnestly responsible in the face of the effects of rapid social, technological, and political change, Victorian literature often represents society not only as a human body but, more specifically, as an ailing human body. Because of the medicinal functions of alcohol and opium, they often serve as metaphors for proposed remedies for the ailing social body. The realist aesthetic of the period also contributes to the popularity of references to drinking and drug taking. Novelists such as Elizabeth Gaskell, Charles Kingsley, all three Brontë sisters, and George Eliot often include such activities in their plots out of an obligation not to prettify the behavior of their characters, whether clergymen, laborers, mothers, or fast young men.

Despite George Eliot's reputation for earnestness, responsibility, and even ponderousness, a remarkable number of her characters stagger through the novels with their perceptions blurred and reason distorted by unwise consumption of brandy, wine, beer, ale, patent medicines, and opium. In 'Mr Gilfil's Love Story,' the lovable clergyman resorts to daily gin to ease his grief over Caterina. In 'Janet's Repentance,' Janet and Robert Dempster drink themselves oblivious every night. In *Silas Marner*, Squire Cass and his sons regularly begin drinking first thing in the morning. George

Eliot's opium users (or occasional experimenters) include Molly Farren, Mr Christian, Mrs Transome, Will Ladislaw, Dr Lydgate, and Hans Meyrick, and Harold Transome is smoking some unspecified but suspicious substance in. the hookah he has brought back with him to Transome Court from Smyrna, one of the biggest centers of the nineteenth-century opium trade (Berridge & Edwards 4). Drug dispensers of varying levels of responsibility include Amos Barton, Lady Assher, Silas Marner, Dolly Winthrop, Mrs Holt, Mrs Transome, Mrs Cadwallader, and all the physicians from Mr Pilgrim of 'The Sad Fortunes of the Reverend Amos Barton' through Daniel Deronda's grandfather. And even normally abstemious characters, such as Mr Tulliver and Mr Brooke, commit some of their most decisive errors when confused by drink. Habitual and occasional users alike complicate George Eliot's plots in the direction of disaster when high, hungover, or just plain drunk

Although the early 'Janet's Repentance' is usually perceived as George Eliot's most important treatment of intoxication, a number of factors resulted in an ever-growing pervasiveness of intoxicant figures as her body of fiction grew. During both the period *in* which she wrote her fiction (the late 1850s through the 1870s) and the period *of* which she wrote (her favorite temporal setting, the years surrounding passage of the First Reform Bill in 1832), intoxication was a popular recreation, a severe social problem, a political and religious issue, an occasion for legislation, a gender matter, and a side effect of the administration of its agents as medicines. George Eliot's fiction represents drugs in all these versions. They also occur at all levels of signification (in particular the mimetic, metaphoric, and metonymic), a circumstance which creates a coherent relationship between, say, Robert Dempster's delirium tremens in 'Janet's Repentance,' a plot event occurring on the mimetic level, and Gwendolen Harleth's metaphorical 'poisoned gems' (407) in *Daniel Deronda*. Indeed, alcohol and opium, the intoxicants to which George Eliot's novels refer most often, form only the kernel of an elaborate complex of related drug figures.

The terms under which to describe and discuss this paradigm

betray an insufficiency that has to do with the multiple ways in which Western culture has responded to such things over the years. Because *intoxication* applies to poisoning by any agent, it denies potential beneficent effects possible from the same substances that can poison their consumers. Although the *OED* limits the word *drug* to medicinal substances, our century has become accustomed to including recreational agents under this term. In addition, although *drug* ostensibly applies to both alcohol and other stimulants and narcotics, many contemporary writers on the subject, probably because of its legality, feel obliged to reiterate that 'alcohol is a drug.' The Greek word *Pharmakon*, especially since Jacques Derrida's 'Plato's Pharmacy,' has a firm association with the written word and its ambiguity, but is largely absent from the nineteenth-century writing under discussion. In addition, although George Eliot aligns writing and drugs, she most often does so in indirect ways: subtextually or metaphorically. Also, she is likely to emphasize the danger more than the conviviality or the euphoria they produce, so that her drugs have decidedly more potential to kill than to cure. For all these reasons, I most often use *intoxication* to describe the effects of consuming such substances, whether these effects include poisoning, drunkenness, anesthesia, or euphoria, and refer to the substances themselves as *alcohol* and *drugs*. To simplify the matter, the particular drugs in question during the nineteenth century were nearly always alcohol and opium.

Physiological Psychology and the Individual Constitution

According to Bruce Haley in *The Healthy Body and Victorian Culture*, John Stuart Mill's 1831 identification of the 'spirit of the age' as a new and dominant idea, together with the typical Victorian's organicist perception of society, made health/disease metaphors inevitable in the social criticism and art criticism of the period: 'The concept of health helped legitimize a moral approach to art by basing it on medical and physiological models. The relationship between morality and physical health, however, was both actual and metaphoric. Immorality was literally a disease of the whole person; but it was also, in its symptoms, progress and effects, *like* a disease of the body. As a result of this dual epistemology we often find a conceptual ambiguity in the language of critics who relied on such models' (67). Such perceptions complicate metaphors which represent attempts to improve the social and moral Condition of England as medicinal drugs for a sick society.

In addition to Haley's 'dual epistemology,' other Victorian social and medical notions guaranteed the trickiness of prescribing remedies for social ills. Haley points out that such prominent Victorians as John Ruskin, J. S. Mill, Matthew Arnold, Herbert Spencer, and George Henry Lewes all agreed on the inextricable complex of mutual influences between the body and the mind (physiological psychology) and also on the interrelationship between the moral and the physical aspects of the human organism, whether healthy or diseased.[2] The resulting blurred distinctions among physical, mental, moral, and social illness decrease the likelihood that any remedy will affect only one aspect of any condition. A drug administered to cure can easily turn out physically salutary but morally or socially poisonous.

The notion of the individual constitution further volatilizes the administration of remedies whether medicinal or metaphorical. According to this theory, chemical mixtures in the system of the consumer, which partly determine the effects of the remedy, differ from individual to individual. Harrison finds the idea of the individual constitution typical of the period: 'It was widely held that each patient had his own peculiar constitution with which the doctor must acquaint himself. Remedies which might cure some might not suit others' (306). In *The Physiology of Common Life*, Lewes advances this belief when he asserts, 'That one man's meat is another man's poison is a proverb of strict veracity. There are persons, even in Europe, to whom a mutton-chop would be poisonous' (59). Indeed he bases his entire project in *The Physiology* on the need for attention to the individual constitution, what he calls 'the necessity of fixing our attention on the organism to be *nourished* rather than on the *chemical composition of the substances which nourish it*' (63 his italics). This individuality of constitution obviates the possibility of a sovereign remedy either for ailing Victorian patients or for whatever complex syndrome is ailing England in a non-physical way, especially since the metaphor of England as patient often disperses into not one but a number of figurative bodies. John Bull, Tommy Atkins, and Britannia are all associated with different groups or different aspects of the so-called national character.

But despite the acceptance of physiological psychology and of the variousness of the individual constitution, writers of the period found hope in the very severity of its condition by viewing disease as a preliminary to health. In *Sartor Resartus*, Carlyle's molting eagle must go through the accompanying sickliness and the ordeal of dashing off its old beak in order to acquire a new one. Like a pregnant woman, the eagle endures an experience which, though natural, brings with it pain and other physical manifestations considered symptoms of illness. Nevertheless, the process culminates in the restoration of health.

Hope for the patient's recovery directs attention anew to possible remedies, and among those proposed for the Condition of England and figured as drugs, many have to do with the written and/or spoken word, including the education of the masses, the distribution of improving literature, and political Reform itself. What makes drugs appropriate metaphors for such language-based cultural remedies is their volatility, unpredictability, and potential to kill as well as cure. At the same time that the urgency of the problems demands instant action, the complexity of the organism and its minute and possibly unguessed-at internal interrelationships call forth elaborate cautions against universal remedies.

Indeed, whoever undertakes to suggest cures for the Condition of England assumes the same heavy responsibility as does the prescribing physician. It was a responsibility from which most Victorian periodical writers did not shrink, as indicated by their frequent drug/disease metaphors. In addition to the passage which heads this chapter, Carlyle's writing depends on the drug/disease metaphor throughout. In 'The Idea of a University,' John Henry Newman specifically parallels 'intellectual culture' with physical health (Norton 979). In *Aurora Leigh*, Elizabeth Barrett Browning's Romney decries the person who can observe social problems yet 'never tease his soul/For some great cure' (Book II, ll. 281-2). Matthew Arnold calls the Condition 'the strange disease of modern life' ('The Scholar Gypsy' l.203). He looks for cure to the work of Goethe whom he calls 'physician of the iron age' ('Memorial Verses' l. 17). Tennyson describes the words of *In Memoriam* as 'dull narcotics' (5, l. 7) for his pain at Hallam's death. These metaphors acknowledge the urgency of the problems involved in Victorian social unease, as well as suggesting the hope located in various kinds of reading and/or writing: of legislation, poetry, Useful Knowledge, fiction.

Alcohol and Opium

Alcohol and opium, the most popular drugs of the period, sustained many complicated and intimate relationships between themselves which encourage interpreting them as two aspects of a single figure. Members of all social classes drank and took opium for the same medicinal and recreational reasons: to achieve euphoria, to cure sickness, and to prepare for or avoid pain. The intoxicants were often available in the same place: Virginia Berridge and Griffith Edwards mention that in some neighborhoods, laudanum and children's cordials were both sold in public houses (33).[3] Both alcohol and opium were subject to adulteration. Of the brandy of Dickens' s time, Hewett and Axton remark, 'The bar brandy that so many Dickens figures take would have been frequently stale and tainted; at the worst, it was often adulterated or faked outright, with a compound of oil of cognac, ammonia, strong black tea, prunes, crushed prune pits, and rose leaves in spirits' (112). Frances Power Cobbe blames the adulteration which transforms 'seas of brandy and gin' into 'infuriating poisons' (Broomfield and Mitchell

302) for 'Wife-Torture in England,' the subject of her 1878 article. Similarly, opium shopkeepers had little expertise in poisons and 'mistakes and tragedies' often resulted from 'bad measuring and mixing' (B&E 27). Both could lead to sudden death from causes other than poisoning: the records of riot-related deaths in the early nineteenth century, for example, always specify intoxication as the cause of death in at least two or three cases.[4] Both opium and alcohol had long sustained ambiguous images as simultaneously stimulant and sedative (B&E ch.2, Harrison 65). Finally, opium and alcohol had a mutually medicinal relationship because opium was used as a remedy for delirium tremens, hangovers, and gout (all alcohol-produced conditions), and alcohol was administered as a substitute for opium.[5]

Especially during the period just before the first Reform Bill, people had easy access to both alcohol and opium. Opium was freely available over the counter, and English people were consuming more alcohol than ever before or since (Harrison, ch. 2). Opium formed the major ingredient in the patent medicines with which nineteenth-century Britons treated their own illnesses and those of their children (B&E 24). Particular medical effects attributed to alcohol included curing indigestion and infection and easing the pain of disease, dentistry, surgery, and childbirth (Harrison 41).

While non-alcoholic beverages such as coffee and milk became more expensive during this decade, gin remained cheap, and its popularity led to the proliferation of gin palaces (which offered child-sized portions for their youngest customers). People considered drinking a necessary preparation for public speaking, courting, getting flogged, or starting a riot (Harrison 41). Opium, too, had a connection with public speaking: Wilberforce and Gladstone both used it to prepare for Parliamentary debate (B&E 66). In addition to their usefulness in stimulating political oratory, opium and alcohol sustained intimate relationships with politics both metaphorically and mimetically. In Victorian journalism and literature, writers often apply metaphors of Reform as nothing more than political opium (Murfin 33) during the same period that treating flourished as an essential component of electioneering. Dual meanings to the word *treat*, both to care for the sick and to buy beer in exchange for support, create one metaphorical slippage between the discourses of drugtaking and politics.

The multiple community roles of public houses during the nineteenth century helped increase the pervasiveness of drinking and drugs on all socio-economic and semiotic levels of Victorian culture. In addition to providing food, drink, lodging, and meeting places, public houses served as banks, libraries, cookhouses, museums, transport terminals, surgeries, morgues, employment bureaus, gambling halls, auction rooms, theaters, and campaign headquarters. In many of these roles they sustained an enduringly intimate relationship with the written and spoken word. In literature, writers of travel, quest, and picaresque tales from Chaucer through Dickens found inns and taverns indispensable settings both in London and on country roads. Drinking places also served literature by providing meeting places for cliques whose members read their latest efforts aloud. Throughout the nineteenth century, brewers and distillers financed publications and other educational projects.

Somewhat lower on the social scale, public ale houses (where oral tradition always has and still does flourish) provided an arena for readings of newspapers, ballads, and chapbooks for the benefit of an illiterate audience. Broadsides decorated the walls. Some public houses, notably the Lord Nelson where Branwell Brontë is supposed to have drunk while in residence at Luddenden, provided more sophisticated literature for their patrons by housing lending libraries. Public houses named for authors (for example, the surviving Shelley's in Mayfair or the Jeremy Bentham in Bloomsbury) exhibited collections of literary memorabilia related to their namesakes. These and other inn signs offered pictorial allusions to historical, literary, and religious narratives for the benefit of the still poorly educated members of the lower classes.

Drinking places in Victorian literature range from sites of

harmless conviviality as in many of Dickens's novels to the threatening 'Dragon on the Heath' in Tennyson's 'The Vision of Sin.' In Mary Elizabeth Braddon's *Lady Audley's Secret*, the ambition to own a public house motivates Phoebe and her ne'er do well husband to blackmail Lady Audley. Later in the plot, Lady Audley burns the lonely, wind-swept Castle Inn to the ground in her attempt to incinerate Robert Audley and his inconvenient curiosity. In *Mary Barton*, the Bartons innocently send the young Mary to the public house to buy refreshments when Elizabeth Gaskell's characters are anticipating visitors. In Christina Rossetti's 'Up-Hill,' the persona takes a tone of ominous inevitability when assuring the spiritual pilgrim, whose journey toward salvation must end in death, 'You cannot miss that inn' (l. 8). Long before Thomas Hardy contrasts conflict on the battlefield with the harmony possible at the 'old ancient inn' (l. 2) in 'The Man He Killed,' he creates the far more ominous Quiet Woman in *The Return of the Native* and Rolliver's where Tess's parents plan mischief for their daughter in *Tess of the D'Urbervilles*. At all levels of social acceptability, from the humble hedgerow ale house to the handsome travelers' inns, the nineteenth-century literary drinking place accommodates both threatening and affirming action.

Although drinking place settings probably occur more frequently in texts authored by men (Dickens alone must account for a substantial portion of these settings in the Victorian novel), authors' attitudes toward their public-house settings do not appear to follow gender lines. During the second half of the century, the alliance between temperance groups and the women's rights movements in the United States and Great Britain institutionalized an opposition between the public house and the private home partly as gendered spaces. Nevertheless, such examples as Tennyson's threatening Dragon and indeed George Eliot's soberly intellectual Hand and Banner deny the possibility that male authors uniformly construct public houses as pleasant refuges while women authors view them as pernicious. Instead, writers of both genders depended on them as versatile settings during a period in which their usefulness extended far beyond the serving and consuming of alcohol.

Alcohol and Opium as Medicines

Because Victorians considered alcohol and opium remedies as well as intoxicants, both drugs relate to the metaphor of the Condition of England. Through this figure, many writers regarded the problems of the times as illnesses in a social body and assumed what they considered the responsibility of devising remedies for social sicknesses. Although seldom described as 'Condition-of-England' novels in the same sense as *North and South* or *Hard Times*, George Eliot's novels address and offer solutions to the problems of the Condition.

Often, the remedies proposed by George Eliot and her contemporaries have something to do with language. Legislation to correct social problems was particularly plentiful during the period of George Eliot's favorite temporal setting, and much of this legislation (for example, the Beer Act and the Anatomy Act), in addition to being written texts themselves, also addressed community health. Early Victorian attitudes toward literacy and education, especially for the lower classes, often won approval as proposed remedies for social ills. In this case, dual attitudes toward enabling the poor to read and write replicated the dual potential of alcohol and opium, as the middle and upper classes often feared the empowerment of their social inferiors at the same time that they encouraged the project through improvements in education for the masses. Consequently the remedial potential of alcohol and opium suits them for their application as metaphors for language-connected strategies, strategies directed at social improvement such as often occur in nineteenth-century political discourse.

Haley's analysis of the Condition of England metaphor in the work of major Victorians acknowledges its prominence in George Eliot's work by opening with a quotation from her partner Lewes and devoting substantial space to the novelist herself. He argues that although she abandoned her early acceptance of phrenology 'in favor of the new physiological psychology,' the new system, like the old, held that 'functions of the mind had their basis in the condition of the body' (197). Because physiological psychology supposes the interrelatedness of mental and physical illness, both sick minds and sick bodies in turn participate in the causal relationships between health and social problems. In the fiction, social problems, for example poverty and political unrest, can lead to physical illnesses, for example cholera. By the same token, physical illnesses, for example cholera, can lead to poverty and/or political unrest.

Perceiving themselves as ill and blurring distinctions between physical and psychological causes and effects, George Eliot's characters often resort to the intoxicating substances themselves, as well as to things represented as intoxicants, to address a range of social/psychological/spiritual/political problems for which the substances may or may not prove efficacious remedies. The metaphorical slippage between medical and political discourses arises from the possibility of dual meanings to such words as *condition*, *disorder*, and *remedy*, all of which can refer to physical as well as sociopolitical problems. The dynamics among the elements of the related metaphors identify aspects of the Condition of England as George Eliot perceives it, specifically uncertain authority, poor education, political corruption, social and political irresponsibility, sudden class mobility, and certain kinds of discrimination against women, especially discrimination connected with marriage customs. In George Eliot's fiction, alcohol and opium, regardless of the semiotic level on which they occur, cluster in plots involving misdirected education, problematic heritage, social ambition, and misguided marriages. As mimesis, metaphor, and metonymy, they cohere to create a figurative complex that pervades all the fiction and affects all its characters, whether or not they frequent drinking places or have ever tasted opium.

Notes

1. Because I am dealing in this work with intoxication as metaphor and theme I make no attempt (as do, for example, Alethea Hayter and Linda Leonard) to establish relationships between intoxication and its author's artistic creativity. Despite an occasional satiric thrust (see Chapter 2, note 14), I found no evidence that George Eliot depended on stimulants or narcotics to encourage her creativity.

2. Rosemary Ashton and Richard Currie place Lewes among the prominent physiological psychologists of the century. Karen Chase explores George Eliot's physiological psychology in more detail in *Eros and Psyche*.

3. Eve Sedgwick observes the importance of the perceptual shift Berridge and Edwards observe in late nineteenth-century England: the change toward regarding the drug consumer as an addict. George Eliot's work meets Sedgwick's timetable well.

4. See Donald Richter's *Riotous Victorians*.

5. As late as 1878 Geoffrey Harding reports 'unlimited amounts of champagne and brandy' as part of the treatment for morphia addiction (1). He notes that not until 1909 did Jennings turn away from treating addiction through alcohol.

A London Marquis O' Granby. Public houses named after this popular hero appear in 'The Sad Fortunes of the Reverend Amos Barton,' *The Mill on the Floss*, and *Felix Holt*.

2

Backgrounds and Landscapes

Branwell declares that he neither can nor will do anything for himself; good situations have been offered him, for which, by a fortnight"s work, he might have qualified himself, but he will do nothing except drink and make us all wretched.

Charlotte Brontë 17 June 1846
The Life of Charlotte Brontë

George Eliot's favorite setting, the English Midlands around the time of the First Reform Bill, permitted her to draw a good deal on her girlhood experience among the people and landscapes of the central provinces to develop the intoxication plots and metaphors in her novels. In addition, she found drug-related figures common among contemporary writers as well as in the works that form the inherited literary treasure (as both she and John Ruskin described it) absorbed into Victorian culture from past ages. Consequently, sources for George Eliot's drug figures range from the dialogues of Plato, possibly the most securely high-culture figure in Western intellectual history, to the public-house culture unavoidably part of the lives of every early nineteenth-century man, woman, and child (whether or not they drank) because of the physical conspicuousness of public houses in the landscape and their diverse roles in nineteenth-century daily life.

Mary Ann Evans's earliest recorded application of the drug metaphor to the written text constructs reading as pernicious rather than redemptive and proceeds from the figure's frequency in religious rather than political discourse. The reference appears in an 1839 letter in which the young Evans describes novels (as opposed to history or biography) as 'poisonous' (*GEL* 1:36) and concludes 'I shall carry to my grave the mental diseases with which they have contaminated me' (22). Such figures occur often among the Evangelical authors of the young devotee's reading material. The young student's letter initiates use of a metaphorical construction George Eliot is still applying forty years later in *Impressions of Theophrastus Such* in such essays as 'How We Encourage Research' in which the writer gets poisoned by 'the gall of his adversary's ink' (39) and 'Diseases of Small Authorship' which compares a book to a 'polypus, tumor, fungus, or other erratic outgrowth, noxious and disfiguring' (126). George Eliot's description of the book as both disease and poison in this last example illustrates how she comes to elaborate her drug figures to achieve a complexity that parallels the complexities of all attempts to elicit stable meaning from language. The figures which associate alcohol, opium, and the printed word begin with the typically Evangelical figure in the young girl's letter, but acquire along the way far more density as she inserts them into her writing as mimesis, metonymy, and metaphor.[1]

Contemporaries: George Henry Lewes and Branwell Brontë

George Eliot's intimacy with Lewes probably contributed to a relaxation of whatever Evangelical attitudes toward alcohol survived her move from Coventry to London in the early 1850s. Lewes included wine and cigars among his daily relaxations, and his ongoing journalistic quarrel with teetotalers such as William Benjamin Carpenter placed him in opposition to the many temperance groups that began their activities in the 1830s.[2] As a pious young Evangelical, Evans had differed strongly with her aunt's belief that 'Mr A.,' a tippling clergyman, was nonetheless in heaven. In the late fifties she records feeling shock at her own rigidity about Mr A. (*GEL* 3:273). Not only did Lewes help relax his partner's rigidity, but his articles provide an important source for her drug figures, for she gained some of her knowledge by living with one of the many Victorians who wrote about addiction for the nineteenth-century periodicals.

Lewes's articles opposing teetotalism suggest attitudes George Eliot was likely to share. His pieces specifically concerned with drinking include 'Teetotalism,' written for the *Leader* in 1855, and 'The Physiological Errors of Teetotalism,' for the *Westminster Review*, also in 1855. In *The Physiology of Common Life*, too, Lewes attacks the bases of nineteenth-century teetotalism. In Lewes's personal life, the convictions he expresses here would permit him to enjoy his wine, despite the alcoholism Rosemary Ashton attributes to his father (10), because of differences between his constitution and his parent's.

The George Eliot/George Henry Lewes collection of the couple's books at Dr Williams' Library contains nine publications by Carpenter, most of which appeared during the 1850s when Lewes was researching *The Physiology*. Lewes's marginal notations in his copy of Carpenter's 'The Physiology of Temperance and Total Abstinence' are often severely argumentative. Most conspicuously, he takes issue with Carpenter's assertion that because even small quantities of alcohol linger in the system, all drinking, no matter how moderate, is lethal. Next to Carpenter's sentence about the moral dangers of 'the habitual presence of alcohol' (47), Lewes writes, 'But it never is habitual.' Later he indulges in an exclamation point to punctuate his response to Carpenter's connections between drinking and gluttony: 'Drunkards not eaters!' (81). Indeed Lewes notes in his journal that when he reviewed Carpenter's *Animal Physiology* in February 1859, George Eliot begged him to restrain his tone. According to Lewes, '[I] rewrote the finale to my article on Carpenter because she entreated me. I had laughed at him for a bit of his usual pretension and nonsense; but she, always alarmed lest people should misconstrue what I do, urged me to cut that out' (*GHL* X, 151). Whether restrained or not, Lewes's criticisms of Carpenter's teetotalism reappear both in his other articles and in *The Physiology*.

But for all his rejection of teetotalism, Lewes expresses in *The Physiology* a caution toward alcohol based specifically on the unpredictability of its effects. He admits to his own bafflement as to why drunkards manage to do without food (147). Although he maintains that large and concentrated doses are poisonous and small diluted doses are not, he specifies no quantity at which curing turns into killing (142). In the end he concedes, 'Terrible is the power of this 'tricksy spirit'; and when acting *in conjunction with* ignorance and sensuality, its effects are appalling' (145 my italics). Like George Eliot's novels, Lewes's articles acknowledge the unpredictability and the volatility of combining drink, not only with other substances, but with 'ignorance and sensuality' (147), moral rather than physical presences in the receiving body. Again like George Eliot's novels, in which such virtuous characters as Adam Bede and Felix Holt enjoy a quart of beer now and then, Lewes's articles do not take up the nineteenth-century teetotalers' crusade against drink.

In 1857 Elizabeth Gaskell, another of George Eliot's contemporaries, published her *Life of Charlotte Brontë*, an event guaranteed to interest Evans and Lewes, for Gaskell devotes much space to Brontë's epistolary friendship with Lewes. Including detailed references to Lewes's letters, the biographer presents him as second only to Thackeray in his influence on Brontë's career: their correspondence discusses such matters as melodrama and the literary marketplace; gender and literature; and (very uncomfortably since Brontë blamed Lewes for destroying her anonymity) the implications of writing under a nom de plume. Gaskell also notes the startling comparison between Lewes's appearance and her sister Emily's made by Charlotte Brontë in 1850. Brontë thought Emily and Lewes looked like twins.

Evans wrote enthusiastically to her friends in Coventry: 'There is *one* new book we have been enjoying—and so, I hope, have you. The 'Life of Charlotte Brontë'! Deeply affecting throughout' (*GEL* 2: 218). According to this letter, however, neither the references to the correspondence with Lewes nor the descriptions of the Brontës' literary struggles account for its being so 'deeply affecting.' Not even the facial resemblance Charlotte Brontë detects between her

sister and Lewes, whose critics seldom fail to describe him as strikingly ugly, draws her notice. Instead, Evans specifies the effects of Branwell Brontë's intoxication to explain the intensity of her response: 'What a tragedy–that picture of the old father and the three sisters, trembling day and night in terror at the possible deeds of this drunken brutal son and brother! That is the part of the life which affects me most' (218). She reserves her strongest sympathy for the alcoholic/opium addict's father and sisters, who live in daily fear of outrage.

Evans raises only one objection to Gaskell's biography: 'She sets down Branwell's conduct entirely to remorse, and the falseness of the position weakens the effect of her philippics against the woman who hurried on his utter fall. Remorse may make sad work with a man, but it would not make such a life as Branwell's was in the last three or four years unless the germs of vice had sprouted and shot up long before, as it seems clear they had in him' (2:218). This comment focuses on the biography's inadequate and misleading description of alcoholism, which Gaskell attributes to 'remorse and agony of mind' (275). In contrast, the metaphor Evans applies, of sprouting and flourishing germs, suggests the inevitable, uncontrollable growth of Branwell's behavior and connects it with a species of vegetation that could be a grapevine. Evans believes that Branwell drank not as a means of forgetting his difficulties with the Robinsons but because his compulsion had developed over a long period.

Aspects of Gaskell's description of Branwell's addiction which Evans does *not* question include the convenience and social attractions of the village public house and the addict's dependence on money to procure drink. Gaskell stresses Branwell's prominence as the most important Haworthian in the company at the Black Bull and the immediacy with which money enabled his drinking: the Brontës can keep Branwell sober only by keeping him penniless. In her own fiction, George Eliot, too, dramatizes the interaction of drinkers in their village drinking places and the various allurements of these settings, many of which, as in

Branwell's case, have to do with gossip, story-telling, oral biography, and other forms of narrative. She also dramatizes the speed with which the drunkard turns money to drink and the negative effects of this rapidity on the family economy.

Indeed, together with the Brontë sisters', George Eliot's novels do much to place the life of the family of the perpetually tipsy wastrel in a quotidian context which diminishes his attractions.[3] Anne Brontë's *The Tenant of Wildfell Hall* and Emily Brontë's *Wuthering Heights* both contain portraits of practicing alcoholics (Arthur Huntingdon and Hindley Earnshaw) who have lost all charm and become the dreariest and most exasperating people to endure. George Eliot carries forth this pattern, creating such characters as Robert Dempster, from whom all raucous charm has fled and also, in 'Janet,' a wife who does not remain piously aloof from her husband's vice as does Helen Huntingdon but, out of desperation, participates in his habits. Her three *Scenes of Clerical Life* and the first two novels take up this theme by depicting families obliged to cope somehow with one member's excessive drinking. Such characters as the hopelessly drunken Mr Dempster and Mr Tulliver, who drinks to excess at holiday time, create serious difficulties in their communities as well as in their families: in the one case legal chicanery and religious factionalism, in the other the litigation that impoverishes his family and forces them to relocate themselves in the St Ogg's hierarchy.

The intoxicants in such plots identify sobriety as part of the earnestness traditional perceptions of Victorianism attribute to George Eliot and to the culture in which she lived. Like many of her contemporaries, notably Thomas Carlyle, she blames some aspects of the precarious Condition of England on the lures of escapism and self-indulgence. George Eliot's early fiction thus deals with social problems that stem from intoxication and with intoxication itself as a social problem. Her fictional representations of drugs and alcohol result from her identification of these problems, her commitment to her realist project, and the interaction between her fictional theory and her first serious attempts at creative writing. Initially positioned, like the Brontë sisters, well out of reach of opportunities for the shared alcoholic 'conviviality' (85) J. A. Sutherland attributes to Victorian author/publisher relations, she, like the Brontës, depends on a thorough knowledge of the taxing details of addiction to tame the imbibing wastrel by confining him within her narratives. Branwell Brontë, of all people, may have played a remote but traceable part in Evans/Eliot's eventual success.[4]

Notebooks and Letters: From Aristotle to 'Jolly Good Ale'

In addition to Lewes's journalism and the Gaskell biography of Charlotte Brontë, George Eliot augmented her own experiences of drinking and drugs by drawing on an entire Western tradition of associating drinking, drugs, and language. In her notes, she refers to a great variety of sources which appeared over a long period, including science, history, poetry, songs, philosophy, and other biography. From such sources she made many notes on drinking and drug taking which manifest her interest in dual effects, homeopathy, the expansion and contraction of the materia medica, and the semiotics (although, of course, she did not call it that) of intoxicants and intoxication, all matters she brings into relation with both social and physical health in her fiction. Among the most important, some of the references directly concern drugs and the diseases they are meant to cure, while some connect drugs and disease with writing.

George Eliot's notebooks contain many entries on drugs, some of which reveal a fascination specifically focused on their dual or multiple effects. In one instance in the Folger notebook she attributes to Emile Littré's 'De la Toxicologies dans l'histoire et de la Mort d'Alexandre' the idea that 'poison and remedy the same thing if we consider, not that which has a hurtful action but that which acts on the system at all' (Pratt and Neufeldt 68). Also in this notebook, she records observations that the editors believe were suggested by her reading about William Cullen in J. Rutherford

Russell's *The History and Heroes of Medicine*: 'Opposite effect of the
same substance e.g. opium sends to sleep, at other times it excites'
(22). A note in her handwriting on the cover of her copy of Francis
E. Anstie's *Stimulants and Narcotics Their Mutual Relationships:
With Special Researches on the Action of Alcohol, Aether, and
Chloroform in the Vital Organism* directs attention to Anstie's
material on the dual effects of opium.[5]

A number of notes on homeopathic drugs also appear. Her
reading of John Ayrton Paris's *Pharmacologia: Being an Extended
Inquiry into the Operations of Medicinal Bodies Upon Which Are
Founded the Theory and Art of Prescribing* provided her with
information on the disease that contains its own remedy.[6] She
notes, 'The rust of the spear of Telephus in Homer cures the
wounds inflicted by the weapon' (59). Among many other notes on
homeopathy are allusions to the notion of the hair of the dog and
to the cure of ills inflicted by witches through the application of
the ashes of other witches recently burned.

Historical readings also prove George Eliot's awareness of the
wide variety of substances considered medicines in various times
and places. Additional pages in *A Writer's Notebook* include
notations on curative powers suspected in honey, gems, music,
bells, and various plants and animals (59-60, 117-8). Another
important note concerns the 'extensive list of animal substances .
. . discarded from the Materia Medica, since it has been known that
they owe their properties to one and the same principle . . .
Earthworms; vipers skinned and deprived of their entrails; human
skulls; dried blood; elks' hoof; urine of a child; of a healthy young
man, etc.' (117). Her habit of perceiving such diverse substances as
medicinal increases the already substantial number of signifiers she
could draw on to create her drug/disease metaphor.

George Eliot's notes also repeatedly excerpt passages about
changing relationships between language and drugs. One of the last
entries in the section of notes from the *Pharmacologia* laments the
'difficulty of identifying plants in the ancient Pharmacopeia because
general names became particular, as cicuta meant not hemlock only

but vegetable poisons in general. Opium meant juice in general. Alkali meant that particular residuum which was obtained by *lixivating* the ashes of the plant named Kell' (118). Her notes on John Wesley include references to the healing effect of sacred language. Wesley concluded he gained good results from praying over his own fever, toothache, and headache, as well as the illnesses of his horse (*A Writer's Notebook* 24).

A further speculation on language and drugs in this notebook concerns Lydgate's confidence that he can work with Mr Bulstrode without becoming contaminated by the banker's religion. Joseph Wiesenfarth identifies the Voltaire allusion by which Lydgate conveys his resolve to concern himself with Bulstrode's 'arsenic' rather than his 'incantations' (130) as one of a series George Eliot made on this topic: 'The words "Incantation" and "charm" appear to be derived from the ancient practice of curing diseases by poetry and music' (59). She also quotes one of Paris's examples of a purely symbolic form of magic consumed as if it were a medicine: 'The precious stones were, at first, only used as amulets, or external charms; but, like many other articles of the Materia Medica, they passed, by a mistake in the mode of their application, from the outside to the inside of the body, and they were accordingly powdered and ministered as specifics' (60). All these notes concern errors as to whether the symbol or the substance has the healing power, the same doubt which impels Silas Marner to give up practicing folk medicine.

George Eliot took similar, although slightly less frequent, notes on alcohol that nevertheless indicate an ongoing interest. Items from John Gardner Wilkinson's book on daily life in ancient Egypt mention the 'privilege' of Egyptian women who were 'not restricted in the use of wine' (6). Another entry from the same source notes how 'Aristotle distinguishes persons intoxicated by wine and beer' on the basis of whether they pass out on their stomachs or their backs (6).

Despite the drinking song's appearance as a bother in the 'Harvest Home' chapter in *Adam Bede*, it also attracted George

Eliot's interest. From the *Gentlemen's Magazine* she copied part of a 'Song for a Curate' which Amos Barton might appropriately sing: 'On some days I drink port with the squire and on some/With the Farmer a cup of brown nappy' (31). From Chaucer's 'The Franklin's Tale,' she copied the lines that begin: 'Janus sits by the fire with doble berd/And drinketh of his bugle horn the wine' (119). To illustrate aspects of English prosody, she chose the ballad from *Gammer Gurton's Needle* whose persona believes he is safe against all kinds of physical threats because of 'jolly good ale and old' (126). In this song the jolly good ale protects rather than undermines the singer's health.

Predecessors: Plato and Burton

If George Eliot's drug figures incorporate a rich mixture of attitudes and information gleaned from her experience as a very young resident of Nuneaton/Griff, her Evangelical background, a series of histories, and contemporary journalism, they also resonate with ideas and attitudes found in the work of the single classical philosopher unpopular even among the elite at Oxford and Cambridge during early and mid-century (Turner, Ch. 8). Plato writes of drugs and language in the *Symposium* and the *Charmides*, but perhaps most substantially in one of George Eliot's favorite dialogues, the *Phaedrus*, which contains Plato's representation of writing as the drug that can either kill or cure.

In her letters and notebooks she has jotted down many Platonic references, but a repeated quotation is 'What motive has a man to live if not for the pleasures of discourse?' (*Miscellaneous Quotations*, Pforzheimer ms. 708: 69). In the same notebooks she summarizes Benjamin Jowett's translation of the story of Theuth and the invention of writing: 'Story in the Phaedrus of Theuth, the inventor of letters, telling the King Thamus that they were the cure of forgetfulness and of folly. Whereupon the king replies that on the contrary this invention will create forgetfulness in the learners because they will not use their memories; they will trust to the external written characters and not remember themselves' (77).

Together with the *Republic*, the *Phaedrus* receives the bulk of Lewes's attention in the Plato section of his *Biographical History of Philosophy* (1845-46, revised 1857), including a substantial analysis of the problems of writing as suggested by the myth of Theuth. The copy of the *Phaedrus* in the collection at Dr Williams' Library re-affirms the interest of the Leweses in this dialogue. Its marginal notations and underlinings reflect at least two careful readings of this edition alone. Like many Victorians' attitudes toward Platonism, George Eliot's improved as the century advanced, and her Platonic allusions increased in frequency.

Like Plato's *Phaedrus*, George Eliot's novels repeatedly employ intoxicant metaphors to deal with the processes by which meaning is embodied in and extracted from language, in particular from metaphorical language. Indeed the metaphors she creates to comment on metaphoricity itself, however they begin, eventually link up with drug metaphors. Such passages occur in *Middlemarch*, and, more extensively, in *The Mill* in the chapter about the failure of Tom's education, and scholars who write about George Eliot's metaphors have made them indispensable references.[7] J. Hillis Miller's famous 1975 analysis of the passage which represents Tom's education through a variety of metaphors, including cures, extends the chain of signifiers far beyond the 'basic' figure of dissemination as a representation of the written word in a state of circulation that permits learning. According to Miller, the final metaphor that 'neutralizes' or 'cancels out' (107) the previous metaphors in this passage is the representation of Mr Stelling's kind of learning as cheese administered to remedy the inability to digest cheese. Miller argues that, despite its attempt to effect a 'cure of metaphor by metaphor, a version of homeopathy' (107), this passage leaves the reader as trapped as Tom in a maze of metaphor.

Miller's Derridean theories about metaphors of dissemination, drugs, and reading refer to the *Dissemination* volume which includes the essay on the *Phaedrus*, 'Plato's Pharmacy.'[8] In this essay, Derrida describes the play of the *Pharmakon* metaphor, the metaphor of language as the drug that can either kill or cure depending on its combination with other drugs administered simultaneously and/or with the materials that are already present in the receiving body. The chain Derrida devises from the *Phaedrus* includes narcotics, poisons, medicines, alcohol, semen, money, paint, dye, perfumes, gems, and ink as metaphors for language, especially written language.

In George Eliot's fiction the chain extends similarly. Metaphors of seed and sowing represent the dissemination of the written word; the occurrence of dissemination in biological reproduction as well as in publication links parenthood (specifically fatherhood) and authorship (and its monetary remuneration).[9] As in writing (in which the son/text inevitably becomes separated from the father/author), the relationship between father and child can become fractured, implying a diversion of the fluid conveying the seed. Like other possible interruptions of orderly descent–such as onanism, loss, adoption, mistaken paternity, disowning, and especially illegitimacy– addiction in George Eliot's novels results in threats to the patterns which govern the non-violent transfer of wealth and power from generation to generation.[10]

Such interruptions in the transfers of power, although often perceived as disruptions, broaden (at the same time they threaten) opportunities for finding competent and responsible political leadership. The political implications of George Eliot's figure arise because the difficulty of finding an alternative to a system largely reliant on hereditary political power constituted the most urgent issue of the Victorian period. When heredity no longer governs who governs, the nation must find other ways of assuring orderly transfers of power, and Evans grew up among disturbances that resulted from failures to do so. In line with the urgency of this issue, clusters of drug metaphors turn up in George Eliot's fiction in plots involving uncertain authority and diverted heritage, whether biological, political, or material, as well as in her comments on or demonstrations of the irretrievable metaphoricity of language. George Eliot's many plots in which parents consume and/or administer intoxicants thus establish connections among drugs, seed, semen, intoxication, and the Condition of England, and also between her novels and the *Phaedrus*.[11]

Midlands self-perceptions also helped shape George Eliot's drug/disease metaphor. Two centuries before her birth, Robert Burton, another author from the Nuneaton area, followed some patterns similar to hers that connect the region of their birth (which often describes itself through a bodily metaphor as the heart of England) with disease and cure. Although frequently described as a medical treatise, Burton's *Anatomy of Melancholy* addresses psychological frailties rather than physical, and it often refers to drugs as both remedies and poisons.

For Burton's persona, the task of writing itself forms a remedy. He writes about 'melancholy, by being busie, to avoid melancholy' (7). (Like most of the passages cited here, George Eliot marked these lines in her edition of the *Anatomy*.) He concludes he will 'make an antidote out of that which was the prime cause of my disease' (8) and later directly describes his book as a cure (22). The danger of the remedy is also emphasized. She places an exclamation point next to the passage: 'Yet one caution let me give by the way to my present or future reader, who is actually melancholy–that he read not the symptoms or prognosticks in the following tract lest by applying that which he reads to himself, aggravating, appropriating things generally spoken, to his own person (as melancholy men for the most part do), he trouble or hurt himself, and get, in conclusion more harm than good' (24). Burton also alludes to the *Phaedrus* (193) and, like Lydgate, believes that a wise physician does not give much medicine (345).

George Eliot makes her most conspicuous use of Burton's idea that study causes illnesses in the motto to Chapter 5 in *Middlemarch*. The passage from the *Anatomy* quotes Burton's listing of a vast number of illnesses generated by the scholar's life to describe Casaubon's deteriorating health. According to Burton, one way to maintain health is to 'avoid overmuch study and perturbations of the minde' (459). George Eliot records her ambivalence about the dangerous amount of writing poured out by the Victorian presses in a marginal note in the *Anatomy*. Next to the passage in which Burton argues 'there is no end of writing of books as the wise man found of old, in this scribbling age especially' (8), she writes: '19th Century.'[12]

Burton's ideas of effective remedies for melancholy emphasize the psychological and the metaphorical. He advises leisure, fishing for example, and relaxed street theater such as he has seen in Italy. In addition, he advises cure of melancholy through merriment. Indeed he personifies his remedies, so that in this case the remedy becomes the doctor, naming 'Dr Merryman, Dr Diet, and Dr Quiet, which can cure all diseases' (453). One remedy suggests that Burton found his (and Evans's) birthplace salubrious. He recommends 'delightsome prospects,' such as 'oldbury in the confines of Warwickshire, where I have often looked about me with great delight, at the foot of which hill I was born' (400).

George Eliot's novels, on the other hand, are more likely to question rather than to recommend Burton's proposed geographical remedies. Although local historian Arnold Bickerstaff notes Oldbury as the site of a 'Roman health resort or spa' (8), George Eliot's character Mr Jermyn fails to revive the healing powers of this area in *Felix Holt* when he attempts to turn Treby Magna into a healing spa similar to Leamington, the most prominent Midlands watering place during the nineteenth century. Furthermore, the 'oldbury' to which Burton and Bickerstaff both refer lies only a few miles from Arbury, the estate on which Evans was born 200 years later in a general area she represented in fiction as sick and sickening rather than healing.

The Leweses: Beer and Wine at Home and Abroad

What we know of Evans's girlhood contains no reason to believe she was sheltered from the drinking around her. The Evanses themselves were not teetotalers. At least one biographer, Marganita Laski, believes Robert Evans's brother 'drank himself to death' (6). The father himself dined often at the George Inn, especially on market day. In 1828, he reports in his journal sharing a 'glass of brandy' with friends at tea. Occasionally he ordered significant quantities of alcohol. In April of 1831, he writes, 'Went to Coventry, Bgt of Mr Whitam 6 gal gin and 6 bottles sherry.' Three months later he 'brought from Mr Whitam 6 Bottles of Porter order three dozen.' A mysterious journal entry in February 1833 reports a trip to the Astley Castle wine cellar from which he retrieved 'to my house 24 Doz and 5 Bottles all safe and sound,' despite losing seven bottles to breakage (16 February 1833). Two months later he notes selling some of this store to Mr and Mrs Johnson, originals for the perpetually drugged Mrs Pullet and her bottle-counting husband in *The Mill on the Floss*, at a price of £15 (9 April 1833). In May Evans again pays Mr Whitam, this time for two gallons of gin and some brandy (13 May).

Mr Whitam (sometimes spelled with two t's) continued to benefit from Mr Evans's custom. Noted in the journal are costs of £19. 6s. 6d. 'for wine etc.' (26 February 1836) and the purchase of a gallon of rum and a gallon of gin a month later (18 March 1836). (As a measure of the size of these amounts, during the same period Evans notes an expenditure of £10. 3s. 6d.. for 'shoes, boots, etc.' [26 February 1836]). In May he distinguishes alcohol destined for Griff from that he has bought for Packington Hall: 24 bottles of sherry go to his own home, while only 12 are destined for Packington (3 May 1836). In 1845 he divides his custom between 'Mr Whittam,' to whom he delivered £10. 2s. for wine, and Mr Waters' competing establishment, where he spent £19. 3s. on wine (16 January).

Robert Evans also participated actively in an economy in which beer or ale often supplemented cash wages (Harrison 56). His journals regularly note his ale orders in amounts of one to three pounds for the workers who unloaded the canal boats on the Arbury estate. At the same time, he maintained the right to regulate consumption of alcohol. On 17 October 1830 he reports joining a Mr Harris and Mr Hake (the clergyman traditionally held responsible for the arbitrary replacement of Mr Gwyther/Mr Barton with a relative of his) in signing 'a paper to discharge all ale sellers and shopkeepers from selling on a Sunday.' In the middle of August in 1836, Evans 'told Mr Hutt I should not keep him upon my Farm as he had fetched Double the Ale that was agreed upon for him to have for the Reaping . . . him and Laken Drank four quarts of Strong Ale, four quarts of Beer each per day.' Whatever Evans's standards, we can be sure eight quarts a day at his expense exceeded them.

And whether or not the Evanses were moderate drinkers, social occasions at Griff House did not exclude strong drink. Mr and Mrs J. W. Buchanan, George Eliot's models for the drinking Dempsters in 'Janet's Repentance,' had tea at Griff House on 23 October 1831. Buchanan appears often in Robert Evans's diary in his professional capacity, notably as a participant in an 1831 dispute involving water rights which associates him with Lawyer Wakem in *The Mill on the Floss*. Despite the connection with Wakem, the neutral tone of Robert Evans's entries seldom conveys any noticeable hostility. Nevertheless, George Eliot's description of Buchanan as more 'disgusting' (*GEL* 2:347) than her character perhaps results from dealings between her father and the lawyer, for it is difficult to imagine a drunkard more disgusting than the wife-beating Dempster. Like the tipsy tea at the Hackit farmhouse which opens 'The Sad Fortunes of the Reverend Amos Barton,' tea with the Buchanans at Griff probably called for pouring beverages other than tea with a generous hand, especially in light of Buchanan/Dempster's habits.

Further evidence of these habits appears in the notice of Buchanan's estate sale in the Coventry *Herald* in 1847. It includes formidable amounts of alcohol in the inventory: 'The Modern and Genteel HOUSEHOLD FURNITURE, Linen, Books, about Thirty Dozen of fine OLD WINE, 100 Gallons of Ale, several Gallons of Spirits, an excellent set of Brewing utensils' (26 February 1847, p. 1). Together with Evans's orders from Mr Whitam, this inventory suggests that middle-class households in the Nuneaton of Evans's girlhood often kept substantial supplies of alcohol on hand.

Later in George Eliot's life, the records kept by Lewes in his journals contain much evidence of moderate drinking. At St Helier in 1857, both wine and beer appeared on their grocery shopping list. Lewes notes sampling Orvieto, 'a light wine like cider' (XI 60) in Rome in 1860. At Paestum on the same trip they enjoyed a picnic lunch packed by their hotel which included a bottle of wine (XI 105). In Como they tried the Vino Santo which Lewes found 'too sweet' (XI 142). In Vidaubin in 1861, he followed a landlady's suggestion to accompany dinner with some Vidaubin wine 'which she had had ten years in bottle; it proved excellent' (XI, 167). In Florence during May of the same year, the couple supped simply but comfortably on 'Brandy and water and biscuits' (XI 182). In September of 1867, in Germany, they sampled a different local wine nearly every night before settling on Hochheimer as 'the most desirable in cost and flavor' (XII 82). In 1871 Lewes instructed his son Charles to have the maid forward '9 or 12 bottles of Claret' to their summer address near Haslemere (*GHLL* 2:168).

Nor do their many purchases of wine mean that they turned their noses up at beer. At Tunbridge Wells in 1853 (where Lewes may have joined her) the holidaying journalist reports drinking beer as a new recreation (*GEL* 2:110). During a period of short rations in 1857, Lewes records an intention to break their routine of habitual frugality by having beer for lunch (Haight 218). On their 1858 German trip, they found themselves at a particularly bad inn which supplied wet sheets and no service and only a humble meal of 'eggs, bread and butter and beer' (X 127). George Eliot writes of drinking beer in Munich in May of 1858: 'We feel already quite at home, sip Baierische Bier with great tolerance' (*GEL* 3:452). Lewes indeed considers himself something of an expert. In Bonn in July of 1866 he comments: 'I had a bottle of Louvain beer and a petit pain for lunch and smoked a cigar. The beer very like ginger beer without its sweetness, but no trace of hops' (XII 20). A few years later at Cambridge, Oscar Browning reports overhearing Lewes trying to dissuade his partner from drinking 'that heavy dark Bavarian beer' (126). These passing references suggest that the couple would have wine in Italy or beer in Germany, according to local custom, and that George Eliot tolerated and even participated in Lewes's habits without disapproval, but that these habits were themselves moderate. In London and on the Continent she saw drinking as a pleasure; in Nuneaton, Chilvers Coton, and Coventry (as in Milby, Shepperton, Treby Magna, and Middlemarch) it was more often a compulsive attempt to escape dullness and a destructive influence on family harmony and civic order.

And the experience with wines noted in Lewes's journal also suggests that, for them, despite being part of their routine, it did possess the ambiguous potential of Plato's *Pharmakon*. Although Lewes notes suffering the morning after some unusually intense wine, as when he visited Epernay in September 1857 (X 80), it does not seem to dawn on him until ten years later that the wine might be causing his discomfort. On Wednesday he enjoys a 'delicious' (XII 26) vin chaud; on Thursday he suffers a headache: 'the vin chaud perhaps' (XII 26). He also attributes cures to alcohol in August of 1857 when he notes that 'dinner and a whole bottle of wine restored us' (XII 79). The beer too is suspected of causing sickness: 'The Vienna beer, or something else, disagreed with me' (XII 138). For the Leweses, their beer and wine could both create and cure health problems.

Lewes's journal additionally reveals that the couple could find amusement in an anecdote concerning alcohol, even at their fellow travelers' expense. In August of 1856, in Berne, Lewes distances himself from his Philistine compatriots when he comments on 'an English party complaining of their wine' (30 August 1856). In 1872, he records an anecdote regarding a physician called to attend a sick child. When the doctor concludes, 'Your girl is drunk,' a second opinion confirms the diagnosis: 'the wet nurse saturated with Irish tea' (2 October 1872). The following year he records the 'story of an Irishman dying offered a glass of whiskey and declining says No, I'll *not face Almighty God with the smell of drink on my breath*' (27 January his italics). The stereotype of the drunken Irishman (or woman) apparently appealed to Lewes.

As for drugs, the poor health of the Leweses obliged them to confront decisions often, and their experience with the results was similarly mixed. In Coventry Marian Evans welcomed the application of leeches for her incessant headaches, calling them 'sweet leeches' ('Bray-Hennell Extracts'). In London she reports dosing herself with a tonic of iron and quinine prescribed by Dr Erasmus Wilson in 1859 (*GEL* 3:54) and in 1860 to 'getting strong in body and mind' (3:359) as a result of his prescription of 'bluepill and hydrochloric acid,' drastic remedies. Both of them benefitted enough from the water cure to visit numerous spas: Harrogate, Malvern, Schwalbach, Bonn, Baden Baden, Tunbridge Wells, Homberg, Plombière. Like the wine and the drugs, the many spas at which they attempted to remedy their illnesses retained the ambiguity of the *Pharmakon*. Although they eventually tired of Schwalbach, Lewes decided his health was 'manifestly improved' (XII 18) after their time there. They drank two glasses of water per morning and another after lunch and enjoyed 'luxurious' baths, including a memorable needle bath, a sort of horizontally constructed shower, on 7 August 1867 (XII 75). On the other hand, their famous trip to Bad Homberg in 1872 elicited the disapproval of the gambling there that George Eliot puts to use in the opening of *Daniel Deronda*.[13] Like wine and doctors, the spas could either kill (especially morally) or cure.

And, although their use of drugs and other treatments seems irreproachably medicinal, the Leweses had some recreational impulses. In 1859 George Eliot writes to her friends: 'If one could but order cheerfulness from the druggist's' (*GEL* 3:79), and she often describes happy moments as an 'intoxication of delight' (3:284, 286). When Lewes delights in the delivery of a new microscope in 1859, she describes him as 'drowned by intoxication' (3:225). The impulse she saw acted on in Nuneaton during her girlhood, the impulse to escape into a more delightful state, never entirely left her no matter how often she portrayed such escapes negatively in her novels.[14]

The quiet provincial market town where Evans spent her girlhood contained many health dangers in addition to public houses of all social levels, the number of which increased dramatically after the passage of the 1830 Beer Act. Local medical men quarreled frequently. Twice the Nuneaton Diarist reports problems involving a local surgeon. In 1834 Mr Lloyd was censured for 'leaving a woman in childbirth' (90); in 1835 the vestry voted to replace him on 'all parish cases' (99). A report on sanitation in Nuneaton in the 1840s returned depressing results. If Burton in the seventeenth century thought 'oldbury' salubrious, in the nineteenth century George Eliot experienced and portrayed the same location as a metonymically sick society. Poor government and cultural tedium lead to both illness and intoxication which in turn further numb the population and create a craving for still more escape into intoxication, a challenge indeed to people interested in ameliorating the Condition of England.

In the late twentieth century, the irony of George Eliot's portrayal of the Nuneaton area lies in the fate of Griff House, her beloved childhood home. Enlarged to three times its original size, the house has itself become a pub and hotel, its sign not a portrait of its famous former resident but rather an endlessly self-referential picture of itself. It still contains the cozy parlour where George Eliot sat Mr Tulliver and Mr Riley down to decide Tom's educational future over their brandy in *The Mill on the Floss*, and today's pub patrons can buy a pint and sit comfortably by the floor-length windows, regarding the pleasant grounds of the ivy-covered, red-brick building where George Eliot grew up.

Notes

1. Rather than attempting to distinguish between 'figurative' and 'literal' language, I rely on the useful Jacobson-based distinctions among mimetic, metaphoric, and metonymic meanings which John Reed applies in 'Victorians in Bed.' Reed applies the term *mimesis* more generally than David Lodge who restricts it to the opposite of diagesis, that is, to dialogue (51). I agree with Jill Matus that metonymy is *not* a species of metaphor, whereas synecdoche *is* a species of metonymy. Nevertheless, I occasionally use *metaphor* generically, interchangeably with *figure* or *trope*. Moreover, I sometimes refer to George Eliot's

entire drug paradigm, which includes literal (or 'thematic' or 'mimetic') versions as a *figure*.

2. See Lilian Shiman's *Crusade against Drink in Victorian England*. Sally Shuttleworth ranks Carpenter alongside Lewes as early psychologists, but differentiates the Leweses' physiological psychology from Carpenter's theory of psychological continuity (257). In *Muttons and Oysters*, Freeman notes that Carpenter considered alcohol purely poisonous (95). Mark Wormald bases his assertion that George Eliot 'admired' (508) Carpenter on an 1853 note to Charles Bray. However, she wrote this note nearly twenty years before the *Middlemarch* passage on the microscope which Wormald believes helps express approval.

3. Barbara Prentis, comparing George Eliot's novels with those of the Brontës, most often bases her comparisons on rigorously traditional interpretations of her life that mention self-loathing and dependence on men more than self-respect and independent achievement. Consequently she makes her best points when she relies on Ruby Redinger's less rigidly patriarchal interpretations. Accepting Redinger's emphasis on Christiana Evans's psychological withdrawal, Prentis parallels this experience with the frequent losses at Haworth Parsonage, thus coming within range of making the proposal I offer in the 'Epilogue' to this work. Regarding Branwell, she notes that Haight parallels Branwell and Will Ladislaw on the basis of their relationships with widows (10).

4. A supplementary work, 'Targeting *Blackwood's*,' summarizes the effects of George Eliot's strategies for achieving publication as they relate to her drug paradigm, arguing that when she included alcohol-related material in her early fiction, the previous contents of her target periodical had offered every reason to believe that John Blackwood would welcome such material. In *The Brontës*, Juliet Barker attributes this same strategy to Branwell Brontë whose literary references to drinking, she argues, proceed less from his own habits than from his obsession with *Blackwood's*. She, too, notes the heavy drinking in both *Noctes Ambrosianae* and in other *Blackwood's* publications (166).

5. Anna Kitchel's edition of George Eliot's 'Quarry for *Middlemarch*' contains notes on a number of similarly ambiguous drugs. Indeed the notes emphasizing ambiguity here are only a sampling.

6. In 'The Genesis of *Felix Holt*,' Fred Thomson dismisses George Eliot's notes on Paris as irrelevant to the novel which Thomson sees as more tragic than political.

7. In addition to Miller, these include Catherine Gallagher, Janet Gezari, Dianne Sadoff, Barbara Hardy, Joseph Wiesenfarth, Daniel Cottom, Jill Matus, Nancy Paxton, David Carroll, and others.

8. In 'Hegel, Derrida, George Eliot, and the Novel,' Gerhard Joseph concedes Miller's point that in *Middlemarch* the narrator's unitary vision metaphors collide with other 'incompatible' (67) metaphors: 'There is no meta-metaphor' (67) for cognition. However, the web, the stream, the text, and the pier-glass Joseph cites as incompatible all relate to the drug/disease/intoxication metaphor if pursued far enough along the metaphorical chain. Through George Eliot's representations of society as an organism, text as web, and web as circulatory system (Miller, Beer), pier-glasses as gems and gems as medicines (Zimmerman, Wiesenfarth), and ignorance as a *disease* of the eyes, all of Joseph's examples associate some aspect of the drug/disease complex not with cognition but with impediments to cognition.

9. Gillian Beer's chapter in *Arguing with the Past* ends by noting how Dorothea's new life demands that she learn the costs of things, but that her 'spending' herself in the river channels is a 'metaphor of expenditure [which] does not here rely on the idea of exchange' (115). Gallagher believes that George Eliot's major metaphor for authorship is monetary, but she also concludes that 'the *Theophrastus Such* essays construct the threat of the prostituting "amusing" author who purveys poison, spreads disease, and generates unnatural passions and excessive appetites' ('The Prostitute and the Jewish Question' 45). Sadoff echoes Miller in 'Bestiary' when she links fatherhood, authorship, and interpretation of metaphor (72).

10. Bernard Semmel's book rightly locates inheritance at the heart of George Eliot's politics. However, he considers it in a Comtean rather than an alcoholic context.

11. Cottom, Gallagher, and Carroll refer to George Eliot's responses to the 'Condition of England' (83), but use the phrase literally as 'state of matters, circumstance' (*OED* 2, 786), rather than as illness. Cottom limits George Eliot's idea of the Condition to communication between authority and populace (83). In *The Industrial Reformation of English Fiction*, Gallagher treats the 'Condition' without alluding to its metaphorical resonance. Carroll centers his discussion of *Felix Holt* on its conformities to and departures from the category: 'Though it contains all the usual ingredients of such novels—working-class hero, aristocratic rival, heroine as heiress, election riot, and so on—*Felix Holt* is, like George Eliot's other novels, a critical examination of the genre . . . carried out by means of a rigorous scrutiny of the phrase "the conditions of life" and its implications. A great many variations are played on the phrase, but the predominant and most abstract meaning refers to that which must be present if something else is to take place or that on which anything else is contingent. Its more restricted sense

is the context or social milieu in which character and event exist' (206). However, in 'The Body Versus the Social Body in the Works of Thomas Malthus and Henry Mayhew,' Gallagher points out that Malthus' recognition that the healthiest bodies, through continued reproduction, still create a major social problem 'ruptures the healthy body/healthy society homology' (85). Although the social body need not be sick to be troubled, George Eliot's heaviest-drinking, most politically volatile communities are sick societies. Gallagher's point explains how such stable, productive, healthy communities as Hayslope and Raveloe can produce such sickly, addicted characters as Thias Bede and Dunsey Cass.

12 In *George Eliot and Blackmail*, Alexander Welsh stresses George Eliot's ambivalence about this torrent of print (120).

13.Comparing George Eliot with Schopenhauer, E. A. McCobb mentions that both writers saw such spas as infernos (537). However, the frequent returns the Leweses made to dozens of spas in both Britain and on the Continent suggest that McCobb may be relying too heavily on the opening chapter to *Daniel Deronda*, and that she saw only the gambling at spas as pernicious while she and Lewes thoroughly enjoyed the health treatments available there.

14. I dismiss as frivolous David Williams' assertion in *Mr George Eliot* that the daily pint of champagne prescribed for her in 1879 somehow led to her passionate note to John Cross. Williams wonders whether its references to Cross's ignorance of 'verbs in Hiphil and Hophal or the History of metaphysics' (Haight 529) make fun of Lewes's scholarship and replies perhaps with excessive certainty: 'Is there a hint of Lewes-mockery here? If there is then beyond question she was drunk when she wrote it' (284).

George Eliot modeled the gallery where Caterina Sarti and Captain Wybrow have their secret trysts on the Long Gallery at Arbury Hall.

3

The Early Fiction

Then drink, boys, drink!
And see ye do not spill,
For if ye do, ye shall drink two,
For 'tis our master's will.'

'The Harvest Supper,' *Adam Bede*

When George Eliot chose the motto for Chapter 2 of *Middlemarch*, she eased the task of mid-twentieth-century genre critics who defined the novel as anti-romance. The motto casts Dorothea as a fuzzy-eyed Don Quixote and Celia as a humbly clear-sighted Sancho Panza able to distinguish a barber's shaving dish from the helmet of Mambrino. The anti-romance definition also fits other characters, such as Maggie, Rosamond, and Gwendolen, who, like the Don, suffer from reading romance and either do or do not progress from harboring romantic notions to achieving a valid perception of something such interpretations called 'reality.' It also applies particularly well to the often-noticed Quixotic allusions in *Middlemarch*. George Eliot's early works support the application of this opposition by presenting a pattern which associates opium with romanticism, especially the romanticism of intense love, and alcohol with realism, especially her detailed and clear-eyed representations of provincial culture. During her early period, she also represents many of her Midlands settings as metaphorically sick societies and alcohol as the remedy to which their members erroneously turn.

Alcohol and Realist Manifestoes

Many of the drinking scenes in George Eliot's early fiction have to do with her realist theory of fiction, the theory which moves

Raymond Williams and Patrick Brantlinger to group her among the novelists who aimed to acquaint the respectable middle classes with the true behavior of their social inferiors. References to alcohol occur in all the manifestoes of realism in the early fiction, most notably in the Dutch paintings passage in Chapter 17 of *Adam Bede*. Of all possible kinds of sordidness that might fulfill the obligation of the mimetic artist, George Eliot chooses tipsiness.

Opium intoxication, on the other hand, has traditionally been associated with George Eliot's realist aesthetic not because of her honest representations of tipsy characters, but because of her representation of romanticism as opium. In keeping with the shorthand formalist definition of the novel as anti-romance, Barbara Hardy (1970) describes *The Mill on the Floss* as Bildungsroman narration of Maggie's erratic and incomplete progress away from romantic self-delusion sometimes figured as opium and toward mature understanding of reality. Quoting a sentence from the 1860 letter which states that 'the Highest election and calling is to do without opium' (*GEL* 3:336), Hardy concludes that *The Mill* is 'about living without fantasy and opiate' (*Critical Essays* 50).[1]

This association between dreamy romance and intoxication occurs in all George Eliot's early fiction. In 'Mr Gilfil,' poisonous drugs (and the sickness they cause) stand for both romanticism in the sense of art located in the long ago or far away, and romanticism in the sense of a passionate, dangerous, illicit love affair. In *Adam Bede*, poisons and intoxication represent the affair between Hetty and Arthur, which again is romantic in both senses. The metaphor recurs in *The Mill* in descriptions of Maggie's passion for Stephen. Associations between intoxication and romance are thoroughly usual in mid-nineteenth-century British literature. The hero of Lewes's 1847 novel *Ranthorpe*, for example, like many of his youthful and romantic contemporaries, is often 'intoxicated' with love, ambition, or the wine of joy.

In such examples, the intoxication representing romantic illusions sometimes results from metaphorical consumption of love represented as opium or poison. Meanwhile alcohol takes its related but opposite role to that of opium when George Eliot launches her manifestoes. As metaphor, intoxication represents romance; at the same time, honest descriptions of drinking and intoxication enhance what George Eliot sees as her realism.

In later fiction, however, George Eliot's intoxicants do not persist in adhering to usual, in fact hackneyed, literary patterns in which they represent the blind foolishness of youthful emotion, nor does she continue to depend on them to prompt reflections on literary realism. As she goes on, her choices of setting, for one thing, result in development of this imagery into an elaborate drug/disease metaphorical complex. The temporal settings offer much potential for varying the kinds of intoxicants portrayed and also varying their effects, especially in her Reform-era plots.

The metaphor owes some of its pervasiveness and semiotic versatility to John Blackwood who reacted strongly, not against George Eliot's conventional metaphorical depictions of romantic love as intoxication, but to its corollary: her insistence on the portrayal of alcoholism as part of her rawboned realism. Although her reading of *Maga* meant that she had every reason to expect Blackwood's approval of such scenes, and despite the editor's efforts to respond to Lewes's warnings to moderate all criticism, when he succumbs to expressing reservations, they often concern her frankness regarding intoxication. George Eliot dealt with his criticism by relegating the drinking in particular to the subtext or the periphery of her plots, a strategy which only increases the metaphorical resonance of all the intoxicants in the novels. It also assures their pervasiveness long past the period when George Eliot had to cater carefully to Blackwood's tastes.

George Eliot's tenacity in the face of Blackwood's objections to the Dempsters' drinking is bound up with her main goal as a writer of fiction, for her early drinking characters, among them Amos Barton, Mr Gilfil, the Dempsters, and, in the novels, the drinking fathers, are deliberate embodiments of her conception of realism. Amos Barton commits blunders with his parishioners which result directly from his fondness for drinking with his flock and which help destroy the community sympathy that might have saved his wife. The children of both Thias Bede and Mr Tulliver have their strength and patience tested by their fathers' drinking. Of these early works, only 'Mr Gilfil's Love Story' lacks a family which must compensate however possible for the errors of at least one member who drinks too much.

But even though 'Mr Gilfil' lacks drinkers and drinking in the main body of its story, in the less long-ago and far-away frame, the narrator emphasizes the gin Mr Gilfil consumes as a daily routine in his old age. In contrast with the Cheverel Manor portion of the narrative (with its Gothic trappings), the frame takes place in early nineteenth-century Milby/Shepperton. This humdrum Nuneaton-based setting supplies much of the realistic detail for all three *Scenes* and highlights the Gothicized manor setting by contrast.[2] Mr Gilfil's drinking helps carry the anti-romantic thrust of the story, for the introductory description of the aged parson uses it as the peg on which to hang one of George Eliot's defenses of realist art. To counter the imaginary objections of 'refined lady readers' (127) to Gilfil's gin, the narrator defends his 'faithful' portrayal over a hypothetical 'flattering' (128) character portrait. By setting her defense in Shepperton rather than at Cheverel, George Eliot locates the gin in the more mundane Milby/Shepperton setting where alcohol is common in the other *Scenes*.

During the writing of 'Janet,' when Blackwood questioned the sordidness called for by her devotion to realism, George Eliot explicitly defended the scenesof Janet's drunkenness. As in 'Gilfil,' although this time addressed to Blackwood rather than to the ladies of her audience, a description of a character's drinking occasions a manifesto. George Eliot's correspondence with her publisher during his first reading of the manuscript confirms the connection between realism and alcohol: of all the sordid touches by which she meant to mirror reality, Blackwood disliked most Janet's drinking.[3] His first letter on the subject objects to Dempster's brutality, but shows more distress 'that the poor wife's sufferings should have driven her to so unsentimental a resource as beer' (*GEL* 2:344). He then turns around and concedes that alcoholism in women is an effective embodiment of realism: 'Still it is true to nature. The case is but too common' (2:345). George Eliot responds with assertions that Milby is considerably pleasanter than Nuneaton, its original, and that the story actually softens reality. Although she acknowledges that, without the changes he calls for, Blackwood might legitimately refuse to publish the story, she refuses to discard Janet's alcoholism. Nevertheless, the revisions recorded in the Penguin edition of the *Scenes* indicate that she did delete drink-related details. Indeed, the notes in the Penguin *Felix Holt* reveal that as late as 1865, George Eliot was still revising her fiction by removing such detail from her descriptions of Midlands towns.

George Eliot's most famous manifesto of realism occurs in *Adam Bede*, and it, too, includes references to drinking. Mr Irwine's pastoral failure with Arthur occasions this narrator's defense of the non-ideal but accurate portrayal of a clergyman. Although, unlike Mr Gilfil, Mr Irwine is not a heavy drinker, alcohol pervades the defense. Delighting in the Dutch paintings, the narrator specifies the quart pots of the homely wedding party as indispensable to the realism and argues that 'heavy clowns taking holiday in a dingy pot-house' (153) also have their place in art. Here the narrator concludes that a faithful representation of peasant characters cannot omit the quart pots in their hands as they celebrate a rustic wedding. Dutch paintings by Jan Steen, Adrian Breuer, David Teniers, and Gerard Dou (whose 'Spinner's Grace' is often named as the specific painting described in Chapter 17 [Witemeyer, Brown]) rely on signs of drinking to illustrate moral lessons.

An anecdote about a publican illustrates the final point of Chapter 17: that 'the select natures who pant after the ideal . . . are curiously in unison with the narrowest and pettiest' (157). Fleetingly, George Eliot presents Mr Gedge, who, unsatisfied with his patrons at the Royal Oak, moves to the Saracen's Head to find better company. Here, however, Gedge is no happier: the patrons of the Saracen's Head are also 'a poor lot' (158). The association between Mr Gedge and the reader who has romantic or ideal expectations warns the audience to accept realism and reject idealism or else deserve the narrator's sarcasm about select natures.

Near the end of the novel, 'The Harvest Supper' chapter, while not itself one of the manifestoes, illustrates the main points George Eliot makes in her review of the third volume of Riehl's *Naturgeschichte des volks* (*Westminster Review* July 1856) so often related to her first efforts in fiction. Repeating the posture of mock shock from 'Mr Gilfil,' the narrator describes the Harvest Home ceremony as essentially a drinking ritual, 'a painful fact, but then, you know, we cannot reform our forefathers' (434). The review acknowledges that the 'delicious effervescence of the mind which we call fun, has no equivalent for the northern peasant, except tipsy revelry; the only realm of fancy and imagination for the English clown exists at the bottom of the third quart pot' (Pinney 269). The pot's recurrence in all the early manifestoes of realism identifies it as essential to George Eliot's idea of the honesty of her portrayal of the peasant.

Alcohol and the Sickness of Society

The medicinal role of alcohol in the nineteenth century connects the drinkers among George Eliot's characters with her version of the Condition of England. Often the characters modeled on her neighbors in Nuneaton guzzle to obliterate the tedium of living in their drab surroundings, choosing a remedy considered medicinal to cure social rather than physical ills (Fenves 427). But George Eliot's heavy-drinking, drug-taking communities suffer both physically and morally and aggravate rather than cure the sickness of society by consuming great quantities of alcohol, the wrong remedy. George Eliot's characters rarely succeed in drawing beneficent effects from alcohol.

In 'Amos,' George Eliot sets up the metonymy of the sick society by structuring the plot around a series of meetings of groups whose physical ills relate to and represent their moral deficiencies. The Hackit tea party, the clerical meetings, and the Workhouse assembly all include a number of sick or sickly members. Mrs Patton is subject to 'the spasms' (88). Mrs Hackit's liver complaint results in her intimacy with Mr Pilgrim who enjoys many friendships with similarly generous patients who offer good port. Attendance is depleted at the clergymen's meeting by 'sore throats and catarrhs' (91). Mr Archibald Duke is 'very dyspeptic' (92), and Mr Baird is distinguished by his fellow-parishioners for 'a sort of cast in his eye, like' (94). At the workhouse, Silly Jim is hydrocephalic; old Maxum is deaf; and Poll Fodge has but one 'sore eye' (62). Amos himself has a perpetual sniffle and badly decayed teeth. Clerical backbiting, drunken gossip, and ineffective poor laws all affect these sickly characters and all are part of the Condition of England as it occurs in the Milby of 'Amos.'[4]

Many other citizens complicate their conditions by heavy drinking which targets both physical illnesses and spiritual ennui, but makes the community ill in both fact and metaphor. Mr Hackit and Mr Pilgrim do not drink tea at the tea party, and Mrs Hackit describes the drinking at the local Benefit Clubs as 'shameful' (50). Alcohol directly sustains the gossip that eventually proves deadly to Milly since it goes forth in the form of 'amusing innuendoes of the Milby gentlemen over their wine' (77).[5] Despite Mrs Hackit's care in providing the port wine prescribed for Milly, the death of Amos's wife results from a moral sickness in this community that its physical ills at once represent and manifest and that heavy drinking aggravates.

Amos's fondness for his drink stimulates him to repeat his social and professional errors over and over, errors often involved with language. Dining at Mrs Farquhar's, he delivers opinions which alienate his audience under the stimulus of 'unwonted gravies and port wine' (85). He enjoys his Sunday supper 'at a friendly parishioner's, with a glass, or even two glasses, of brandy-and-water after it' (85), and the narrator connects Amos's brandy with Amos's language when he observes that, like the drinking, the faulty grammar is itself mediocre. Described as 'not at all an ascetic' (85), Amos helps neutralize his potential effectiveness by drinking with his flock and so further befuddling his already poor ability to predict the effects of the words of his conversation, his sermons, or his lending-library books.

Although Amos (like Silas Marner after him) has the power to cure his neighbors of their physical ills, his drinking and his social ambition help convert him from a healer to a killer. He is so good with medicinal herbs that he steals one of Mr Pilgrim's patients, thereby setting himself up for Pilgrim to spread the gossip about the Countess to every farm that he and his colleague Pratt visit in their medical rounds. Partly because of the medical men's willingness to spread gossip, even Amos's effective healing eventually contributes to the deterioration of Milly's health. As sick as Milly (and with a name a single synecdochic letter away), Milby, the mixed-up receiving body, deflects the positive power of Amos's herbs. George Eliot curtails the positive, healing potential of her herbalist just as she curtails the healing potential of her drugs by concentrating on alcohol and opium, drugs which in her novels are more likely to intoxicate than cure.

Amos's effectiveness with the more primitive healing also reinforces the dangers of class mobility, if not a component of George Eliot's Condition of England, then one of its symptoms. Amos's move from carpentry and Evangelicalism to an Episcopalian ministry by way of Cambridge and the Clerical Book Club (Knoepflmacher *The Limits of Realism 47*) has unsuited him to communicate effectively by distancing him from his audience, and George Eliot expresses the ineffectiveness in a metaphor of distillation: Cambridge 'is not apparently the medium through which Christian doctrine will *distil* as welcome dew on withered souls' (21 my italics). The reputation of Cambridge, situated on the edge of the Fens, as a center of opium distribution further volatilizes the metaphors representing Amos and his unhappy effects on his parish.

'Janet's Repentance,' set close in time and place to 'Amos,' also presents a sick society, again a heavy-drinking society.[6] The narrator attaches strong irony to his description of the Milby drinking as a remedy for imagined ills: 'Milby might be considered dull by people of hypochondriacal temperament; and perhaps this is one reason why many of the middle-aged inhabitants, male and female, often found it impossible to keep up their spirits without a very abundant supply of stimulants' (254). George Eliot continues to emphasize Milby's drinking but culminates the description by cautioning that to some extent the town's dingy appearance belies the reality of 'the human life there, which at first seemed a dismal mixture of griping worldliness, vanity, ostrich feathers, and the fumes of brandy . . . looking closer, you may have found some purity, gentleness, and unselfishness, as you may have observed a scented geranium giving forth its wholesome odors amidst blasphemy and gin in a noisy pot-house' (262). The representation of Milby as pothouse, noisy with spoken sin and polluting gin, suggests that alcohol in Milby acts with great volatility to toxify language into deadly forms such as blasphemy and gossip. In combination with alcohol, this language both causes and aggravates what is wrong.

One of George Eliot's departures in *Adam Bede* from the rawboned realism of the *Scenes* is that she does not represent Hayslope as a metonymically sick society. The physically sick characters, Mrs Poyser and Miss Irwine, are not necessarily morally or spiritually sick. Instead, Irwine's sickly sister, who herself dispenses drugs to the people in Hayslope, is a symptom of a flaw in a social order which finds nothing to do with superfluous women (a Wollstonecraftian aspect of the Condition). The sickness in Mr Irwine's family forms a pocket of disease in an otherwise healthy community. In addition, descriptions of Hetty's condition as a sickness emphasize that Arthur has spread illness from his own environment across class lines. Superfluous women and illegitimate children thus assume status as part of George Eliot's version of the social problems that make up the Condition of England.

George Eliot's identification of her favorite audience also suggests the importance of her intoxicants. Although, as I have argued elsewhere, her subtextual debt to Mary Wollstonecraft suggests that she also targeted young women as an audience, she reports most pleasure when she believes herself able to influence young men, in particular young men in need of reform. Because youthful profligacy demands leisure, the composition of this group supposes she was aiming at people with at least middle-class status as the most important part of the audience to whom she hoped to present an unsentimental and non-pastoral version of peasant life. Both profligate young men and the peasants depicted in Dutch paintings are assumed to drink heavily, therefore intoxication links George Eliot's didactic objectives and her designated audience.

Drugs, Romanticism, and the Sickness of Society

Although in the *Scenes* drinking is a symptom and a cause of social sickness, other kinds of drugs also poison the settings of these tales, manifesting one of the ways in which a canonical Victorian at once reacts against and carries forth the practices of literary Romanticism, practices which persist throughout the century in more popular forms such as sensation fiction. In 'Mr Gilfil,' George Eliot's representations of romantic love as a drug make exotic Cheverel Manor as poisonous to Caterina as humdrum Shepperton is to Milly Barton. The romance represented as drugs and poisons thoroughly toxifies Cheverel Manor figuratively and literally. Since Gilfil's later drinking and pastoral laxity result from this toxicity, the romanticism encourages the alienation of the disaffected clergyman, one of many in George Eliot's fiction who stand idly or impotently by, unable to improve things.

   In 'Gilfil,' poisons and the sickness they cause stand for the romanticism of Caterina and Arthur's love affair. Caterina Sarti begins playing with poison early in life. The infant left at the foot of her father's deathbed 'held an empty medicine bottle in her hand, and was amusing herself with putting the cork in and drawing it out again to hear how it would pop' (151). Her play with the medicine bottle prefigures her relationship with Captain Wybrow in which she alternately controls and indulges her passions of love and jealousy.

Drugs and poisons apply to both Wybrow's and Caterina's romantic susceptibilities. Wybrow finds the habit of trifling with his uncle's ward produces 'an agreeable sensation, comparable to smoking the finest Latakia' (164). Caterina perceives the irresponsibility of Wybrow's trifling as a 'poison' (194). Indeed the narrator constructs Wybrow himself as a poison, in contrast with his rival Mr Gilfil who uses only 'nature's innocent opium: fatigue' (181). When Gilfil discovers that Wybrow has not abandoned his attentions to Caterina, he craves the vengeance of being able to 'pound him into paste to poison puppies like himself' (191). Wybrow's mimetically sick heart kills him; his figuratively sick heart combines with Caterina's romantic Italian essence and the other manifestations of extreme romanticism at the Manor to help kill Wybrow, Caterina, and eventually Caterina's baby.

In addition, in 'Mr Gilfil,' George Eliot goes beyond the usual associations of romance and poison to add a metaphorical layer of associations specifically between words and poisons. At Cheverel Manor, language, love, and drugs form combinations that aggravate Caterina's condition of 'diseased susceptibility' (198). 'Intoxicated' (180) by the renewal of Anthony's affectionate whispers, she wrenches herself from his embrace 'with the desperate effort of one who has just self recollection enough to be conscious that the fumes of charcoal will master his senses' (180). Mr Bates's conversation about the heir's love story combines with his habitual indulgence in 'that obvious and providential antidote, rum-and-water' (182) to aggravate Caterina's jealousy.

Later, the neo-Gothic renovations turn the metaphor to metonymy by physically sickening the inmates of Cheverel Manor. When the Baronet returns from Italy full of enthusiastic plans, the servants express their fear of side effects: 'We shall be pisined wi' lime and plaster' (155). Eventually Sir Christopher suffers a relapse of his asthma that justifies his servants' fears because it has been brought on by the plaster dust scattered by the renovation.

Consequently, although at Cheverel Manor George Eliot does not create an alcoholically aggravated sick society like that in Milby/Shepperton, the romantically and linguistically linked poisons at Cheverel Manor sicken this environment, too.

In *Adam Bede*, despite the surface health of Hayslope, images of poisons and drugs again represent the dangers of a romantic affair. Adam fails to produce in Hetty 'the sweet intoxication of young love' (86), but her earliest awareness of Arthur creates 'a pleasant narcotic effect' (86). She is in a 'pleasant delirium' (87), and she spins her hopes into 'a rancorous poisoned garment' (212). After the fight in the woods, Adam accuses Arthur of raising hopes that can 'poison' (252) Hetty's life. Late in the story the narrator still refers to her affair with Arthur as 'short poisonous delights' (282).

Arthur, for his part, dawdles in the Chase in the dappled light of 'an afternoon in which destiny . . . poisons us with violet-scented breath' (111). He tells Mr Irwine that being overcome by love no more suggests a flawed character than a good constitution prevents 'small-pox' (146). But Mr Irwine elaborates didactically on Arthur's metaphor: 'Yes; but there's this difference between love and smallpox, or bewitchment either–that if you detect the disease at an early stage, and try change of air, there is every chance of complete escape without any further development of symptoms. And there are certain alternative doses which a man may administer to himself by keeping unpleasant consequences before his mind' (146). Arthur's failed attempts to follow this advice only returns him to the powerful attractions of narcotic love.

George Eliot's notations on the traditional medicinal powers of gems, and her other novels, in which the metaphor recurs, suggest an additional signifier in the metaphor of romance as drug, for from *Adam Bede* on, gems, too, often represent the toxicity of romantic love. Dinah reproaches Chad's Bess for her pride in her ear-rings which Dinah argues 'are poisoning your soul' (28). Earrings with false gems recur as a sign of vanity when Hetty dons them as part of her imitation-lady outfit in 'The Two Bedchambers' chapter. Later, at the birthday feast, earrings signify both Hetty's vanity and

Arthur's love: he has bought her a pearl-and-crystal pair she can never wear in public. Hetty's other gift of jewelry from Arthur, an enameled locket containing wreaths of their hair, has a more directly stated capacity for toxicity. The birthday party occurs after Arthur and Hetty have begun their sexual activity, and it goes forth in a poisoned atmosphere that questions the entire ritual celebrating the fitness of the heir for the authority he will inherit (this novel's indirect dramatization of the recurring Victorian political problem). Mrs Poyser refuses to leave the Hall Farm unguarded during the festivity because tramps might poison the dogs. The sense of things all wrong is emphasized by 'the poppies that nodded a little too thickly among the corn' (214). Finally, Adam sees Hetty's tell-tale locket fall off at the dancing and the night is 'poisoned' (243) for him, too.

Arthur's keg of birthday ale, which matures exactly when he himself attains his majority, forms an alcoholic equivalent for the young heir. Like Wybrow, the lover is a poison. Arthur's failure to inherit, his susceptibility to pleasure, and his contrast with Adam pose the question of whether heredity or merit should determine who manages little Hayslope.[7] George Eliot examines the same question in the contrast between Wybrow and Gilfil, one the heir, the other the responsible chaplain who could administer Cheverel Manor better than either Wybrow or Sir Christopher. Like the Brontë sisters in the characters of Arthur Huntingdon and Hindley Earnshaw, George Eliot involves drugs in the irresponsibility of the squirearchy. Hence her conservatism does not reject the need to question heredity power. Still, she continues to associate radicalism and potential chaos with drinking as well, especially in the public house settings in such novels as *Felix Holt* and *Middlemarch* where the drinking places serve as campaign headquarters.

Instabilities and Ambiguities

The gems and other versions of the pharmaceutical complex proposed by Plato, elaborated on by Derrida, and associated with ambiguous language by both, permit George Eliot some complex metaphors even at this early stage. In some cases, signifiers Derrida associates with drugs that can operate as killers or healers maintain the drastic ambiguity of his *Pharmakon*. In others, George Eliot expresses her ambivalence toward writing itself through a version of the metaphor which reverses its terms. In 'Amos,' for example the figure reverses: instead of drugs representing language, language represents drugs when the narrator asserts that 'In some of the ale-house corners the drink was flavored by a dingy kind of infidelity, something like rinsings of Tom Paine in ditch-water' (60). *The Rights of Man*, the most potent and ubiquitous of ale-house political literature, represents the theology imbibed in public houses in a double image: a piece of writing combines with ditch-water to represent still another mixture, infidelity and ale. A disease metaphor reverses when the narrator summarizes the innocence of the Barton children in terms of writing as a representation of the fatalities: 'They had not learned to decipher that terrible handwriting of human destiny, illness and death' (110). In this example, instead of disease representing society and/or drugs representing writing, writing represents illness. The third variation evokes the power of both the written and the spoken word, for in it George Eliot represents the spoken word of gossip as spilled ink: with 'inky swiftness did gossip now blacken the reputation of the Reverend Amos Barton' (88). Out-of-control ink, which represents gossip, destroys a manuscript and a table cloth, objects linked by their own traditionally metaphorical relationship in which the literary task is envisioned as woven material.[7]

George Eliot also applies more usual Platonic drug metaphors in the *Scenes* as when the narrator describes the volume of sermons Lady Cheverel supplies as a remedy for Caterina as 'medicine for the mind' (195). In the first three examples, language represents drugs or disease; in the last, more typically of Western tradition, drugs represent language, in this case, the (written) sermon.

In general, the pastoral settings of the first two full-length novels detoxify both alcohol and language. In this pastoral community, wine can produce beneficial effects. A positive use of wine (and, as Knoepflmacher notes, an allusion to the Last Supper) occurs when Bartle Massey offers Adam Bede some restorative wine in the 'upper room' (356) in Stoniton during Hetty's trial. It revives Adam after his ordeal and represents the bond of fellow feeling between the two men. In *The Mill on the Floss* the narrator concedes to the robber-barons of the Rhine an alcoholic zest. The barons, despite being 'drunken ogres . . . had a certain grandeur' (237) in contrast with the humdrum and presumably sober residents of the Rhone valley. Also in this novel the narrator describes Mrs Tulliver's standing by Maggie after Tom's brutal post-elopement rejection as a 'draught of simple human pity' (424). In the later fiction, the word *cordial*, a kind of liqueur as well as a reference to the heart, creates warm effects. When Lydgate comes to confide in Dorothea after the destruction of his reputation in Middlemarch she offers him a 'cordial' look, which 'softened his expression' (557). Indeed the motto to Chapter 55 of *Middlemarch* compares Dorothea herself to good wine: 'Hath she her faults? I would you had them too./They are the fruity must of soundest wine' (399). Although less prominent than the poisonous potential of intoxicants, the positive effects of George Eliot's drinking and drugs sustain an ambiguous potential that can, occasionally, include pleasant warmth and good feelings.

And the ambiguity applies even to such clearly remedial social solutions as the acquirement of literacy by working-class characters. In the chapter 'The Night School,' in which Bartle Massey teaches reading, drug signifiers proliferate. Of the three backward students, a sawyer, a poacher-turned-Methodist, and a dyer, the last is the most promising and the one surrounded by pharmaceutical associations. Not only does his occupation connect him with dye, one Platonic version of the language-connected drug, but he gets his advice from 'the druggist at Treddleston' (199) and also resolves to send his son to school.

The interests of a dyer who receives advice from a druggist and wants to make sure his son also has the opportunity to achieve literacy place him among a number of George Eliot's later characters similarly occupied with their children's achievements of skills more highly developed than their own, Mr Tulliver, in particular. The dyer's interest in 'strange secrets of color' (199) also evokes the powerful magician who appears briefly in the first paragraph of *Adam Bede* as an equivalent for the narrator. A strong contrast with the Chapter 17 narrator who is devoted to realism, the magician helps emphasize the mystery, unpredictability, and volatility of the narrative task by equating it with sorcery. Through him and despite the manifestoes of realism calling for a down-to-earth approach to the creation of plots, George Eliot acknowledges the subtler dangers as well as the possible benefits of sophisticated literacy and the difficulty of any attempt, including her own, to represent life accurately through narrative.

Indeed, *Adam Bede* is the last narrative in which George Eliot inserts a manifesto of realism. Accordingly, the peasant with his quart pot and the tippling clergyman appear less didactically in the later fiction. Mr Lingon's drunken agreement to support his nephew's Radical candidacy in *Felix Holt* and Farmer Dagley's drunken attack on Mr Brooke in *Middlemarch* occasion no expressions of realist literary theory. The set-to with Blackwood guaranteed that, after 'Janet,' George Eliot would relinquish her settings of rawboned realism. Having accepted that Blackwood did not want his clerical stories to treat issues raised elsewhere in many of the articles in *Maga*, she abandons these themes and compromises with the more pastoral settings in *Adam Bede*, *The Mill on the Floss*, and *Silas Marner*. She then chooses an even more remote setting in *Romola*, before returning to her Warwickshire settings with *Felix Holt* and *Middlemarch*. But, although she relegates the theme of alcoholism to the periphery or the subtext in the pastoral novels, she does not abandon it.

Notes

1. It is this passage that connects the metaphor to Marx's. As Nancy Cervetti points out, the sentence occurs in a paragraph about

Catholicism in a letter to Barbara Bodichon ('Mr Dagley' 89).
2. Indeed, as U. C. Knoepflmacher has argued, the settings in 'MrGilfil' only confirm George Eliot's realist bias. Knoepflmacher concludes that the story is an 'anti-romance romance' in which she 'creates Sir Christopher's extraordinary world only to affirm the power of the ordinary' (15).
3. See Roland Anderson for additional comments on the Eliot/Blackwood dialogue on which he bases his agreement with W. J. Harvey that Chapter 17 does not intrude awkwardly on the narrative as has often been argued.
4. In a 1980 article, David Carroll describes the Milby of 'Janet' as a social organism in a state of decay. In *Conflict of Interpretations*, he elaborates on Janet's synthesis of material and spiritual rescue, linguistically connected by the pun in which *spirit* refers both to the human soul and the drink that can destroy it (71).
5. As Steven Marcus observes, gossip scenes make up nearly half of this story.
6. Carroll's analysis of organicism in 'Janet' assigns a synecdochic relationship between Milby and its citizens. On this basis, Janet's recovery signals Milby's vanquishing of 'the demon of indifference, epitomized in alcohol' (346).
7. Michael Wolff believes that the 'Epilogue' accomplishes precisely this shift. After meeting Arthur, Adam returns 'from the old seats of power, from that is, a visit to Arthur and Irwine, to the new center, that is, his home' (7).
8. J. Hillis Miller points out this relationship in 'Narrative and History'; Sandra Gilbert applies it specifically to *Silas Marner* in 'Daughteronomy.' Indeed these traditional perceptions of the text as woven material help incorporate women characters and women writers in the pharmaceutical metaphor, for which Derrida allows only the essentially male version suggested by the father/author, son/text relationship in which sperm signifies ink.

A composite: three Nuneaton drinking places.

4

Public Houses:
Unstable Language in Dangerous Places

'The Wager, A New Song'

'Tother night, 'twas Saturday last
Released from the plague of the Shop
All Labour and care being past
Away bounded I like a Top
To enjoy a cool Tankard and Pipe
And Feast on Society's charms
At the House of a Jolly good wight
And y-cleped the Newdigate Arms.

A few chosen spirits I found
The juice of John Barleycorn quaffing
And the glass and the Joke went round
'Midst laughter and smoking and chaffing
At length of a sudden there rose
A riot of Tongues like a Babel
As to which of the present gay Beaus
To eat their raw meat was best able.

'Occurences at Nuneaton' 1826

Because Mary Ann Evans wrote the earliest letters in Gordon S. Haight's collection in the mid-1830s, we know very little about her life between 1828 and 1833, the years that form her favorite temporal setting in her Midlands fiction. Apart from Robert

Evans's terse diary, the major document providing details of the area's daily life during this period is 'Memorandum Occurences at Nuneaton' (sic), a chronicle of local events between 1810 and 1845 said to be written by John Astly. In contrast to surviving portrayals of Nuneaton by Mary Ann Evans and her father in fiction and journal, the Diary describes activities such as boxing matches, balloon ascents, and hangings, events perhaps too vulgar for the attention of a seriously Evangelical young person or the notations of an estate agent with heavy responsibilities and a need for maintaining careful records and unassailable authority.

At the same time, George Eliot in her fiction and the Diarist in his journal assign public houses a prominent place in their descriptions of Warwickshire.[1] While the Diarist notes many business transactions involving public houses and expresses opinions regarding related commercial, moral, and political issues, George Eliot mentions numerous drinking places in her fiction, even when she sets little action there. In most of her stories, the drinking places bear names drawn from common Warwickshire signs which she carefully suits to the events that occur in these settings and to the characters who frequent them. George Eliot's choices for their names usually call attention to a variety of relationships characterized by instabilities in the political, financial, and familial relationships of her characters, instabilities that help create the Condition of England.

The public houses themselves often accommodate scenes in which sons and daughters deal with their parents' irresponsibility either effectively or inadequately. Most of the irresponsible parent characters have habits which must be redeemed by the acts of conscientious children or by substitute parents who assume the duties abandoned by delinquent fathers or mothers. Adam Bede, often criticized as excessively idealized, reveals his major fault, a priggish streak similar to Felix Holt's, in his interactions with his irresponsible father.

Adam's change from judgmental to sympathetic becomes more dramatic when viewed in terms of his father's drinking habits and the places where Thias enjoyed his many pints. In the case of Mr Tulliver, the difficulties of the father point directly to his daughter's crisis, a crisis that climaxes with a moral decision delivered at an inn and commented on by the narrator in a metaphor of wine pressing.

The Beer Act in Nuneaton

During the period of George Eliot's favorite temporal setting, the ubiquity of public houses in the Midlands and elsewhere increased dramatically because of passage of the 1830 Beer Act.[2] The eleven-year-old Mary Ann Evans, who was already acquiring the Evangelical seriousness that would persist for ten years, must have cringed as beer sellers proliferated in the neighborhood of Miss Wallington's school in Nuneaton.

William Howitt, writing in 1844 of the *Rural Life of England*, lamented that a 'new class of ale houses has sprung up under the new Beer Act, which being generally kept by people without capital, often without character, their liquor supplied by public brewers, and adulterated by themselves, have done more to demoralize the population of both town and country than any other legislative measure within the last century' (491). The newly licensed houses were, according to Howitt, 'low, dirty, fuddling places' (491), many of them created in rooms of people's homes. In the Nuneaton area where Evans spent her girlhood, they brought the number of ale sellers within a radius of a half mile from 28 to 37. In outlying villages (Robinson's End, Stockingford) the number of ale houses was likely to double.

Over the 35 years covered in his journal, the Nuneaton Diarist identifies drinking, the major although not the only activity pursued at nineteenth-century public houses, as a pervasive community problem in his reports of public drunkenness and criminal acts committed by drunkards. The Diary also contains a copy of the ballad which includes the two stanzas which head this chapter. Indeed, the goings on narrated in subsequent stanzas of the

1826 ballad conclude with a climactic regurgitation of raw meat which proves that in the early nineteenth century, great vulgarity could be found among the guests even at Nuneaton's most respectable drinking places. The Newdigate Arms served as a market-day meeting place for the respectable middle-class males of the town as well as serving as the site of the raw-meat-eating competition as narrated in 'The Wager' above.

The importance of Nuneaton's public houses and of the activities that occurred there appears in the Diarist's description of passage of the Beer Act. He lists the names of both old and new ale and spirit sellers and reports: 'On the tenth of this month came into operation the Ministerial Acts of throwing the Beer Trade open and the taking off the whole of Beer Duty (ab't 2/8 per Barrel). It excited great interest among the people and was anticipated with no small degree of satisfaction and consequently a drink'g enjoyment was the order of the day.' The joy of this event to the people of Nuneaton suggests that other local historians are correct in agreeing that in the 1830s Nuneaton was a heavy-drinking town of nearly legendary stature.[3]

The Diarist also chronicles a steady stream of drink-related mishaps in Nuneaton during the early part of the century. In 1816, there were charges filed involving adulterated brandy and at least one arrest for selling gin without a license. In 1822, a drunken coachman rode his horse into the butcher's shop, killing the animal and wounding the butcher's boy. In 1824, the Old Victuallers group voted to petition against a homeowner selling beer and ale on his premises. Two years later, the Diarist describes 'the Annual Clubs Feasts ab't as usual–not quite so much parade, but as much drunkenness.' At the 1827 Assembly, 'intoxication was disgracefully conspicuous.'

A more recent local historian, Arnold Bickerstaff, often refers to the oddly frequent intersection of education and drinking in Nuneaton in his thesis, *History of Education in the Nuneaton Area* (University of Nottingham 1964). As early as 1808, he notes disturbing reports of drinking at the meetings of the Governors of the Old Grammar School, Nuneaton's oldest and most important boys' school (founded in the sixteenth century). Totaling up costs for the supplies consumed during these meetings, Bickerstaff provides a figure of over £15 for wine, negus, brandy, rum, and gin. More than one early nineteenth-century master at the grammar school eked out his pay by also keeping a drinking establishment.

And then, somehow, in the 1830s, money intended for the building of a new Sunday School 'was really going to the purchase of a public house' (154). The role of J. W. Buchanan, George Eliot's model for the drunken Lawyer Dempster in 'Janet's Repentance' (Haight 8), as secretary of this enterprise (the 'Nuneaton Market House and Sunday School') not only suggests Buchanan's power in the town but also provides a hint that he might have been a key figure in the diversion of funds from a Sunday School to a bar room.

After the 1832 Reform, many incidents involving alcohol also involved politics. In 1832, the Diarist notes that candidate Dempster Heming, prototype for Harold Transome in *Felix Holt*, transported between four and five hundred men to swell his vote. Like the voters in the 1866 novel, they 'were regaled with Bread and Cheese and Ale' (68). In 1837, at the Tory dinner for M.P.s Dugdale and Wilmot, the guests 'numbered about 150, [it] was badly conducted, drunkenness, thievery, and other disorderly conduct.' Indeed this party appears to have been a complete brawl at which drunkenness and politics blended to provide opportunities for a great variety of petty crime.

Other local historians support both Bickerstaff and the Diarist. In a 1936 series in the *Nuneaton Chronicle*, Edward Nason describes Sunday at the Plough, an inn located all too close to the church: 'It was here that the bell-ringers from the Parish Church, when they had finished their "chime" . . . repaired to quench their thirst in home-brewed ale. It was thought to be rather a scandal at the time, but not much earlier I am afraid it was not *very* unusual for some members of the congregation to slip across the road for a little refreshment. As this morning sermon was seldom less than an hour in length, there was some excuse for this' (79 his italics). Peter Lee's series on 'Old Nuneaton,' which appeared in the 1983-84 *Nuneaton Chronicle*, emphasizes heavy drinking in its headlines: 'Town Brewery produced 23,000 gallons a week' and 'Old Abbey Street: A Drinker's Paradise.' The Diarist's list of 19 drinking establishments in Old Abbey Street, a thoroughfare no more than half a mile long, suggests the accuracy of Lee's Edenic headline. With a different quality of home-brewed ale available from house to house, the Old Abbey Street drinker would have a great range from which to sample. Ale was equally plentiful one street over in the Market Place, where, as Lee notes in a tone of perverse pride, three taverns stood side by side in a row: the Ram, the Hart, and the Castle.

In the fiction, George Eliot's drinking places, from the most uncomfortable hedgerow ale houses through the most prestigious inns, serve as settings of political and familial volatility. Nineteenth-century British public houses not only provided food, drink, and lodging, they also served as meeting places, banks, libraries, museums, transport terminals, surgeries, morgues, employment bureaus, gambling halls, auction rooms, cook houses, theaters, and campaign headquarters. Here customers exchanged money for drink, and, in the practice universally accepted as 'treating,' drink for votes. At the Newdigate Arms or the Bull Inn a Nuneaton resident could lose all possessions at a selling up, win an election, see a dramatic performance, suffer an amputation, or gamble away a heritage.

In stable, well-ordered communities, public houses performed a variety of useful functions that disposed them to contribute to community harmony. According to Brian Harrison, 'Only gradually during the nineteenth century did respectability become suspicious of the pub, which housed improving institutions of all types–reading rooms, debating societies, museums, discussion groups, and meeting-places' (*Kingdom* 181). In George Eliot's novels, too, drinking places can facilitate communication, sustain order, and provide valuable services, as do the Rainbow in *Silas*

Marner, the pleasant coaching inn in the opening to *Felix Holt*, and the Hand and Banner in *Daniel Deronda*. But despite the pleasant memories of travelers' inns George Eliot notes in her journals, she most often sets scenes threatening to property, order, and meaning in drinking places.[4]

Because George Eliot never once names a character, a town, a village, a home, or a drinking place carelessly, her inn signs carry much resonance. When she chose names for the drinking establishments in her fiction, she drew most of them from the Warwickshire houses familiar to all residents of the Midlands from ratcatchers to Baronets. The Green Man ('Janet's Repentance'), the Ram (*Felix Holt*), and the Royal Oak (*Adam Bede*) all appear on the Diarist's list of Nuneaton ale sellers at the time of the passage of the Beer Act, and names such as these still appear on pub signs in Warwickshire and elsewhere.

Histories of inn signs agree that the ale stake announcing a new tap ready for testing was among the first commercial signs in England, and that, like other pre-nineteenth-century signs, public house signs were designed to appeal to a largely illiterate population. Michael Brander observes that pub names have always and still do change constantly (91). After Henry VIII dissolved the monasteries, for example, iconophobia compelled many publicans to remove the religious elements from the signs. Such houses as the Angel and the Cross Keys typically lost the Virgin recipient of the Angel's annunciatory message in the one case and St. Peter holding the keys in the other.

Other signs changed according to the political fortunes of the honoree and the whim of the owner. A dab of paint could turn a hero fallen into disfavor into a more current celebrity. The Marquis of Granby, for example, whose military heroism assured that he appeared on many signs, is often a refurbishment of an earlier, more transient hero (Larwood & Hotten 45 hereafter L&H). Nevertheless, his own popularity was durable. In 1870, a hundred years after his death, there were still 18 Marquis O' Granbys in

London alone (L&H 43). In George Eliot's fiction, drinking places named after the Marquis of Granby appear in 'Amos Barton,' *The Mill on the Floss*, and *Felix Holt*.

Like the public houses of Reform-era Warwickshire, George Eliot's drinking places often go by several names, which emphasizes both polysemous language and other sorts of instability. The Markis o' Granby in *The Mill* is known 'among intimates as Dickison's' (71). The Tankard in *Middlemarch* is more commonly known as Dollop's. The Sugar Loaf in *Felix Holt* is also called Chubb's or the New Pits. In George Eliot's 1832 settings, houses that go by different names serve customers of potential class mobility and changeable politics who drink and read and talk together under equally unstable signs.

Besides being subject to frequent change, public house names are liable to be deceptive (Delderfield 86). The Britannia often commemorates something other than Great Britain, for example, perhaps a ship or a train. Dual names such as The Crown and Anchor, rather than implying a relationship between the two pictured objects, more often combine unrelated objects from the signs of two earlier establishments on the same site (L&H 19). Less-than-general literacy resulted in mispronunciations of words and misinterpretations of both words and pictures which in turn created inexplicable oddities, the corruption of the Star and Garter into the Leg and Star being the most often mentioned. The multiple roles of the houses correspond to the instability of their representations in their own names and, in turn, on the signs hanging outside. This linguistic volatility proceeds partly from synecdoche. One drinks, for example, at the Carpenter's Arms, but also, in common parlance, at *the sign* of the Carpenter's Arms, so that the sign represents in yet another way the establishment as a whole.

In addition to being linguistically volatile, inn signs could be physically dangerous. Nicknamed 'gallows signs,' many seventeenth- and eighteenth-century signs attached to the wall of the building but also stretched all the way across the road. They obstructed traffic and were eventually forbidden by law. An incident in 1718 when one such Fleet Street sign fell and killed 'two women, the king's jeweller, and a cobbler' (L&H 28) conclusively decided the fate of these texts which could so easily turn into missiles of real danger to people's health and soundness.

Finally, because artists sometimes painted the signs to pay an outstanding balance owed the publican, the signs, like the ale and beer sold within, could usurp the role of money as a medium of exchange, further complicating the representational relationships involved. For the sign, the owner exchanged coins or bills, which, like a banner representing a nation or a heraldic coat of arms, take purely symbolic roles vis à vis the signified. The events occurring in George Eliot's drinking places often involve rapid exchanges of money which destabilize social organization: drinkers seal bargains, trade horses, and gamble. Reputation and economic status shift quickly in these environments.

Progress, Meaning, and the Replacement of Signs

George Eliot chooses public houses as important setttings throughout her fiction. 'Janet's Repentance' opens in the Red Lion, and Dempster's agents organize the protest at the Green Man and the Bear and Ragged Staff, both names which correspond to the lower-class status of the patrons. 'Green Man' refers to the woodsman/ruffian/vegetable-god archetype often present in architecture and literature throughout England and, in some forms, the rest of Europe (as lovingly described by William Anderson in *Green Man: The Archetype of Our Oneness with the Earth*). This sign also specifically suggests Robin Hood, a hero local to the Midlands. Another Milby public house, the Bear and Ragged Staff, a sign of the Earls of Warwick, is also appropriately local and appropriately ferocious. Its picture of the climbing bear prepared for bear-baiting with a muzzle and chain emphasizes the animal's savagery and implies a similar potential in the people who drink there and respond to Dempster's rabble rousers.

In 'Janet's Repentance,' George Eliot makes the public house signs vehicles to convey her acknowledgments of linguistic instability. In 'Janet,' the narrator spends most of Chapter 2 describing Milby in imagery of clothing and drink, one an element of outward appearances, the other both a symptom of and an intended cure for the dull materialism that ails the town. The chapter begins with two Carlylean similes: clothing and, not drink itself, but a representation of drink, the sign of the Two Travellers public house.

As Michael York Mason has pointed out, the irony of George Eliot's passages on the temporal distance of her settings ultimately emphasizes the similarities between her settings and the time of writing rather than the differences.[5] As in *Middlemarch* and the other Reform-era fiction, ironies about progress and the perfection of mid-Victorian society link the faults of her characters with those of her readers. The opening to the chapter establishes the temporal distance of the early 1830s partly in terms of alcohol and ignorance:

> More than a quarter of a century has slipped by since then, and in the interval Milby has advanced at as rapid a pace as other market-towns in her Majesty's dominions. By this time it has a handsome railway station, where the drowsy London traveller may look out by the brilliant gas-light and see perfectly sober papas and husbands alighting . . . There is a resident rector, who appeals to the consciences of his hearers with all the immense advantages of a divine who keeps his own carriage . . . The gentlemen there fall into no other excess at dinner-parties than the perfectly well-bred and virtuous excess of stupidity; and though the ladies are still said sometimes to take too much upon themselves, they are never known to take too much in any other way . . . In short, Milby is now a refined, moral and enlightened town; no more resembling the Milby of former days than the huge, long-skirted, drab great-coat

that embarrassed the ankles of our grandfathers resembled the light paletot in which we tread jauntily through the muddiest streets, or than the bottle-nosed Britons, rejoicing over a tankard in the old sign of the Two Travellers at Milby, resembled the severe-looking gentleman in straps and high collars whom a modern artist has represented as sipping the imaginary port of that well-known commercial house (252-3).

Having placed the reader on a train observing mid-Victorian Milby's sober commuters, the narrator adds irony to the passage by citing as one of the manifestations of progress the rector whose carriage enhances his preaching.

Now the irony broadens. Milby's church and school are bigger, but the sobriety previously admired coexists with a stupidity that denies the alleged intellectual progress. The narrator concludes by paralleling the differences between the contemporary town and the 1832 Milby with differences in fashions in winter coats over twenty-five years and then in the same sentence to the differences between the old and the new signs at the Two Travellers. George Eliot's comparisons of progress in Milby to winter coats and tavern signs confirm similarity between the two ages rather than difference partly because of the ambiguity of clothes and the instability of inn signs as signifiers.[6]

Thomas Carlyle's enormous influence on nineteenth-century life and literature reached George Eliot early and survived his highhanded refusal to read *Adam Bede*. Like Caterina's name (*Sarti* is Italian for tailors), this passage in 'Janet' evokes the clothes metaphor basic to *Sartor Resartus* and also the advertising sign to which he objects in *Past and Present*.[7] Like the wardrobes in *Sartor Resartus*, George Eliot's winter coats, whether the 1832 greatcoat or the 1857 paletot, at once reveal and conceal essences. Their representational value, consequently, is ambiguous.

But the signs of drinking places are even slipperier: changeful and arbitrary symbols that cast suspicion on the estimate of Milby progress, for the replacement of two bottle-nosed tankard-hoisters by a respectable port drinker accurately represents only Milby's steadily ongoing consumption of alcohol. Contrary to the narrator's assertion, the interval of 25 years has not reduced the liquor trade, at least not at the Two Travellers which has continued to thrive.

Consequently the signs suggest that external changes, such as the replacement of one sign by another, do not necessarily indicate any change in the reality, in this case the reality that alcohol is sold and consumed within. At the same time, because the gentleman on the sign, both in his clothing and in the activity of traveling, evokes the supposedly sober commuter visible at the train station, the sign implies that these sober papas are not necessarily totally abstemious despite their improvement in social status.

Both the old and the new Two Travellers signs, which replace one signifier by another (and the name itself emphasizes duality), in the end invalidate what the narrator ostensibly wants them to prove: the progressive sobriety of present-day Milby. Hence they assert the arbitrariness of signification itself. Over the years, Milby's bourgeoisie has replaced its farmers and artisans; port-wine glasses have replaced ale tankards; and knowledge (education, literacy) ostensibly has replaced ignorance, but all in only non-progressive substitutions. The town's signs, both tavern and linguistic, replace each other without progress. Like a text in which infinite substitution occurs within a closed set, Milby/Shepperton and its drinking places are the sites of multiple linguistically connected replacements that can yield meaning or withhold it, but always assure its instability.

In 'Amos Barton,' the public houses contribute to the Bartons' sorrows in ways directly connected with language. In this story, and in later characters such as Mr Stelling and Mr Sherlock, the state of the clergy plays its part in the Condition. As Knoepflmacher points out, Milly's death occurs partly because of Amos's faults, faults which proceed from class ambitions nurtured by his Cambridge education: 'Instead of following the example of his father, 'an excellent cabinet-maker and deacon of an Independent church,' Amos's imperfect training at Cambridge leads him to regret his past and to snub the 'ordinary minds' of his flock (*Limits* 47). Most often in George Eliot's fiction, the superior social status of the clergyman isolates him, as with Mr Irwine, Parson Jack Lingon, or the Reverend Augustus Debarry. In other examples, such as Mr Stelling or Amos, their ambitions reduce their effectiveness.

Arguments regarding the threats of Catholicism, the factionalism resulting from Dissent, and the education and status of the clergy (as in *Blackwood's* 'The Old and New Style at Oxford,' 1856) occupied many pages of nineteenth-century periodicals. These problems also mean that George Eliot's clergyman characters seldom perform effectively to reduce the malaise. Like Mr Gilfil, many of them like to drink. Mr Lingon agrees to support Harold Transome's Radical candidacy only after consuming his after-dinner port. Mr Irwine bears an alcoholically resonant name.

Amos Barton enjoys his drink, and although he does not frequent public houses, the activities there help bring on the story's catastrophe. The narrator mentions three houses where the lethal gossip about the Bartons and the Countess goes forth: Granby's, the Jolly Colliers, and an unnamed 'alehouse in the village' (59) from which a tippling shepherd brings news of Milly's mortal illness to Mrs Hackit. Amos loses his reputation among the clergy and eventually becomes a widower partly because of the gossip which is then fulfilled in the shepherd's message.

Although most of the drinking in 'Amos Barton' happens in homes (the Farquhars', the Hackits', Mr. Ely's) the role of the Shepperton taverns as centers of gossip confirms the lethal power of both drinking and language. In 'Mr Gilfil,' taverns and ale houses again supply an arena for gossip, notably gossip about Mr Gilfil's quarrel with Mr Oldinport, information 'as good as lemon with their grog' (73) to the local farmers. In this case, the gossip adds to Mr Gilfil's effectiveness, despite his own heavy drinking, because of the farmers' dislike for Oldinport.

In 'Janet's Repentance,' George Eliot moves the hazards of

drinking and its associations with language to the center of her plot. The opening scene occurs in The Red Lion, Dempster's house, and the name is carefully chosen. The red lion is the sign of John of Gaunt (L&H 119), fourteenth-century Duke of Lancaster and pretender to the throne of Castile who, like Dempster, has a record of being constantly at odds with clergymen. The lion is rampant, suggesting Dempster's absolute power in his house, as well as his own animalistic tendencies.[8] Like Branwell Brontë, whose conduct corresponded to the name of his favorite local drinking place, the handily located Black Bull in Haworth, Dempster drinks at a house whose name describes his own unmanageable temperament. Consequently the inn setting and its signs can yield accurate meaning, in these cases information concerning its patrons. But, because sketching the personalities of its patrons conflicts with the ostensible purpose of the signs, they succeed no better at conveying the intended meaning than does the letter from Bulstrode Raffles accidentally finds in *Middlemarch*.[9]

The Red Lion is the stage for Dempster's control of Milby's attitudes toward the religious/political change represented by Mr Tryan's Evangelicalism. The narrator describes this change as a disease: 'a murrain or a blight' expected 'as little as the innocent Red Indians expected smallpox' (263), one of numerous references to Evangelicalism as disease among George Eliot's Midlanders. Such references place the opponents of Evangelicalism into the role of attempting to find a remedy for the disease, in Dempster's case a combination of alcohol and language.

In the opening scene, Dempster drafts the petition against Tryan's Sunday night preaching while drinking what his associates regard as awesome amounts of brandy. He demonstrates his aggression by outshouting Luke Byles's accurate definition of Presbyterianism, arguing entirely from his own authority through an attack on the reliability of Byles's encyclopedia.[10]

Dempster's attack is a flight, the unique form of oral alehouse rhetoric immortalized in Samuel Johnson's famous retort: 'Sir, your wife, under the pretext of keeping a bawdy house is in fact a receiver of stolen goods' (quoted in Jackson 132). The flight labels Byles's book 'a farrago of false information, of which you picked up an imperfect copy in a cargo of waste paper' (184). Dempster ends his flight by describing Luke as fit only 'to sit in the chimney-corner of a pot-house, and make blasphemous comments on the one greasy newspaper fingered by beer-swilling tinkers' (185). His signature 'would be a blot on our protest' (185). Dempster's public-house rhetoric labels Byles a prater, drinker, companion to other drinkers, blasphemer, and, ultimately, a small ink spill, a blot.

In this first chapter of 'Janet,' Dempster both consumes and distributes alcohol, manipulates both the written and spoken word, and applies metaphors of both body fluid and ink in his characterization of Byles as blot, a figure through which ink represents a heavy-drinking blasphemer named after a body fluid. In the Red Lion, drink promotes irresponsible language meant by Dempster as a remedy and accommodates elaborate linguistic play in which signifiers exchange figurative roles with referents, and multiple slippages occur.

Both Dempster and his adversary have intimate relationships with language: Mr Tryan dispenses the spoken word in his sermons, lectures, and parish visitations and the written word in his religious lending library. Dempster's campaign against Tryan makes use of both oratory and printed placards. Having accumulated his money by manipulating the law, that most fixed and paternally connected of all kinds of writing, Dempster calls on the oratorical skills apparently developed in the courtroom to transform the Milby crowd outside the Red Lion into a mob.

Whereas Dempster is saturated by alcohol, law, and money, Tryan, though dying of tuberculosis, is free from polluting combinations. The word he delivers is untainted and life-giving. When Mrs Linnet offers him some wine, he reminds her that he is a 'Rechabite,' a name eventually connected with a flourishing nineteenth-century temperance group (Harrison *Kingdom* 181). His self-description then recalls to him an unexpected meeting with Janet, of whose reputation as a drinker he is well aware, at the bedside of a dying consumptive. It thus anticipates his future relationship with Janet in which he struggles to supplant her addiction through a process of sponsorship and reliance on a higher power that helps locate the origins of twentieth-century twelve-step programs in dissenting and evangelical religious practices.

But despite his current freedom from literal pollutants, Mr Tryan suspects it is his preaching that is killing him. Dempster is both morally and physically sick; indeed, his moral weakness has led to his physical ills. Although Tryan is physically sick, and his sickness has come upon him as a result of his guilt over a seduction, he cures Janet. Thus even Tryan's effect is ambiguous: he can benefit Janet but in the effort only harms himself through self-neglect, overwork, and too much preaching. His mobility, unlike Amos's carries him downward on the social scale: from Cambridge to an Evangelical ministry carried forth in humble surroundings. Upon the death of his Nuneaton original, Mr Jones, the Diarist accuses him with great harshness of having created 'more division and quarrels on a religious score in the Town among the church people and Dissenters than had taken place during the last half century' (12/31). In Milby, even the dedicated Mr Tryan provokes community strife.

Sobriety and Responsibility in Adam Bede

In *Adam Bede* and *The Mill on the Floss*, George Eliot deals with problems of inheritance she will later treat more explicitly in the 'Address to Working Men by Felix Holt.' At a time when succeeding Reform Bills were dispersing uninherited power among the social classes, George Eliot argues for the development of a paternal responsibility that will guarantee a heritage of education and sobriety for the newly enfranchised groups. Both Adam's father and Maggie's destroy rather than protecting their children's inheritances. In 1867, the 'Address' clarifies George Eliot's attitudes towards the effects of such behavior as aggravations of a dangerous Condition.

The public houses of Hayslope accommodate scenes that often turn on questions of paternal responsibility. The name of the Holly Bush, where Wiry Ben drinks when there is good company, is of ancient origin, associated both with the Roman sign for the availability of wine and the medieval ale garland. The traditionalism and pastoralism of this name go along with the general innocuousness of drinking in Hayslope. The organicism of the Bush makes it appropriate to a community George Eliot consistently represents through such imagery as roots, branches, and flowers.

But despite the traditional, pastoral name of the Holly Bush, its mention provokes Adam. In the opening scene of the novel, Ben is making fun of Seth for forgetting to install panels in his door. When Ben jokes about Seth's Methodism and suggests that, for all his tolerance, Mr Irwine is 'none so fond o' your dissenters' (9), Adam responds: 'Maybe; I'm none so fond o' Josh Tod's thick ale, but I don't hinder you from making a fool o' yourself wi't' (9). Adam's defensive sermon allows him to vent his anger at his father's drunkenness on Wiry Ben, who is, like Thias, a 'loose fish,' nineteenth-century slang for a drunkard. In addition, his sermons link him with the professional preacher, the person who, as Seth points out, 'empties the alehouses' (10). Because emptying the alehouses would bring Thias back home to his responsibilities, this goal would supply Adam with an unconscious motive for his sermonizing.

Wiry Ben's estimate of Adam receives almost instant support from another character also intimately associated with a drinking place, the landlord of the Donnithorne Arms. Describing Adam as 'lifted up and peppery-like' (16), Mr Casson becomes one of the first characters of the novel to criticize Adam accurately for this moral deficiency.

Indeed the sign of Mr Casson's Donnithorne Arms raises other questions involving paternal power and responsibility by alluding to a conspicuous fatherly failure, a failure in the ancestors of the Donnithornes and in Arthur's grandfather, the current representative of the family. The 'promise of good feed for himself and his horse' (13) indicated by an abundance of land attached to the inn must serve the traveler as consolation 'for the ignorance in which the weatherbeaten sign left him as to the heraldic bearings of that ancient family, the Donnithornes' (13). The lack of arms on the sign of the tavern indicates that in the wake of the dissolution of the monasteries, the Donnithornes have failed to take up the tasks of the monks who offered hospitality, food, and lodging to belated travelers. Its shabbiness represents the poor stewardship of Arthur's grandfather.

Arthur intends to supply his grandfather's lack as soon as he can after the old squire's death: he wants to install a sign that testifies to his improvement over his paternal predecessor by making Hayslope 'like Treddleston-where the arms of the neighboring lord of the manor were borne on the sign of the principal inn' (369). Like Adam, Arthur must make up for the deficiencies of a male progenitor who fails to do his job. But, unlike Adam, Arthur will never be able to assume his place as heir nor to claim his own heir (or heiress). The death of his bastard child by Hetty results in his spending most of his life away from Hayslope, leaving the management of the estate to agents and the inn unadorned by the Donnithorne heraldry.

Although events at the Holly Bush and the Donnithorne Arms both measure the deterioration of Adam's relationship with his father, within the action of the story the father drinks at neither house. Thias's alehouse is the Waggon Overthrown, a name George Eliot drew from her memories of Nuneaton. (Although not on the Diarist's 1830 list of ale sellers, it appears in the journal of her father who notes paying his workers there.) Like Dempster's Red Lion, the name of the Waggon Overthrown strongly suggests the nature of the man who drinks there. With its representation of a ruined or upended working vehicle, it describes the fate of Thias since he has taken to drink.

And of the three drinking places, the Waggon Overthrown provides the most potent threat to orderly replacements by legitimate descent. Adam's heart hardened against Thias on 'the night of shame and anguish when he first saw his father quite wild and foolish, shouting a song out fitfully among his drunken companions at the "Waggon Overthrown"' (43). The shame of this vision of his rollicking father causes the teenage Adam to run away, although his feelings for his mother and brother prompt him to return before he gets too far.

Adam's escape from Hayslope would interrupt a normal pattern of descent in which he would replace Thias as village carpenter and assume the rank in Hayslope that belongs to this position when Thias dies or becomes feeble. Adam decides to return to his duty to his family acknowledging that burdens are for those healthy enough to bear them. Like Mr Tryan's role in Janet's recovery in the third *Scene*, Adam's attitudes toward his father demonstrate another similarity with twentieth-century twelve-step programs. Whereas Dinah and Seth rely on the text, 'Take no thought for the morrow' (40), Adam dwells bitterly on his childhood pride in Thias during his sober days, and looks ahead to the many tasks he will need to perform for the drinking Thias in the future. He does not take life one day at a time.

Finally, Adam's painful development of fellow-feeling begins at the very house where he has first rejected his father. Returning from Snowfield with the frightening knowledge that Hetty is missing, he gets only as far as Treddleston where he 'threw himself without undressing on a bed at the "Waggon Overthrown"' (334). His severe judgments begin to abate in this location when he first shows generosity of spirit toward Hetty. Moreover, the sacramental sharing of wine with Bartle Massey in the 'upper room' during Hetty's trial, the scene in which he resolves to 'never be hard again' (360), is a drinking ceremony between Adam and a surrogate father (Knoepflmacher *Limits* 112). Drinking with Bartle occurs simultaneously with Adam's forgiveness of the faults of his recently dead drunken father.

The habits of such upright characters as the Poysers demonstrate the innocuousness of drinking in Hayslope. The family has freshly drawn ale with dinner, and Adam, although he specifies a preference for whey, drinks mead and ale as well. But when conflict, danger, and possible sudden change in the social order threaten the community of Hayslope, drinking often has something to do with it, whether or not it acts as a direct cause.

The Birthday Feast, at which Hayslopers spend a good deal of time trying to sort out the various levels of the village hierarchy, is troubled with secrets and danger represented by imagery of poppies and poisons. Like most young men of his social position, Arthur includes drinking among his pleasures, one of a catalogue with which to beguile idleness, a catalogue in which the routine seduction of a milkmaid would not be out of place. Arthur not only drinks his usual wine with dinner before he meets Hetty at the Hermitage, but he carries a flask along with him. During the incident that culminates in the fist fight with Adam, Arthur's attempts to deceive the righteous carpenter succeed only partly because 'he had tried to make unpleasant feelings more bearable by drinking a little more wine than usual at dinner today, and was still enough under its flattering influence to think more lightly of this unwished-for rencontre with Adam than he would otherwise have done' (250).

Indeed an undercurrent of danger troubles the atmosphere of all the drinking scenes in *Adam Bede*, many of which feature Hetty, who harbors social ambitions encouraged by her affair with Arthur. The scene in which she takes advantage of the ale-tapping at dinner to dress up in Dinah's clothes de-stabilizes her identity in a transformation George Eliot associates with spilled ale. The appearance of Hetty in Dinah's clothes creates a 'contagious' (193) influence on the ale jug which slips from Mrs Poyser's hands when she catches sight of Hetty's face replacing Dinah's under the Methodist cap. (Hetty secretly does want to change costumes, but with Lydia Donnithorne rather than with Dinah.)

To restore order after the incident, the Poysers and Adam discuss 'the new tap,' the 'hopping,' and the disadvantages of making one's 'own malt' (195). The drawing of the ale sets the stage for Mrs Poyser's predictions of inflammation for herself, St Vitus dance for Mollie, and murrain for the cattle. The instability of Hetty's identity combines with the threats of coming disease to add an ominous undercurrent to the domestic comedy of the scene.

Adam Bede thus links intoxicants with disease, language, romantic love, squandered money, and diverted descent. Like George Eliot's subsequent fiction, this novel associates threats of illegitimate or premature replacement of paternal authority with drinking or drug taking by irresponsible parents: Thias, Arthur, and, on the metaphorical level, Hetty.

The 'Onward Tendency'

Having created an only superficially sober and healthy community in *Adam Bede*, George Eliot goes on to attribute an unhealthy volatility to the community in *The Mill on the Floss*. Bassett, the home of the Moss family, is a stubborn pocket of sickness, and the illnesses of many residents of St Ogg's, most importantly the Tullivers, worsen as the novel advances. Again the drinking establishments are places of social and economic volatility, and when intoxicant metaphors occur in clusters in any particular scene, they usually accompany threats of bewildering transformations and violations of orderly patterns of descent.

At the outset, the community of St Ogg's is fairly healthy. Mr Tulliver is 'not dyspeptic' (69). Mrs Tulliver is 'stout and healthy' (82). Mrs Glegg is attractive and robust despite the 'drug-like odors' (110) in her cupboard and the mutton-bone she carries in a pocket of her gown to guard against cramp (107). One reason for the relative health of St Ogg's is its methodical resistance to change. The Dodsons flourish during 'sober times when men had done with change' (106).

Consequently the community has avoided the volatility Haley assigns to societies likely to be represented as diseased in *The Healthy Body and Victorian Culture*. Nevertheless, the pockets of illness in the settings of the novel eventually spread to encompass the Tullivers who become sicker as the novel advances. Tom injures his foot; Yap develops a fatal lump in his throat; Mr Tulliver has a stroke; and Mrs Tulliver becomes 'feeble' (246). Maggie's elopement with Stephen plunges both Lucy and Philip into serious illness.

Moreover, a number of locations in *The Mill* accommodate much heavy drinking. Although Mrs Pullet's survival attests to her good physical health, the quantity of her medicines indicates that she must remain constantly drunk on mixtures composed substantially of alcohol and opium. She lives at Garum Firs, a most attractive and orderly establishment, but named after a medicine for horses.[11] Mr Riley and Mr Tulliver decide on Tom's school during a night of brandy drinking, and Tom's accident to his foot results directly from Mr Poulter's drunkenness.

Members of this community apply alcohol metaphors frequently. Mr Tulliver tells his wife, 'Never brew wi' bad malt upon Michaelmas-day, else you'll have a bad tap' (21-22). Mr Glegg outrages his wife by observing, 'You're like a tipsy man as thinks everybody's had too much but himself' (111). The narrator describes Mrs Tulliver's un-Dodsonian weakness with a beer/ale metaphor: in the company of her sisters she becomes like 'small beer' (40). Alcohol is often on the minds of George Eliot's *Mill* characters.

Most importantly, the three drinking places in this novel–the Marquis O' Granby in Bassett, the Black Swan in King's Lorton, and the Golden Lion in St. Ogg's–are all associated with sickness, wounds, social mobility, money, and/or disturbed relationships between parents and their children.

The Bassett public house, the 'Markis o' Granby,' is ironically named and located at the heart of the community: all roads lead thither. Its landlord has a 'melancholy pimpled face' (71); its smells of tobacco and beer make it 'fatally alluring' (71) to Mr Moss's neighbors. Although Mrs Moss can brag of her husband 'that he didn't spend a shilling at Dickison's from one Whitsuntide to another' (71), he is also 'a man without capital, who, if murrain and blight were abroad, was sure to have his share of them' (70). Mrs Moss is often 'laid up so' (74), a possible allusion to her frequent confinements that equates childbirth and sickness.

King's Lorton, the location of the Black Swan, is another unhealthful environment. Mr Stelling's ambition tempers his health and strength, and he has married somewhat beneath his Oxford background in choosing the lovely Louisa Timpson. Like Amos Barton's, his social ambition results in an unhealthy situation, especially for Tom. With unconsciously ironic self-description, Stelling terms any education other than the traditional classical curriculum he employs 'charlatanism' (123).

Tom, who is also at King's Lorton for social advancement, rapidly loses his vitality in this environment. George Eliot's famous passage about shrew mice and metaphor describes Tom's experience under Mr Stelling's regimen and forms one of the bases for J. Hillis Miller's most extensive description of her metaphors ('George Eliot's Bestiary' in *Reading and Writing Differently*). In this passage, the narrator of *The Mill* directly represents Tom himself as a remedy: he is 'in a state of as blank unimaginativeness concerning the cause and tendency of his sufferings as if he had been an innocent shrewmouse imprisoned in the split trunk of an ash-tree in order to cure lameness in cattle' (125). Represented as a cure, Tom comes to need a cure as much as do the cattle whose lameness calls for the imprisonment of the shrewmouse. As Miller argues, Tom, the cattle, and the shrewmouse exchange figurative roles in an elaborate semiotic dance.

The chapter in which Mr Poulter's drunkenness contributes to the injury to Tom's foot concludes with a pun that also emphasizes linguistic instability: the narrator accounts for Tom's childishness in wanting to keep the sword by noting that 'it is doubtful whether our soldiers would be maintained if there were not pacific people at home who like to fancy themselves soldiers. War, like other dramatic spectacle, might possibly cease for want of a "public."' (156). At the King's Lorton public house, Mr Poulter spends the money Tom gives him for the loan of the sword.

To entertain Tom during the lameness inflicted by Mr. Poulter's sword, Philip tells him the story of *Philoctetes*, an appropriate text for these products of Stelling's classical curriculum, thus supplying an allusion through which George Eliot increases the complexity of the relationships among her characters. Like many of her allusions to illness and intoxication, this one occurs subtextually. *Philoctetes* offers various equivalents for the characters in the novel. Odysseus, like Mr Poulter, is an aging warrior. In his inheritance of the enmities of his father, Neoptolemus, the son of Achilles, is like both Tom and Philip. Like Tom, Philoctetes is wounded in the foot; like Mr Tulliver and Tom both, he cherishes his enmities. Both George Eliot's novel and Sophocles' drama are concerned with sickness, cure, medicine, and doctors.[12] In addition, both concern marvelous weapons, false friends, and inheritance. Because nearly all the characters in *Philoctetes* are sons and fathers, the allusions associate the shifts in these relationships with the physical and moral condition of George Eliot's sons and fathers, and, in turn, with the resulting social order or lack of it in nineteenth-century Britain.[13]

Back in St Ogg's, the Golden Lion is connected with all of the disasters that befall Dorlcote Mill, disasters which result in dramatic changes in the Tullivers' socioeconomic status and in the family order. When Mr Tulliver seeks advice on Tom's education, both he and Mr Riley are drinking more brandy than usual. Mr Tulliver's educational ambitions for his son involve turning Tom into a man who is quick enough with language to defeat the lawyers who threaten the mill. But he also fears premature replacement and consequently wants Tom to choose a different occupation from his own.

Mr Riley bases his advice largely on his conviction that Mr Tulliver has extra money on hand, a community perception which Mr Tulliver encourages during his market-day lunches at the Golden Lion: 'He had been always used to hear pleasant jokes about his advantages as a man who worked his own mill . . . They gave a pleasant flavor to his glass on market-day' (69). Actually, the mill is heavily mortgaged, and Mr Tulliver's drinking increases with the progress of the lawsuits involving the mortgage. When Tom returns from King's Lorton for Christmas he finds that 'Mr Tulliver got louder and more angry in narration and assertion with the increased leisure of dessert' (137). It is seeing Mr Wakem 'on market-days' (140) that fans his ire.

Mr Tulliver's health deteriorates as his obsession grows. His hasty litigiousness results in the losses with which he is trying to cope when he gets the letter saying that the mortgage on Dorlcote Mill has been transferred to Wakem. Like a poisonous draught, this letter precipitates his illness. Maggie tells Tom: 'It was the letter with that news in it that made father ill, they think' (177). But the letter is also the remedy for his illness, a truly ambiguous Platonic *Pharmakon*. Instead of prescribing a literal medicine for Mr Tulliver's sickness, the doctor calls for the same letter that has made him sick to be 'brought and laid on the bed, and the previous impatience seemed to be allayed' (175). Here again, the *Pharmakon* reverses: instead of drugs representing writing, a piece of writing assumes the role of the drug.

To discuss the crisis of Mr Tulliver's loss and illness, the entire Dodson family gathers at the mill. At this meeting Mrs Tulliver indulges her horror over the potential dispersion of her domestic goods, in particular to the Golden Lion. When the auction actually occurs, she listens as 'one thing and then another had gone to be identified as hers in the hateful publicity of the Golden Lion' (209). The land and mill are also to be sold 'in the proper after-dinner hour at the Golden Lion' (215). Finally, Mr Tulliver regains his economic status at the Golden Lion during the jubilant afternoon on which, with Tom's help, he triumphantly pays off his creditors.

The inn's name emphasizes the leonine temperament of Tulliver himself and the materialism of his tragedy. *Golden* is an adjective applied more often to calves than to lions. George Eliot discovered this suitable name on her 1859 trip to southwest England during which she was also searching out useful mills and rivers. Although she judged the Frome River too insignificant to power the kind of mill she had in mind for her novel, she retained the name of the Golden Lion, the excessively 'commercial' establishment where the Leweses lodged, for her then-novel-in-progress (*GHL* X 31). Located at the corner of St Mary and St Edmund Streets in Weymouth, the inn emphasizes the gilded rather than the tawny aspects of its namesake by means of a rampant leonine figure above the entrance The couple's time there made Lewes sick: he 'went to bed with a racking headache' (*GHL* XI, 31). The next day they moved to quieter private lodgings a short distance away.

Finally, like that of her mother, father, and brother, Maggie's status changes dramatically at an inn where she not only makes the moral decision most often located as the novel's climax, but also makes a mistake that clinches her reputation in St Ogg's. She waits to confront Stephen with her decision against marrying him until they arrive at the inn at Mudport where she couches her rejection in a wine metaphor: she refuses to marry him because the hurt to Lucy and Philip will be like savoring joys 'wrung from crushed hearts' (414). When she flees his presence she solidifies her loss of reputation by taking the wrong coach to yet another inn where she lies ill for a day before she regains enough energy to return home.

By the time Maggie is able to return to the mill, her reputation is irretrievably gone and she gets treated by the young men of St Ogg's like 'a friendly barmaid' (431). The settings which accommodate events leading to the destruction of Maggie's reputation are the same settings in which her father has indulged his truculence. The resulting financial losses help ripen Maggie's appetite for pleasure and so bring on her degradation in the town of St Ogg's.

More significant than any inn setting in this story, however, is the mill of the title. The local legend in which it figures, the legend that a change in ownership causes floods, makes it one of the most powerful locations in St Ogg's. Selling the mill to Wakem doubly (perhaps trebly) interrupts the orderly process of descent by which the mill has stayed in the Tulliver family for generations, for not only does the mill go out of the Tulliver family but Wakem gives its supervision to his illegitimate son Jetsome, a drunkard. Mr Deane is able to buy the mill back for Tom because Jetsome mismanages it and because Wakem decides to sell it after his bastard son falls from his horse in a drunken stupor.

The mill's production of malt as well as flour gives it an important place in George Eliot's complex of figures of intoxication. By supplying local brewers, it participates in the manufacture of beer and ale. The addition of the malting, a process which arrests the germination of seeds (thus creating an opposition between beer and biological insemination), has formed a major event of Mr Tulliver's childhood. His later fears of replacement by Wakem and by his own son interfere with Tom's participation in normal processes of maturing and postpone, as it happens forever, the possibility of Tom's own seed bearing the fruit of offspring. Absorbed with making money, Tom dies before he can marry.

On the day Tom goes to St Ogg's to ask Uncle Deane for a job, he faces a series of reminders of his unhappy situation along his way. On his walk into St Ogg's, he is obliged to confront a series of drug-connected signifiers that impress him with the weight of his inherited debts. First, a friendly publican, 'one of his father's customers' (200), offends him by inquiring after Mr Tulliver's health 'with a confused, beery idea of being good-natured' (200). The incident precedes the unpleasantness of his talk to Uncle Deane, a talk during which Deane is 'not distinctly aware that he had not his port-wine before him' (203). Uncle Deane hurts Tom's feelings by putting his handsome King's Lorton handwriting at small value, and the Latin acquired so painfully from Mr Stelling leads him to suggest pharmacy as a likelier career than work at Guest and Company. The day concludes with Tom's recognition of a handbill announcing the coming sale. It is a day on which malt, beer, pharmacy, paternal sickness, port wine, and a printed handbill all mingle to bewilder a son forced to begin his adult life prematurely by assuming his father's debts.

When Tom finally recovers enough money to satisfy his father's creditors, the Golden Lion becomes the setting for some of the events of Mr Tulliver's final day on earth. But, having portrayed Mr Tulliver bragging about his wealth at the Golden Lion, entertaining Mr Riley with brandy and water, and increasing his consumption as the lawsuit goes on, the narrator does a sudden turnabout and makes a point of Mr Tulliver's sobriety in the chapter that narrates his death.

The chapter begins with the assertion that 'Mr Tulliver was an essentially sober man--able to take his glass and not averse to it, but never exceeding the bounds of moderation' (310). But after 'the party broke up in a very sober fashion at five o'clock' (311), Mr Tulliver is still stimulated. Again the narrator emphasizes his sobriety: 'The air of excitement that hung about him was but faintly due to good cheer or any stimulus but the potent wine of triumphant joy' (311). Soon, however, the pride in Tom that has made the health drinking so satisfying to Mr. Tulliver yields to his irritation that he does not chance to meet Wakem on the ride home. Instead, Wakem confronts him at the mill with accusations about his farming and his sobriety: 'You have been drinking, I suppose' (311). Tulliver first denies this accusation then attacks Wakem. A few hours after the attack he dies.

The abrupt emphasis on Mr Tulliver's sobriety distinguishes his beating of Wakem from a similar incident in 'Janet's Repentance,' in which Dempster dies partly from delirium tremens after whipping a servant during one of his daily bouts. Were Mr. Tulliver also drunk, George Eliot would have been repeating a sequence from the story that, of all her fiction, troubled her publisher most, largely because of the alcoholism. And because Maggie's addiction (to Stephen's love) is also metaphorical and thus differs from Janet Dempster's literal addiction, George Eliot is applying the same technique of relegating the addiction from the mimetic level to the metaphorical in both the father's and the daughter's plots.

The painful acquirement of literacy dramatized in this novel (Welsh 118) also relates to the rapid changes that both cause and result from aspects of the Condition of England. If Maggie achieves a moral victory when her father does not, it is partly because of the education she has scraped together from Philip's knowledge and from the copy of *The Imitation of Christ* which haphazardly falls into her hands to provide moral guidance.[14]

Mr Tulliver dies by the word, but this book saves Maggie: she thinks of it only seconds before she feels the waters of the flood. It serves her in her final crisis when the remembered words of Thomas à Kempis ease her away from a temptation, not for the bottle, but for Stephen's intoxicating love.[15] Mr Tulliver's conflict, on the other hand, is the conflict of the man who spells poorly, judges a book by its cover, and whose favorite--and indeed his last--word is *puzzling*. In the world of change St Ogg's has become, Tulliver takes for his enemy the law, that most fixed kind of writing.

The narrator emphasizes that the problem is generational in the chapter 'A Variation of Protestantism Unknown to Bossuet' which discusses the cost and necessity of a society's accommodating change while retaining a spiritual life and fellow-feeling.

Maggie and Tom Tulliver typify the 'young natures in many generations, that in the onward tendency of human things have risen above the mental level of the generation before them, to which they have been nevertheless tied by strongest fibres of their hearts' (239). This model duplicates George Eliot's view of the progress of democracy in the nineteenth century. Voters prepared by education replace a politics based on heredity, in a progress that destroys at the same time as it builds. In George Eliot's scheme, literacy may prepare people for political responsibility, but it also divides them from their parents.

In the second of her 'pastoral' novels, George Eliot has changed the father's enemy: no longer, as with Thias Bede, is it the bottle. Instead, being in conflict with the law he is at odds with himself (because of the Freudian identification of the father with the law) and, more importantly, with the written language that mystifies and ultimately kills him. In changing the father's enemy from Thias Bede's bottle to Mr Tulliver's law and literacy, George Eliot's metaphors of intoxication allow her to adopt addiction themes she has used since the *Scenes* but to do so in a way to which Blackwood could not take exception.

Nevertheless, in George Eliot's next novel, *Silas Marner*, an opium-taking mother (Molly Farren) and a heavy-drinking father (Mr Cass) partially restore the addiction theme to the literal level on which it occurs in the earliest fiction. This novel's setting forms a part of a progress that eventually, in *Felix Holt*, will return George Eliot, by way of Raveloe and Florence, to the Midlands settings of her early fiction, settings crowded with drinking places, drugs, diseases, doctors, and irresponsible parents and subject to abrupt political change.

In these later Warwickshire novels, having fulfilled her promise to Blackwood (and succeeded wildly in her writing of fiction), George Eliot regains the confidence to restore drinking and drugtaking to the mimetic level, but also sustains the metaphorical roles of her intoxicant signifiers. She continues to suggest linguistic and social volatility through metaphors of intoxication and public house signs that, like linguistic signs, can both yield and threaten meaning.

Because of the community importance of the Newdigate Arms and the other public houses of Nuneaton, Chilvers Coton, and Griff, young Mary Ann Evans had much experience connected with the drinking places of Warwickshire at the time of passage of the 1830 Beer Act. Despite her gender and her age at the time, she accumulated knowledge of events there that remained among her memories of her early home all her life. Her experiences resulted decades later in a recurring motif throughout her fiction which suggests a creative imagination formed at a time and in a place where drinking powerfully affected the community, a community where three ale houses–the Ram, the Hart, and the Castle–stood side by side in a row in the Market Place.

Notes

1. The fragment William Baker identifies as 'George Eliot's Napoleonic War Novel' mentions an innkeeper character who promises to fit among George Eliot's usually scurrilous publicans (Smith 15). Like the

opening to 'The Spanish Gypsy' in the Moorish tavern, her plan for
such a character testifies to her continuing fondness for the drinking-
place setting.
2. Lilian Shiman notes that the Beer Act, devised to reduce drunkenness
   by reducing consumption of spirits, most often effected the opposite
   by increasing consumption of beer. Norman Longman describes the
   results of the Act: 'The beer-shop explosion was felt in every corner
   of the country' (24).
3. Valerie Dodd describes both Nuneaton and Coventry as hard-drinking
   places; the latter was 'notorious for ignorance, immorality and
   drunkenness' (7)
4. Wolfgang Schivelsbusch emphasizes both the community and the
   lawlessness of the drinking place, when he observes that 'all rituals in
   pubs and bars issue from a collectivity, a *we*' (177 his italics) and that
   'somehow the rules of the outside world don't govern here' (167). He
   also points out that the drinking ritual of the *potlach,* a gift giving or
   sacrifice, 'creates an unstable social equilibrium' (173).
5. Mason makes this point in '*Middlemarch* and History.'
6. Peter Fenves' analysis of this passage largely coincides with mine,
   especially when he notes that Milby does not progress; it only repeats
   (429). See Chapter 5 on repetition and George Eliot's theory of
   alcoholism.
7. Haley draws attention to Carlyle's use of bodily disease as a metaphor
   for social sicknesses (59). The advertising signs Carlyle deplores sustain
   a long and flourishing relationship with alcohol and other suspect
   remedies (Altick *Presence* 549).
8. David Williams opens his biography of Lewes with a reference to the
   Bloomsbury pub of this name, 'long a favorite meeting place for
   unorthodox thinkers' (7), where Lewes met his medical-student friends
   during the 1830s.
9. In this section of *Middlemarch,* George Eliot alludes to the
   discrepancies between author's intentions and interpretations of the
   unstable text when Raffles interprets the business letter from Bulstrode
   accidentally found in Rigg Featherstone's fireplace. Rather than
   decoding whatever message Bulstrode may have intended at the time
   of writing, Raffles interprets only its address, from which he deduces
   that Bulstrode has accumulated wealth and position enough to be a
   suitable blackmail victim. Alexander Welsh depends partly on this

episode in his discussion of how the 'theme of blackmail in the later nineteenth century can be tied to developments in communication and in literacy itself' (7). David Carroll's examinations of George Eliot's *Conflict of Interpretations* extends the problem exemplified in the passage to all her fiction.

10   Fenves does a good job of relating Dempster's profession, his control over language, and the similarity of his role to the narrator's. He argues that in the character of Dempster George Eliot 'draws upon the analogy between language and society' (425).

11.   In her discussion of Maggie's book, Oliver Goldsmith's *Animated Nature*, Beryl Gray also notices this meaning to the name of the Pullets' home although she associates it more with a recipe from Roman times before it became a veterinary remedy (142).

12   Both Susan Sontag and Howard Brody describe *Philoctetes* as an important early text in which sickness forms the motif. The ninth volume of *Literature and Medicine* is devoted to other literary embodiments of this motif.

13   William Cohen observes that in the Biblical story, the motto to *The Mill*, 'in their death they were not divided,' applies to the deaths of Saul and Jonathan on the battlefield, rather than to any sort of sibling or romantic indivisibility. As a result, it adds emphasis to the questions concerning generational replacements George Eliot confronts in the relationships between the Tulliver children and their father.

14.   Michael Ragussis attributes Maggie's success to her development of metaphorical rather than tautological ways of naming. Whereas Mr Tulliver cannot progress beyond definitions that depend on repetition (most importantly, that water is water), Maggie develops fellow feeling by escaping a tautological definition of self. Ragussis argues persuasively that metaphors are necessary to fellow-feeling in that to develop sympathy the 'I' must be defined not as the 'I' but in terms outside the ego. Consequently, to be a Feuerbachian sympathizing being, one must be able to metaphorize, in particular one's self (130). See Chapter 5 of this work regarding tautology and addiction.

15.   In the scene in which Maggie first reads the *Imitation* the narrator contrasts 'enthusiasm' (256) with other methods of dealing with the hardships of poverty, conditions under which 'some have an emphatic belief in alcohol, and seek the *ekstasis* of outside standing-ground in gin' (256). Thus, unlike some kinds of religious texts such as the

sermons she describes as 'medicine for the mind' in 'Mr Gilfil,' the *Imitation* stimulates rather than stupefying.

When George Eliot and George Henry Lewes visited Prague, a setting in 'The Lifted Veil,' they were reading the works of Thomas DeQuincey.

5

Parables of Addiction

Do we not while away moments of inanity or fatigued waiting by repeating some trivial movement or sound, until the repetition has bred a want, which is incipient habit?

Silas Marner

When in *The Mill on the Floss* George Eliot removes the addictions of the characters from the mimetic level on which addictions occur in 'Janet's Repentance' to the figurative addictions of the father (to litigation) and the daughter (to passionate romance), George Eliot initiates a pattern she sustains in three more works of fiction: 'The Lifted Veil,' 'Brother Jacob,' and *Silas Marner*. In these three works, drinking/drug-related substances or activities represent habits which characters either do or do not conquer and help reveal the sophistication of her conception of addiction. By this time, George Eliot has expanded the related activities to involve not only drinking and drugs but also compulsions stemming from weaving, hoarding, gambling, and story-telling, particularly as associated with political volatility and diverted heritage. Indeed, all three of these narratives deal with compulsion and demonstrate an expertise on the topic of addiction unusual for her period. In light of D. A. Miller's description of reading itself as addictive, it is interesting that these parables include George Eliot's shortest works. They do not encourage a continued involvement with themselves.

'The Lifted Veil': Clairvoyant Ease

The oddities of 'The Lifted Veil,' written just before The *Mill on the Floss*, and George Eliot's ambivalence toward it, have evoked much speculation, begun by Sandra Gilbert and Susan Gubar, who see it as a parable of female creativity and identity, and continued by scholars who often employ genre, biographical, feminist, and/or psychoanalytic approaches.[1] In addition to responding well to these approaches, the story also works as a parable of addiction. Bertha Grant attracts Latimer despite his knowledge that she is poisonous and capable of killing him.   Latimer's behavior is clearly compulsive: he persists in courting Bertha despite his knowledge of her deadliness.   Young Latimer early succumbs to metaphorical intoxication. Released from the scientific curriculum inflicted on him at home as a corrective to his weak constitution, he describes his subsequent happy period in Geneva as 'a perpetual sense of exaltation, as if from a draught of delicious wine' (8). Nevertheless, like drinking alcohol, imbibing exaltation results in sickness. Powers of foresight he will repeatedly identify as 'diseased' (19, 21, 26) develop during his recovery and culminate in his prevision of Prague (where the Leweses read the work of Thomas DeQuincey during their 1858 visit [*GHL* X 129]). Soon afterward, he has his second prevision: of Bertha Grant whom he will persistently perceive as poisonous.

Initially, the problem the narrator associates with Latimer's previsions is that they are an easy shortcut, devoid of meaningful effort. He contrasts his second vision with a true remedy: his application of reviving *eau de cologne*, from which he draws delight 'because I had procured it by slow details of labor, and by no strange sudden madness' (17). Gradually, Bertha herself becomes an addictive intoxicant. After first seeing her in his vision Latimer behaves 'like a man determined to be sober in spite of wine' (17), though her acts 'intoxicate' him (24, 26, 44, 46) over and over. She 'besot[s]' (44) him, becomes his 'hashish' (45), and her lamia presence, especially the association with the Lucrezia Borgia portrait, makes him feel 'poisoned' (28). Even though Latimer knows in advance the outcome of marrying Bertha, he states, 'The fear of poison is feeble against the sense of thirst' (30). The confused dénouement of the story pits the doctor/friend's efforts at reviving the dead servant against Bertha's deliberate attempt to poison her husband to death.

Only a few weeks after finishing 'The Lifted Veil,' George Eliot wrote to Mrs Congreve of her desire to order 'cheerfulness from the druggist's' (3:79). Both the writing of 'The Lifted Veil' and this impulse toward escape through ease procured at the druggist's occurred during the period of the Liggins affair which occupied much of the spring of 1859.[2] Like any successful Victorian writer whose texts were subject to such hazards as misattribution, piracy, plagiarism, and unauthorized sequels, George Eliot had reason to fear the dangers of print Derrida and Plato attribute to the conditions of writing texts. But the first hazard, misattributed authorship, was especially close to George Eliot's experience. The Liggins difficulty, in which various Warwickshire neighbors proposed an obscure clergyman as the author of her early works, forced her to risk her tenuous reputation still further in claiming the authorship of her text and the money due her. Liggins was a notorious drunkard.

The burdens of pseudonymity, together with the interpretation of Bertha as an intoxicating substance against which Latimer struggles, help account for George Eliot's touchiness about 'Veil,' for once more this theme brought her into conflict with John Blackwood who detested many things about this story. She returned to the writing of *The Mill*, with its suddenly sober parent and only metaphorically addicted daughter, then went on to disguise Silas Marner's addiction as miserliness rather than portraying it as opium- or drink-related. Nevertheless, scholars connect Latimer and Silas through their similarities as being subject to many of the conditions usually associated with nineteenth-century women: introspectiveness, powerlessness, and, in Silas's case, engaged in incessant weaving.

'Brother Jacob': Sugary Ease

'Brother Jacob,' written close in time to 'Veil,' has also earned a good deal of interest from psychoanalytic critics, in particular Ruby

Redinger who sees an important similarity to *Silas Marner* in its concerns with money and family. The stolen guineas in 'Brother Jacob' place this story, too, among George Eliot's plots of intoxication and addiction because David Faux gains his money by selling innutrient sugared confection. George Eliot's notes on medicines, as quoted in Chapter 2, which include honey among the substances with medicinal uses, encourage the interpretation of sugar as a drug. When the idiot brother Jacob interrupts David Faux as he is burying his mother's stolen hoard, the narrator strengthens the link through an allusion to *The Tempest*. Offering Jacob a yellow lozenge produces 'as great an ecstasy at its new and complex savour as Caliban at the taste of Trinculo's wine' (8). Later, David eludes his brother's embrace and manages to slip off to Liverpool to make his escape to the West Indies only by getting the burdensome Jacob drunk on beer.

On his return from the West Indies, David sets himself up as a purveyor of sweets who caters to the Grimworth housewife's desire to avoid the 'slow details of labor' (17), a desire opposite to the effort Latimer values when he contrasts his labor in securing the *eau de cologne* with the ease of his previsions. David Faux resembles George Eliot's publican characters in that on his return he continues to try to reach his goals by plying other characters with liquor as a way to seduce the suspicious people of Grimworth and to solidify his position among them. As suitor to Penny Palfrey, he presses on her father the Jamaican rum he has brought back with him from the West Indies and reminds Mr Palfrey of his expectations of a continuing supply. His other techniques for ingratiating himself include claiming a false ancestor, and he frequents the Woolpack, whose name, associated with fibers, anticipates the weaving metaphor of *Silas Marner*. When Jacob turns up to embarrass David and destroy his reputation, the confectioner attempts to squirm out of the situation by attributing Jacob's witless affection to drunkenness. Thus characters and metaphors from both stories develop out of plots involving addiction, Latimer its victim and David its agent. In the character of Silas, George Eliot synthesizes some of these elements. As a weaver, Silas gains his living in one of the occupations most important in the Warwickshire of George Eliot's youth, where weaving and drinking interacted. She grew up in and near towns where both men and women operated their noisy handlooms at home rather than in mills. According to most reports, the weavers scarcely began their week's work until they had stretched their Sunday drinking as long as they could. Exhausted and hungover, they staggered to their looms at midweek and worked without stopping until they began the desperate cycle again. In *Silas*, George Eliot draws on aspects of the these conditions in characters and plots related to weaving, writing, and intoxication.

Silas Marner *and the 'Logic of Habit'*

The play of the intoxication metaphor creates three new ways of looking at *Silas*: as a parable of addiction similar to 'The Lifted Veil,' as a comment on the dangers and possibilities inherent in the workings of language, and as a proposal and a warning regarding solutions to the sociopolitical problems regarded as the Condition of England in the nineteenth century. A number of important scholarly descriptions of *Silas* as a fairy tale or a fable depend partly on its comparative vagueness as to time and remoteness as to place. But George Eliot's settings in *Silas*, though spread over decades rather than years and less precisely geographically located than the *Scenes*, nevertheless include Reform-era temporal detail and Midlands physical detail at the same time that the remoteness fulfils her plan to move her action out of Warwickshire.[3]

As a recovery parable, the novel narrates how Silas overcomes his addictions, not to drink or drugs, but to the seductive repetitiousness of two acts: weaving and counting a hoard of money. It also demonstrates a model of responsible parenthood whose rights come to outweigh those of the biological parents.[4] Finally, the novel raises questions about various kinds of volatile and addictive forms of language and, politically, offers hope for tranquillity in England through its peaceful and orderly replacement of the privileged irresponsibility of Godfrey by conscientious Silas, whose fatherhood to Eppie replaces a fractured hereditary model without creating disorder. In this plot, several aspects of the intoxicant metaphor interrelate to dramatize ways of dealing with addiction, problematic meaning, and political disorder.

In *Silas* George Eliot offers her most complete theory of addiction to date. With hoarding, weaving, opium taking, and drinking, she groups a kind of ritual talk often found in protoliterate societies such as Raveloe, all of which offer the seductive charms of repetition with little or no variation. When Dunsey steals his money, Silas is obliged to go cold turkey from his evening ritual of counting his guineas, a ritual during which 'their form and colour were like the satisfaction of a thirst to him' (68).

After the theft results in unavoidable variations in his only two activities, weaving and counting money, which both repeat one small action over and over, Eppie arrives to aid in his recovery by creating further constant daily variation for him, for, as the child grows, each new challenge of parenthood differs from its predecessors. The incident with the coal hole, for example, demonstrates how little Silas can anticipate Eppie's capers. His consultations with Dolly Winthrop not only help him develop ever-changing strategies for dealing with Eppie, but in contrast with the repetitiousness of his previous activities, they nourish sociability rather than the isolation of the solitary addict. Indeed during his hoarding days Silas has regarded his money as his offspring.[5]

By the end of the novel, Silas even finds the mild stimulation of his pipe unappealing and unnecessary. In contrast with Molly and Godfrey, the responsible parent earns his paternity through conquering his addiction, in his case not to opium or alcohol, but to repetition itself. At the same time, the orderly village hierarchy survives despite numerous threats, many of which have to do with language, and many of which originate at the Rainbow.

Traditionally seen as an important center of Raveloe community, the Rainbow, in addition to unifying the villagers by providing a place for drinking and conversation, helps affirm its hierarchy.[6] But the marriages that have anything at all to do with the drinking place all suffer in some way. The narrator blames the widowerhood of Squire Cass for his willingness to drink there with his inferiors. The narrative of a second abruptly ended marriage, that of Godfrey to Molly, also has associations with the Rainbow. The marriage is a plot through which Dunsey hopes to replace Godfrey as heir when the Squire discovers the existence of his daughter-in-law, a plot which, if it succeeds, will thereby disrupt the pattern of descent which depends on primogeniture. After Dunsey and Godfrey decide to sell Wildfire to make up the rent money, Godfrey concludes his very bad bargain with the brother who wants to replace him by going to the local drinking place, where bargains are often sealed, but going without the other party.

The Rainbow and its product also play a part in some of the worst decisions Dunsey makes regarding the sale of Wildfire. After he agrees with Bryce on the terms of the sale, 'a draught of brandy' (84) prompts his decision to join the hunt rather than to deliver the horse to its buyer right away. He stakes the horse when he is rushing to catch up with the pack after a stop to adjust a stirrup. But it is rather language (Dunsey's angry curses) that delays his rejoining the hunt, and the delay then necessitates the careless haste that kills the horse. He decides to abandon the dead horse and walk to Silas's cottage where he hopes to negotiate a loan that will replace the rent money, and the narrator attributes this decision to his anticipation of telling the story of his feat to 'a select circle at the Rainbow' (86). Thus its potential narrative value at the public house helps motivate him to persevere in his trek, so that he ends up in the vicinity of Silas's cottage just on the very night that the weaver has gone out and left the door unlocked.

The third marriage associated with the Rainbow, the wedding of Nancy Lammeter's parents, dramatizes the problematic of language and meaning and also has to do with narrative. On the night of the theft of Silas's gold, the Rainbow forms the setting for a recital of the wedding anecdote, part of a repeated ritual of local oral tradition. In the wedding anecdote, Mr Macey confronts serious issues when he tries to identify the agent responsible for formalizing the marriage: the spoken word of the preacher, the intentions of the participants, or the written register.

As a result of some heavy drinking to combat the cold of the winter morning, the preacher has bungled the wording, reversing the couple's genders. Afterward, Drumlow reassures Macey that it is the 'regester that does it' (102). But the audience is left to suspect that something is wrong somewhere for, although the marriage turns out fine, the bride dies early, so that Macey's anecdote ultimately confirms the binding power of neither the spoken vows, the written register, nor the couple's intentions. In Mr Macey's metaphor, none of them works effectively as glue.[7] By this point, George Eliot has assembled the elements she usually includes in her intoxicant complex. The problematic weddings affect orderly descent. The tailor conducts discussions about language in a public house.

But Mr Macey's tale of doubtful marriage is not the topic that immediately precedes Silas's interruption, for the group moves from talk of the wedding incident to their reminiscences about the previous owner of Mr Lammeter's estate: 'A Lunnon tailor, some folks said, as had gone mad wi' cheating' (102). Mr Macey contrasts this tailor, believed to be ashamed of his origins, with himself, the last of a family proud of being tailors. He points out that his own pride results partly from having inherited his trade and partly from the manifestation of this inheritance on the sign over his door. Meanwhile an inheritance plot enters in the story of the London tailor, Mr Cliff, whose motivation in building up his stables stems from a desire for his son to gain an important badge of class status: a good seat on horseback. When the weak boy disappoints his father by dying, the tailor bequeaths his estate to the charity which then sells it to Mr Lammeter.

The stables are the setting for the ghost story, a legend of restless horses and restless corpses named in honor of absence. According to Mr Macey, 'Cliff's Holiday' has been the name of it ever sin' I were a boy; that's to say, some said as it was the holiday Old Harry gev him from roastin, like' (103). The London tailor replaces the original owner of the Warrens; the tailor's son dies before he can replace his father; Mr Lammeter replaces Cliff, none of them a direct inheritance. Evidence of ghosts suggests another incomplete replacement, for the ghost of Cliff continues to make appearances in the stables of Mr Lammeter.

Then, after a gap created by a chapter break, the image of Silas appears among the drinkers at the Rainbow so suddenly and palely that the drinkers suspect he is of the same species as the ghost of the tailor. When Silas bursts in on the discussion, his loss replaces a number of absences that have gone before.

During this part of the novel, George Eliot juxtaposes the vacancies that concern the people in Raveloe with the linguistic problems that turn up in such episodes as the Lammeter/Osgood wedding story. By presenting a series of vacancies (absences) in the center of her novel, George Eliot emphasizes repetition and replacement, two processes that can either generate or obliterate meaning, partly by associating them with politics and alcohol.

George Eliot drafts the problem of inherited versus merited privilege and power mainly in Godfrey's plot. When Godfrey abandons his paternal duties, Silas is there to assume them. The aged weaver replaces the young squire as father to Eppie, a replacement the young girl endorses, indeed votes in favor of, when Godfrey tries belatedly to re-replace Silas. Less obviously, he becomes father-in-law to Aaron Winthrop, thus replacing Dolly's husband, himself (as Kristin Brady has noted) 'a man who drinks' (110). Under similar circumstances, elected politicians should replace hereditary rulers only if they are sufficiently responsible. Part of Silas's responsibility consists in overcoming an addiction.

Repetition, Vacancies, and Language

In 'Plato's Pharmacy,' Derrida notes that one condition for the interpretation of the written word is the absence of the author:

unlike speech, writing circulates at a distance from its author/father who then loses the opportunity for modifying or correcting interpretations of it. Absence therefore both permits and imperils the meaningful interpretation of written language. In *Silas*, George Eliot presents a series of absences throughout the narrative which permit the instabilities that grant latitude for both interpretation and for the fluidity of parental roles that occurs when Silas replaces Godfrey as Eppie's father. The absences in *Silas* include: Silas's money, Cliff's Holiday, some significant chapter breaks, and the absent father, all mutually echoed in the other absences both physical and metaphorical.[8] On the topic of absence, even the landlord of the Rainbow and Dr Kimble agree. When the company suggests that the inharmonious Mr Tookey should get his Christmas money for *not* singing, Mr Snell feels an alarm 'that paying people for their absence was a principle dangerous to society' (99). The publican agrees with Kimble the apothecary on the undesirable economic results of absence.

And the absence most riveting to the attention of Raveloe is the loss of Silas's gold. According to Dunsey, cottagers hide their hoards in only three places: the bed, the thatch, or a hole beneath the floor. Because Silas has chosen the space under the bricks, he learns of the theft by confronting the absence of his gold, signified by the empty hole.[9] After the loss of the gold, announced of course at the Rainbow, a gap occurs in his life before the arrival of Eppie who is repeatedly described as a replacement for his guineas.

The loss of the gold necessitates that most of the community adjourn to the Rainbow to try to solve the crime. Outside in the yard, Mr Macey and his friends ponder about the tinder-box discovered near the Stonepits, while inside Mr Snell remembers a suspicious, foreign-looking peddler and connects him with this provocative clue. The arcs of the narrative provided at the Rainbow to solve the mystery conduct its talkers only to a totally insubstantial end, the non-existent peddler.

Metaphors involving both gaps and threads also connect Silas with his product. Despite the apparent narrowness of his humdrum life, the narrator tells us, the gold has formed its center: 'the object round which its fibres had clung' (129). The equation of Silas's life with these fibers combines his weaving and his lost money. The gold he earns now acquires a new significance: no longer a means of marking empty time, it acts as a 'fresh reminder of his loss' (129).[10] Silas needs to fill his 'blank with grief' (129). The anticipation of an 'empty evening-time' creates agonizing mental 'chasms' (130).

By Chapter 11 more absences are conspicuous. Dunsey is gone, though unlamented; Molly will soon follow him. The New Year's Eve setting suggests great temporal instability. The Red House, with its inn-like name, celebrates with an Open House (allowing the lower classes to look on, though not participate) which puts it into a community role similar to the Rainbow's.[11]

Silas's gap fills on New Year's Eve when Eppie arrives to replace the gold. Just as Silas has run to the Rainbow to report the theft, he rushes to the Red House to report the death of Molly, the arrival of Eppie, and the need for a doctor. On this night of Godfrey's decisive rejection of his wife and child, the Red House is already a maelstrom of drug signifiers. Indeed these have surrounded the Cass family from the beginning of the novel.[12] Described throughout as 'tankards' (73, 121, 211), the family has two sons: Dunsey, whose neighbors believe he is likely to 'enjoy his drink the more when other people went dry' (73) and Godfrey, defended at the party by Ben Winthrop who applies an alcoholic metaphor when he refers to the heir as 'a pot o' good ale' (160).

But the most narcotic of all metaphors applied to the Casses lies in Godfrey's name.[13] The young man who has succumbed to marriage with an ex-barmaid opium addict shares his name with the most popular brand of children's opium, Godfrey's Cordial, a name, in fact, which by midcentury had become generic for sweetened tincture of opium, of which 12,000 weekly doses were estimated swallowed by the children of Coventry during 1862 (Parsinnen 33, 42). Godfrey's wife is full of opium on the literal level; he, on the figurative level.

George Eliot's narrator emphasizes Molly's conscious

responsibility for her addicted state: 'Molly knew that the cause of her dingy rags was not her husband's neglect, but the demon Opium, to whom she was enslaved' (112). She cannot engage in self-reproof because these are not sentiments likely to 'make their way to Molly's poisoned chamber, inhabited by no higher memories than those of a barmaid's paradise of pink ribbons and gentlemen's jokes' (164). Whereas Janet Dempster's literal addiction gives way to Maggie's figurative craving for Stephen, in *Silas Marner* George Eliot restores a woman's addiction to the literal level.

The scenes leading up to Godfrey's rejection of this already poisoned wife and their daughter (drastic interruptions of proper descent) contain much drinking as well as other examples of the metaphor. During the holidays the villagers wake up with toast-and-ale and the ritual language of the Athanasian Creed (141). At the Red House the Christmas guests again engage in ritual language: 'the annual Christmas talk' (141) of Mr Kimble's experiences 'when he walked the London hospitals thirty years ago' (141), all accompanied by 'a strong steaming odor of spirits-and water' (141). Meanwhile, Godfrey carries on an anxious inward dialogue about Molly that persists despite 'much drinking' (143).

Habit and Language

Not only do these events go forth amid usual Victorian imagery of language and social problems as drugs and diseases, but George Eliot continues to emphasize linguistic processes. Repetition without replacement stultifies meaning rather than producing it. And repetition without variation explicitly equates with addiction.

The narrator of *Silas* attributes Silas's hoarding to repetition: 'Do we not while away moments of inanity or fatigued waiting by repeating some trivial movement or sound, until the repetition has bred a want, which is incipient habit?' (67). Repetition afflicts scholars as well as weavers: 'instead of a loom and a heap of guineas, they have had some erudite research, some ingenious project or some well-knit theory' (69). Here weaving metaphors mix with actual weaving: Silas's loom is a traditional symbol of a wine press (and therefore associated with the printing press); the scholar's theory is 'well-knit' (69). But, unlike the scholar's, Silas's repetitions are drained of significance. The gold that he has formerly equated with possibilities for generosity is now only a marker of passing time. The narrator's description of Silas's hoarding as 'golden wine' (72) to him, draws attention to both its attractiveness and its addictiveness.

Repetition also accounts for Silas's loss of his gold. The night that Dunsey is lurking about with the guineas on his mind, he feels safe leaving his door unlocked because of the force of habit and repetition: 'The lapse of time during which a given event has not happened is, in this logic of habit, constantly alleged as a reason why the event should never happen, even when the lapse of time is precisely the added condition which makes the event imminent. A man will tell you that he has worked in a mine for forty years, unhurt by an accident, as a reason why he should apprehend no danger, though the roof is beginning to sink . . . This influence of habit was necessarily strong in a man whose life was so monotonous as Marner's' (90). Silas goes out on his errand, leaving the meat on his key and his door unlocked, and creates the opportunity for the theft.

George Eliot also associates alcoholism with repetition. She attributes the heavy drinking of 'our rural forefathers' (such as the Casses) to their monotonous lives. When they drink they 'say over again with eager emphasis the things they had said already any time that twelve-month' (80). On New Year's, the Squire's drunken hospitality also manifests itself through repetition: 'In higher spirits' (152) than early in the day, he 'felt it quite pleasant to fulfill the hereditary duty of being noisily jovial and patronizing: the large silver snuff-box was in active service and was offered without fail to all neighbors from time to time, however often they might have declined the favor' (152).

George Eliot here is reviving a description of drunkenness from 'Janet.' After the boisterous night at the Red Lion when Dempster

returns with the news that the bishop has decided against Mr
Tryan's sermons, the company at the Red Lion celebrates until
'several friends of sound religion were conveyed home with some
difficulty, one of them showing a dogged determination to seat
himself in the gutter' (283).[14] The narrator sums up the Raveloe
attitude toward the traditional holidays, hallowed by custom: social
duties consist of exchanges of 'visits and poultry with due
frequency, paying each other old-established compliments in sound
traditional phrases, passing well-tried personal jokes, urging your
guests to eat and drink too much out of hospitality, and eating and
drinking too much in your neighbor's house to show that you liked
your cheer' (158). Repetition with variation allows meaning;
repetition without variation is both cause and effect of intoxication.

Among the most serious offenders among George Eliot's
characters, her publicans engage in constant repetition, often in the
form of narrative. Nineteenth-century teetotalism blamed publicans
for intemperance. Brian Harrison quotes a characterization that
depends on an identification of publicans as diabolic (but also
paternal), a parody of the Lord's Prayer called 'The Publican's
Prayer,' which begins, 'Our Father which are in Hell' (426). George
Eliot's publicans from Mr Casson through Mrs Dollop conform to
nineteenth-century perceptions not only by distributing drink but
by engaging in meaningless talk. In *Silas Marner*, Mr Snell makes the
most meaningless statement in the novel to a group of drinkers
gathered in his public house. When he asserts to the group around
the fire that 'the Rainbow's the Rainbow' (97), he articulates a
sentence almost entirely empty of significance because of its
repetition without variation or replacement.[15] Even the house with
the pastoral name succumbs to a troublesome meaninglessness and
ultimately is no more a center of stability than Dempster's Red
Lion, Tulliver's Golden Lion, or, indeed, Nello's Apollo and Razor.

But replacement is the remedy that restores order and provides
meaning. Both Godfrey and the Squire look forward to acquiring
Nancy Lammeter's dowry and to her replacement of the long-dead
women of the family. Eppie takes the place of the stolen gold, and

this replacement then validates the most important replacement of the novel. On the one hand, Silas's triumph over Godfrey reaffirms the Victorian value of responsibility; on the other, the narrative clearly favors the interruption of biological descent in the replacement that occurs when Eppie chooses Silas. By favoring the rights of the adoptive father, the narration suggests the value of a process essential to generating meaning through language and at the same time acquiesces to the necessity for a new, non-hereditary political order.

Considering issues of meaning also helps make sense of Silas's unfulfilling return to Lantern Yard. The trouble with the people of Lantern Yard is that they overinterpret. Silas's fits cannot be purely physical: they must convey some divine meaning. The lots are not merely lots: they must indicate Silas's guilt. And money carries specific significance of the Divine Will, too. Because of its potential use for charitable purposes, 'for twenty years, mysterious money had stood to him as the symbol of earthly good' (19). So accustomed is Silas to the overinterpretation typical in Lantern Yard that he gives up his herbal healing because of his doubts about the necessity of the herbs to the cure. According to Silas's speculations, the word of prayer ought to be able to do it all. He concludes that 'herbs could have no efficacy without prayer, and that prayer might suffice without herbs' (11). Unable to resolve this doubt, he abandons a medical role he is suited for and breaks a link with his mother who has bequeathed him this knowledge.

When Silas and Eppie visit the site of Lantern Yard to gain some explanation of Silas's expulsion, they find that the building and the congregation have disappeared without a trace and have been replaced by a factory. Thus the narrative punishes the overinterpreters of Lantern Yard with oblivion. But this visit also directs attention ahead to the other yard, the yard of the Rainbow where the wedding party gathers to celebrate not only Eppie's wedding but also Silas's fatherhood.

In *Silas*, George Eliot exploits every detail of the drinking place setting: the sign displaying its name, as well as the organization of space inside and the yard outside, all of which help affirm the Raveloe social hierarchy. Although Squire Cass and his sons drink at the same house as do their neighbors, they drink in hierarchically subdivided spaces of parlour and kitchen. Among the humbler drinkers, the hierarchy continues downward as the drinkers distance themselves from the fire according to the price they pay for their tipple. Drinkers of spirits have more prestige and a warmer seat than ale drinkers. Like the stripes of a rainbow that mingle only slightly around their edges, the social classes maintain their identity and mingle very little at the Raveloe public house.

The Rainbow accommodates the ambiguity of the *Pharmakon* perhaps better than any of George Eliot's other public houses. The action at the Rainbow results in diverted heritage and meaninglessness, specifically through their connections with fractured marriages and volatile absences. At the same time, the political conservatism attributed to George Eliot accords with the happy ending in which the marriage of a contented working class couple reaffirms order in the village which escapes strife. She expresses her wariness of the consequences of class mobility in her desire for people to just accept, indeed to choose, the duties of the station into which they were born. The Rainbow, consequently, is simultaneously healer and threat even though it avoids the greater potential for evil connected with most of the drinking places in George Eliot's fiction. In *Felix Holt*, another working-class character professes to choose the class into which he was born over the mobility George Eliot finds threatening. Meanwhile, in *Romola*, she creates her most unstable community to date.

Notes

1. Following the earlier lead of U. C. Knoepflmacher and Elliott Rubenstein, these include Carroll Viera, Millie Kidd, James Diedrick, Peter Allan Dale, June Szirotny, and Beryl Gray.
2. The Liggins affair, in which a Nuneaton man fraudulently claimed to

have written George Eliot's fiction, demonstrates one of the hazards of authorship.

3. Local histories associate Raveloe with both Marston Jabbett and with Bulkington, two villages which lie within a few miles of Griff House. Patrick Swindon also locates Raveloe in Warwickshire (47).

4. In *George Eliot and Herbert Spencer*, Nancy Paxton approaches the replacement of the biological parent with the responsible parent as George Eliot's critique of Spencer's belief in the biological fitness of women, and most naturally beautiful women, as parents. Because Silas replaces Godfrey as well as Nancy as the responsible parent to Eppie, the gender of the failed parent is, I believe, less important to my argument than to Paxton's. Bernard Semmel focuses on this replacement to prompt a discussion of the 'politics of national inheritance.'

5. To Jeff Nunokawa, Eppie's arrival frees Silas from what George Eliot casts as an illicit, masturbatory contact between his body and his coins, from 'the intercourse between gold and bodies that makes Silas Marner a purely sensuous subject' (289). In both his interpretation and mine, Eppie replaces the money and acts as therapy, though for differing conditions. I am willing to concede, although not to deal with, the masturbatory quality of Silas's evening joys partly because of the repetitiousness of that activity.

6. Although generally seen as a source of unity, the public house scenes have elicited mixed estimates from George Eliot scholars. Henry Auster believes the villagers at the Rainbow are 'argumentative' (174); Jerome Thale believes 'the famous Rainbow scene may suggest community, but it also suggests dullness and bad temper' (quoted in Auster 194). Writing on 'The Lifted Veil,' Carol Viera includes a note observing that the Victorians did not always find rainbows encouraging and that, because Silas does not find his gold there, this Rainbow yields only false promise. Felicia Bonaparte ('Carrying the Word of the Lord'), U. C. Knoepflmacher (*Limits of Realism*), and Henry Alley ('Balance of Male and Female') are among those who emphasize the positive aspects of rainbows in connection with the Raveloe public house

These scenes also tantalize readers who cannot fathom how a Victorian woman could gain enough knowledge of these gendered spaces to represent public house culture so accurately. One author, writing in 1931, the high point, as I have argued elsewhere, for biographical absurdities, depends on the Rainbow scenes in *Silas* to assert that they 'could not have been done by man or woman unfamiliar with the inward inspiration of inns. She liked inns. She liked to sit in them and listen to the gossip and she, by some mixture of masculine ease and feminine dignity, was accepted by the company when a woman in a bar-parlour was an outrage on the company and on womanhood' (Burke 29).

7. Gilbert argues that Eppie's function as commodity supplies the marital glue Mr Macey desires.

8. In connection with Carroll's identification of this novel's hermeneutic struggle in its characters' desperation to 'bridge chasms' (145), he mentions a number of its gaps: social gaps among its characters, the duality of its plot structure, and the 16-year interlude in the narrative. Alan Bellringer also notices *Silas's* 'large time gaps' and places them among the 'interesting narrative effects' (63) in George Eliot's shorter fiction. Like Carroll, Stewart Crehan counts class differences on the list of 'discrepancies and fault-lines' in *Silas* and draws attention to its concern with periods of silence

9. See the Introduction to J. Hillis Miller's *Fiction and Repetition* regarding such vacancies. In *The Classics Reclassified*, Richard Armour focuses on this passage in his parody of a *Silas Marner* quiz. His suggested Question Five reads: 'If you were looking for a cottager's hoard and it wasn't in the thatch, in the bed, or in a hole in the floor, would you: a. give up, b. call Sherlock Holmes, c. go straight.'

10. Gilbert argues that Silas's gold is empty of social meaning ('Daughteronomy'). But to Silas the gold has signified good because, although only potentially, it could allow him to perform acts of charity. Indeed, he does not acknowledge the meaninglessness of his gold until Eppie's arrival.

11. Brian Swann links the Red House with the Rainbow as sites for choral comment by the community (118).

12. Regarding the breakfast ale drinking part of the daily habits of the Casses (which I mention in Chapter 1), Swindon acknowledges that ale for breakfast would not necessarily singularize the Squire during much of the eighteenth century. By the time of the temporal setting of *Silas*, however, tea had become the 'established breakfast drink' (66). He also believes that the Squire's breakfast ale helps suggest he is 'overfond of

the bottle' (66). Swindon connects the Rainbow scenes with Adrian Brouwer's canvas, 'Peasants Playing Cards in a Tavern,' and Teniers's 'The King Drinks.'

13. Although this interpretation of Godfrey's name differs from Bonaparte's in 'Carrying the Word of the Lord,' i.e, 'God-free,' it does not conflict.

14. According to Carroll, in 'Mr Gilfil' repetition goes forth mainly in the frame (along with most of the drinking) which 'consists of repetition, recurrence, and choric songs' (57). Earlier he argues that for the narrative to proceed 'repetition has to give way to difference and Gilfil has to be separated from the community' (47).

15. Michael Ragussis makes a similar point about Mr Tulliver who creates such tautological definitions for 'water,' 'river,' and 'Wakem.' But Bonaparte believes Snell's talk is a model of 'Hegelian synthesis' (45).

Santa Croce, with its piazza and the 1863 facade.

6

Romola: *San Buonvino*

> . . . for bating Covent Garden, I can hit on
> No place that's called 'Piazza' in Great Britain
>
> Byron's 'Beppo'

It is frequently said of British pubs that they are uniquely British. They are not like American bars or French cafes or Italian wine shops. In *Romola*, George Eliot, perhaps acknowledging the quintessential Britishness of one of her favorite settings, does not attempt to substitute Italian wine shops for her public houses. Instead, she disperses activities she has heretofore located in inns and taverns and their yards among three settings: Nello's barber shop, a variety of *piazze*, and the monasteries of the religious orders, especially San Marco. Volatile political action; rearrangements of biological, economic, and political heritage; and dramatizations of all kinds of instabilities occur in all three locations. The patterns among the drug figures elsewhere in the fiction help create related patterns within this novel, often considered a failure because of its creaking historical machinery. 'The Florentine Joke' chapter, in particular, fits less awkwardly in *Romola* in light of its participation in the complex of drug/disease figures.

Public Houses, Inns, and Monasteries

George Eliot's conversions of public houses and their yards into Florentine settings that accommodate similar kinds of action support the traditional scholarly notion of *Romola* as costume drama: nineteenth-century Positivists all dressed up as early Renaissance Florentines.[1] Although scholars locate these similarities mainly in the Comtean philosophy expressed or implied in *Romola*, other similarities between George Eliot's 1832 English settings and her 1492 Florence include a common political volatility, a medium of print newly powerful in both cultures, and a common dread of an anticipated pestilence. But George Eliot gets even more specific in drawing her parallels between nineteenth-century England and fifteenth-century Florence, for she repeats some of the specific social, economic, and political conditions from the Midlands England of her own childhood in her version of the Italian setting so popular in Victorian fiction and poetry.

In early nineteenth-century Warwickshire, as in Renaissance Florence, the economic and political stability of the community depended on the state of its cloth and ribbon industry. Consequently, George Eliot's childhood in Warwickshire gave her every reason to associate economic and political volatility with textiles.

Romola's Florentines are also weavers and dyers.[2] Two merchant guilds of fifteenth-century Florence, the *Arte della Lama* (wool) and the *Arte di Calimala* (dressing and dyeing) were, at the time of George Eliot's setting, making good profits from selling the red wool cloth they produced on international markets. In 1861, on the trip taken specifically to research *Romola*, the Leweses made repeated efforts to visit a silk weaver working near the Porta San Niccolo in the Oltrarno. The poverty of his living conditions corresponded to the economic insecurity of weavers in the Midlands, a matter often referred to by authors dealing with the Condition of England.

The Rucellai family, among the most prominent in Florence both then and now, also gained their success from textiles, specifically from transformations achieved by dyeing. Their name, according to the narrator, is 'prettily symbolic' (402). It refers to a species of lichen which 'having drunk a great deal of light' (402) yields the dye which the Rucellai transform to money and power.

As in *Middlemarch* (one of George Eliot's most clearly identifiable Warwickshire novels), in which Bulstrode turns profits from dyeing and weaving and banking into such projects as the Middlemarch Infirmary, many of the thirteenth- and fourteenth-century buildings of Florence–Santa Croce, Santa Maria Novella, the Duomo itself–were built through alliances between the banking and textile businesses.

The monasteries scattered throughout every area of Florence resembled the inns of Warwickshire in a number of important ways. Like travelers' inns, monasteries offered hospitality. Indeed, they served as direct ancestors of public houses since many British inns came into being when Henry VIII's disestablishment of the monasteries left travelers stranded without a drink, a meal, or a bed for the night. On their 1861 research trip, the Leweses lodged at monasteries at LaVerna and Camaldoli on their journey through the rugged hills southeast of Florence, despite problems created by her gender.

In addition to letting rooms, monasteries, like English inns, were multi-purpose buildings in which, as in public houses, medical treatment and surgery occurred. They often distilled and brewed, and they contained pharmacies and libraries, two features of which George Eliot and Lewes had direct experience. When they wanted to see the Ghirlandajo frescoes at Santa Maria Novella in 1861, they secured permission from the '*Direttore della farmacia*' (*GHL* XI 180). Because the Dominican pharmacy, the *Officina Profumo-Farmaceutica*, produced perfumes as well as medicines, it conveys the intimacy of the relationship between drugs and the perfume version of the *Pharmakon* George Eliot will stress in connection with Esther's attar of roses in *Felix Holt*. At Camaldoli, Lewes visited the pharmacy and submitted his cold to the treatment of the '*Padre Speziale*' whose potion calmed and refreshed him.

Finally, like the alehouses that disseminated information by means of circulated and displayed chapbooks, handbills, placards, broadsides, and oral tradition, monasteries were centers for the transmission of culture, in particular narrative: their inmates worked at illuminating and copying manuscripts and applying colors to wood, canvas, or wall, often-poisonous colors purchased from the pharmacist. Again like some nineteenth-century public houses, monasteries contained libraries. Two of these in particular won George Eliot's admiration during her travels in Italy: Michaelangelo's library at San Lorenzo in Florence and the Ambrosian library in Milan.

And, like the public houses, the monasteries in George Eliot's fiction accommodate conflict, instability, and manipulations of language. Dino reports his fearful dream of Romola's marriage in the Chapter Room just off the outer cloister in San Marco. In Savonarola's cell, Tito manages to trick the monk into self-betrayal. In the large and graceful Michelozzo library at San Marco, Savonarola, along with the other monks who refuse to arm themselves, succumb to Dolfo Spini's attack. Consequently, George Eliot's monasteries do not serve as a detail in a reassuring affirmation of a divinely ordered way of life for a Victorian writer envious of the supposed stability of the Middle Ages (as often occurs elsewhere in Victorian literature in the medievalism of Tennyson and Morris). Instead, George Eliot's monasteries in *Romola*, like her drinking-place settings elsewhere, accommodate action that emphasizes conflict and instability.

The Apollo and Razor and the Florentine Piazze

The Apollo and Razor, Nello's barbershop on the Piazza San Giovanni, also resembles the inns in George Eliot's fiction. Traditional connections between surgery and barbering parallel with the medical and more conspicuously the surgical functions of British public houses. The sign of Nello's shop (a dual image like, for example, the Crown and Anchor) depicts Apollo and a shadowy hand that represents the First Barber. Nello's grandiose connection between the physician god and the barber has Apollo 'bestowing the razor on the Triptolemus of our craft' (78). As the prototypical farmer, Triptolemus participates in George Eliot's metaphors equating the dissemination of the word with the sowing of seed. Nello's sign carries as many diverse implications as do those of the Two Travellers or the Rainbow.

Furthermore, Nello himself resembles the publicans of George Eliot's fiction. Her *Romola* notebooks confirm that in this character she turns Burchiello, the barber who absorbed much of her interest during her research for *Romola*, into a Warwickshire publican. Like Mr Casson of the Donnithorne Arms, he is pretentious. Like Mr Snell of the Rainbow, he takes refuge in non-committal: 'Heaven forbid I should fetter my impartiality by entertaining an opinion' (82). Mr Snell says, 'I'm for holding with both sides; for, as I say, the truth lies between 'em' (105).

Although he runs a barber shop and not a wine shop, Nello derives his own metaphors from the language of intoxication. His loquacity is 'like an overfull bottle' (73), and he considers his own understanding 'good wine' (184), but himself an 'empty cask' (184). Again as in nineteenth-century England, the competition is the druggist down the street where 'a dull conclave' meets at 'the sign of the Moor' (80), an image that, as Moor's or Turk's or Saracen's Heads, appears on signs all over Britain and which dates from the era when Crusaders used the inns as points of assembly and departure.

The third comparably volatile setting in *Romola*, the *piazza*, like the yards and market places of Warwickshire, is essentially an absence: a space that gains its shape from the surrounding buildings. In the 'Proem' that opens *Romola*, the Florentine Spirit considers the current state of his city from the San Miniato Hill: the domes, the towers, and the Arno. But the only locations he is interested in revisiting are 'the Piazze where he inherited the eager life of his fathers' (46). He yearns for the politics and language of the *piazze*: the voting, the jokes, and the 'significant banners' (46), all of which change with the changing political winds.[3] Consequently they are suitable settings for all the unstable signification that occurs in Florence as its citizens strain to interpret an environment choked with signs, including the *palle* of the Medici, the pyramid of vanities, the plentiful religious icons, the frescoes and paintings that form its glory, and the written works produced by its new printing press.[4]

Like all of these signifiers, God's word is polysemous: according to Florentines, 'When God above sends a sign, it's not to be supposed he'd have only one meaning' (62). And political change is seen as mere replacement without progress: Bernardo del Nero fears that the change following Lorenzo's death will consist only of 'knocking down one coat of arms to put up another' (121). Rapid political transformations, such as those precipitated by the death of Lorenzo, make the need to locate and stabilize meaning urgent but also nearly impossible.

The relative effectiveness of peculiarly Florentine symbols such as the flags and banners representing Guelf, Ghibbeline, and guild (articles which, like money, have a purely symbolic function by nature) especially challenges the spectators to the parade, as do the *ceri*, the outsized candlesticks loaded down with tiers of icons. The Florentine penchant for semiotic excess eventually culminates in Savonarola's Pyramid of Vanities and his abortive attempt to stage a walk through the fire. Rather than being saved by signification as Cennini believes, George Eliot's Florence is deteriorating, sinking in a flood of meaningless, ugly, tawdry, ineffective signifiers.

An especially threatening condition under these circumstances is the possibility and then the eruption of pestilence which results in constant efforts to ward off disease by means of one symbol or another. Many citizens of Florence, including such variously positioned characters as Bardo, Bratti, and the powerful Bartolommeo Scala, credit the medicinal role of gems.

But often, as in *Silas*, the healing agents do not work unless accompanied by prayers, a kind of language sometimes created specifically for repetition. In other cases, the metaphor reverses again as when the parchment breve worn around the neck has a medicinal purpose. Tessa wears a 'scrap of scrawled parchment' (163) next to the coral Tito gives her. Various other drug/poison metaphors include Bardo's representation of printed manuscripts as 'poisonous mud' (96); Dino's description of his father's learning as both poison and wine; and the narrator's more conventional representations of Baldassare's vengefulness as a poison (284, 333, 376).

Weddings, Medicine, and 'The Florentine Joke'

Images of drugs and disease form especially thick clusters in the scenes in which the Florentines try to sort out their environment and deduce principles for the imposition of political order. Savonarola, an indecipherable text himself, twice describes the Florentine Church as 'polluted' during his Advent sermon and four times promises a literal pestilence as the consequence. He also describes the city's wickedness as 'wine' (290). According to Bardo, Florence without Lorenzo is like an 'alchemist's laboratory' (121) without the alchemist.

The authorities who exert power over the city have peculiar associations with disease and drugs. Both Piero di Medici, the putative successor to Lorenzo, and Bartolommeo Scala, Secretary to the Republic, suffer from gout, and Pope Alexander is the Borgia Pope, associated by his name alone, but also by George Eliot's narrator, with poisons. Cennini sums up the situation by saying that Florence has been 'over doctored by clever Medici' (141). Like Milby/Shepperton, Florence is a morally and metaphorically sick society whose physical health is also deteriorating.

The *piazze* of Florence, in addition to accommodating political and symbolic events, also serve as settings for events involved with marriages, all of them fraudulent or truncated.[5] On the Piazza Santissima Annunziata, Tito has the conjurer at the carnival 'marry' him and Tessa. After her betrothal ceremony, Romola encounters the ominous masquers on the Piazza Santa Croce. The *piazze* sustain action likely to result from false weddings as well as the weddings themselves. When Tito sunders his relationship with Baldassare on the Piazza del Duomo, a false son cuts himself off from an adoptive father. There are no marriages with orderly successions among the main characters in *Romola*, a circumstance conjoined with the problems of eliciting meaning and imposing order.

The weddings on the *piazze* soon give way to more overtly ominous events to which Florentines respond with further desperate attempts to sort out meanings. On the Piazza San Marco, Savonarola's challenge to God succeeds, but only temporarily.

Florentine doubts revive almost as soon as the flash of sun they have taken as God's blessing dies away. The Piazza della Signoria accommodates the pyramid of vanities, the trial by fire, and the execution of Savonarola. Radically unstable signification pervades all these events.

One effect of adding the semiotic layer of the intoxicant metaphor to Jan Gordon's classic analysis of textual, filial, political relationships is to draw into the drug/disease paradigm some of the apparently troublesome parts of the narrative, for example the chapter George Eliot calls 'A Florentine Joke,' a chapter often taken as a demonstration of her difficulties with historical fiction.[6]

Having introduced Tito fresh from the sale of the onyx supposed to represent his devotion to his father, the narrator begins the chapter with one of her comments about the coercion of character-transforming deeds.[7] She draws her metaphor, the death of a child, from the events of the previous chapter in which Tito sells the onyx: 'Our deeds are like children that are born to us; they live and act apart from our own will. Nay, children may be strangled, but deeds never' (219). This simile–with its implication that Tito, who has disowned his adoptive father, would be capable likewise of infanticide, the ultimate disowning of a child–combines with Dino's death and the false marriage to enlarge the family group susceptible to Tito's betrayal. With the introduction of the Florentine Joke named in the chapter title, the theme of baby-switching acquires its metaphorical medical overlay.

The joke begins because of Nello's aversion to the quack who has begun to see patients and sell remedies on Nello's turf, the Piazza San Giovanni. A typical caricature of the greedy physician common in the popular culture of both Britain and Italy, Maestro Tacco introduces himself in the act of calling for disease rather than cure for his raw-mouthed steed:'The vermocane seize him!' (179). Nello then pretends to try to please Tacco by comparing him with Antonio Benevieni, 'the greatest master of the chirurgic art' (228). Indignant at the implication of equality between surgery and medicine, Tacco labels the latter as the science of Galen,

Hippocrates, Avicenna–and himself.

Now Nello pretends to warn Tacco against some gossip circulating the report that Tacco makes 'secret specifics by night: pounding dried toads in a mortar, compounding a salve out of mashed worms, and making your pills from the dried livers of rats which you mix with saliva emitted during the utterance of a blasphemous incantation' (229). Claiming to be providing the opportunity for Tacco to refute these reports and verify his medical skill, Nello introduces the Florentine Joke: the conjurer disguised as a *contadina* cradling a monkey disguised as a sick infant. Frightened by the sudden appearance of the simian substitute for the peasant baby, Tacco flees, leaving Nello satisfied to have 'cleared my piazza of that unsavory fly trap' (233).

Because this sequence depends on the substitution of an interloper for a legitimate infant, as well as the substitution of one kind of medical practitioner for another, it continues the pattern of usurpation begun with Dino's death in the previous chapter by means of a medical metaphor acted out on a *piazza*. Through its repetitions of events involving legitimate and illegitimate parenthood and its applications of metaphors from the drug/disease complex, 'The Florentine Joke' chapter is also united to the chapters that immediately precede and succeed it.

Preacher, Teacher, Tailor, Spy

In addition to converting drinking places into Florentine settings, George Eliot includes in *Romola* many characters who qualify as *Pharmakoi*, distributors of drugs. From her earliest fiction through *Daniel Deronda*, her characters administer various kinds of drugs and various versions of the written and spoken word. Literal dispensers of drugs include pharmacists, physicians, apothecaries, publicans, brewers, distillers, maltsters, quacks, and women. Dispensers of the written and spoken word also occur often: lawyers, preachers, teachers, librarians, politicians, rhetoricians, and writers. A final category would include professions with a metaphorical association with the written and/or spoken word: a weaver whose task typically represents that of the novelist; a farmer who sows seed as does a disseminator of the word; a banker who, like an author, exchanges written or printed representations, in the banker's case currency, checks, drafts, deeds, and mortgages.[7] Fortune tellers and seers, pawnbrokers, gamblers, magicians, painters, perfumers, and jewelers also buy, sell, or exchange products that represent language and/or depend on it for part of their own value.

All of these characters participate to some degree in the archetype of the *Pharmakeus*. In writing about the pharmaceutical metaphor, Derrida lists similarities between the Egyptian god of writing, Thoth (according to Will Ladislaw, one of the subjects of Mr. Casaubon's scholarship in *Middlemarch*), and the Theuth of Plato's dialogue. The *Phaedrus* portrays Theuth as a subordinate: a technocrat, an engineer. Like the Egyptian Thoth, he is 'engendered' (87), that is, a son-god. (George Eliot introduces such characters as Adam, Tom, Philip, Tito, Felix, and Will specifically as younger male relatives.) Like Hermes (sometimes proposed as his Greek equivalent), Thoth is often a messenger, as are Tito Melema and Will Ladislaw. His role as 'secretary to Ra' again would include Will himself as well as the secretaries to whom Mr. Brooke compares Will. As 'god-doctor-pharmacist-magician,' the Theuthian archetype would also apply to some degree to Lydgate of *Middlemarch*, the Egyptian sorcerer who opens *Adam Bede*, and all the doctors as well as the women healers.

Theuth, a 'clever intermediary' (88), is primarily an agent; like Christian in *Felix Holt* or Lush in *Daniel Deronda*, he is an agent capable of manipulations and thefts. Derrida's description of the character as 'a *joker*, a floating signifier, a wild card, one who puts play into play' (his italics 93) suggests such gamblers as Farebrother, Fred Vincy, Gwendolen Harleth, the Cass brothers, and the desperate Lydgate as similarly Theuthian.[8] In *Romola* in particular, participants in the Theuthian archetype are many.

On the literal level, spurious doctors include such quacks as Tacco and the magician who unites Tito and Tessa. George Eliot alludes to historical doctors, including Hippocrates, Galen, and Avicenna, but also to Boccaccio's Maestro Simone, a fictional physician who is conceited, wealthy, and, like Maestro Tacco, the victim of a violent joke. The name of the Medici, who were originally in the pharmacists' guild, links the sick society with the people who attempt to use their power to cure its problems and increase their wealth. The Medici family patrons were Sts Cosmos and Damian, doctors represented often in Florentine art and especially prominently in the Fra Angelico fresco on the wall of the chapter room in San Marco where Romola's brother Dino delivers the warning conveyed by his vision, a vision that concludes with an image of Romola lost in a mass of parchment.

In addition, a huge number of the characters of this novel distribute the written or spoken word in some form or another. Professors of Rhetoric include Tito, Poliziano, Pietro Crinito (Tito's successor), and Domizio Calderino, Professor of Rhetoric at Rome, considered a rival of Tito. Librarians and founders of libraries also occur often: they include Boccaccio; Pope Nicholas V, founder of the Vatican library; Callimachus; Cosimo de' Medici; as well as most of the religious orders in Florence. Although Tito's supreme betrayal of Bardo is the sale of the library, a sale that is irrevocable because documents have sealed it, he schedules one of his trips out of Florence so as to serve as consultant on the new collection in Rome.

Characters still more directly associated with the distribution of the printed word and therefore with the Theuthian archetype swell the crowd at San Giovanni, which includes, besides Tito and Nello, Francesco Cei, who is a poet, and Pietro Cennini, the printer. This society, led by orators, and, as Gordon notices, defined by scholarship, is dominated and manipulated by the greatest *Pharmakoi* of all: Tito and Savonarola.[9]

And of all George Eliot's characters, perhaps none fits the archetype so well as Tito Melema. Tito is entirely double. He has two of everything: two wives, two fathers, two children, two names, two political allegiances, two T's in his name, and, as Alison Booth points out, he dies two deaths (189). As rhetoric professor, scholar, and secretary, he spends nearly all of his time manipulating the written word and almost none originating it. He forges letters that trap Savonarola at the same time that he depends for his own safety on a written guarantee of immunity. Derrida writes, 'When Thoth is concerned with the spoken rather than with the written word, which is rather seldom, he is never the absolute author or initiator of language' (88). Tito translates the Latin of Savonarola for the illiterate crowd. When he delivers the good news of the arrival of grain-laden ships from France, he usurps the glory of the original messenger whose horse fails just at the town gates.

In linking Thoth and conspiracy Derrida mentions more details which occur in Tito's plot: 'It is not in any reality foreign to the "play of words" that Thoth also frequently participates in plots, perfidious intrigues, conspiracies to usurp the throne. He helps the sons do away with the father, the brothers do away with the brother that has become king' (89). Dolfo Spini calls Tito a 'necromancer' (603), and Ser Ceccone calls his favors an 'opiate' (608). Finally, before his marriage to Romola, Tito lives at the Apollo and Razor, the barber shop on the Piazza San Giovanni that has much in common with an English public house.

But George Eliot narrows the Theuthian archetype still further in attaching Tito specifically to its archetypal embodiment in Bacchus. Bonaparte's placement of Tito in a pagan tradition rests largely on an elaborate set of Bacchic allusions that also allude to Thoth. Tito characterizes himself as Bacchus in the wedding picture he commissions from Piero: a god of joy who brings with him the wine of joy. Bonaparte's description of Tito warns that the Bacchic archetype provides 'no mere drunken god for Eliot, and indeed there is not the slightest hint of dissipation in Tito. The corruption of Bacchus is far subtler, to be found not in the scenes of revelry but in the very nature of joy. The vine that brings relief also brings oblivion' (68-9). Tito is singing a hymn to Bacchus when Baldassare interrupts the party in the Rucellai gardens with his futile attempt to discredit him, thus he repudiates his father for the second time in public at a party Bonaparte describes in detail as a Bacchic *speragmos.*[10] Its setting, the Gardens of the Rucellai family who produce their dye in the red color associated with Bacchus, stresses this construction of Tito (Bonaparte 171). But if Tito in the beginning has the potential for either good or evil, he quickly chooses his side and embraces the evil side of the *Pharmakeus* despite his sobriety.

As with Mr Tulliver in the earlier novel, the narrator twice draws attention to Florence's reputation for sobriety. Nevertheless, on two important occasions, drunkenness intensifies the volatility of the action: at 'The Supper in the Rucellai Gardens' and on the night of 'The Masque of the Furies.' George Eliot originally intended to call the chapter about the supper 'A Political Supper in the Rucellai Gardens' (Sanders 720). Even after having dropped this adjective, however, she begins the chapter by noting Tito's awareness 'that the object of the gathering was political' (409) and that 'good dishes and good wine were at that time believed to heighten the consciousness of political preferences' (409). In addition, the Rucellai, purveyors of the lucrative red dyes, are noted in Florence for their devotion to 'Madonna della Gozoviglia and San Buonvino' (409). Although Bernardo Rucellai warns his guests against talking politics until 'we can drink wine enough to wash them down' (411) the talk becomes political prematurely (just after the fish) despite Rucellai's warning. Normally sober out of caution, in the political atmosphere of the supper Tito drops his guard and drinks enough to befuddle his response to the sudden appearance of Baldassare. Together with the wine, the suddenness prompts his second repudiation of his father.

As Tito destroys one family bond after another, George Eliot consistently represents his moral deterioration as an illness. His guilty desire for Baldassare's death creates an 'unwholesome infecting life' with 'contaminating effects' (151). His betrayal becomes a 'poison' (170), and his fear of Romola's discovery of his secret induces an 'intoxication of despair' (205) and a 'sickening' (234) feeling. After the first rejection of Baldassare he feels 'smitten with a blighting disease' (287), and he deflects Romola's suspicions about his new armor by telling her he is 'not well' (314). More specifically, George Eliot compares Tito's guilt to a toothache which resists cure no matter how unscrupulous the methods employed to get rid of it. In addition, he shares with such characters as David Faux, characters prominent in the parables of addiction, his contriving of the easiest ways of achieving the most effortless life.

Like Tito, Savonarola is poised to deliver either good or evil for Florence. He is a controller and dispenser of the spoken word, who also is 'double' (578, 621, 665). The narrator several times describes his character as one 'in which opposing tendencies coexist in almost equal strength' (612). Savonarola is thought to have 'enchanted' (623) Fra Domenico, and he tells himself: 'Thou hast cured others: and thou thyself hast been still diseased' (666). His youthful period as a medical student in Ferrara identifies him still more closely with the archetype.

Romola's attempts to decipher Tito take up the early years of her marriage, and her effort to locate the meaning of Savonarola occupies the three final chapters that precede the epilogue. But Romola's final act of interpretation does not occur until after her return from the plague village.[11]

Savonarola dissuades her from going on with her first escape attempt by appealing to her respect for signs. He invokes 'fidelity to the spoken word' (431) of her marriage vows. Savonarola also applies metaphors of money and wine in this scene. To flee Florence would be to deny her inheritance as a daughter of the city. Like Tom Tulliver, she bears inherited debts, notably 'the debt of a Florentine woman' (430). The sacrifice of returning to Florence and Tito will be an ambiguous drink: 'The draught is bitterness on the lips. But there is rapture in the cup' (436). Romola is well aware of the sacramental nature of marriage and that her escape from Tito is a rejection of a connection between sign and meaning. Her decision to return rests on her intellectual acknowledgment of the power of the symbols Savonarola invokes and on her emotional responses to this power.

By the time of her second escape attempt, Romola has modified her belief in the power of Florence's signs and abandoned her submission to that power. She resumes the nun's habit, 'in her heart-sickness' (586) explicitly rejecting any concern for its being a disguise: 'Why should she care about wearing one badge more than another' (587). In the plague village the metaphor falls away as she confronts a community suffering from literal illness and in need of literal remedies. Romola replaces remedies such as the breve, gems, processions, prayers, and charms popular in Florence with more direct efforts that quickly dispel the effects of the plague in the village on the coast.

In the plague village Romola enters an environment where the sickness eliminates the moral and linguistic complexities of life in Florence. Throughout George Eliot's fiction, characters' sicknesses simplify difficult moral problems. In 'Janet,' when Dempster enters his final illness Janet is able to set aside her conflict over the violence in her marriage.[12] In *Middlemarch*, when Dorothea learns from Lydgate of the seriousness of Casaubon's state, she too finds new certainty that enables her to abandon less selfless attempts at fulfilment. Because of the peremptory needs of the sick villagers, Romola's life there acquires the simplicity required by the demands of life-and-death situations and loses the instability of existence in a nightmare maze of deceptive surfaces laden with problematic meaning. George Eliot's depictions of sickness as a preliminary to health, a pattern that occurs throughout her novels, suggests hope for England's recovery from its Condition.

On the night of Tito's death, drinking contributes to the political violence as it does in 'Janet' and again with still greater emphasis in *Felix Holt*. Dolfo Spini issues his orders from a room where he keeps 'abundant wine on the table with drinking-cups for chance comers' (631). Here he and his cohorts finally detect Tito's duplicity, a duplicity Dolfo finds especially audacious because 'he's got that fine ruby of mine' (63). When Spini issues the orders that result in Tito's death, he is 'on his guard against excessive drinking' (631); nevertheless, he 'took enough from time to time to heighten the excitement' (631). Consequently Tito, who attempts to divert the intentions of Spini's mob by scattering diamonds before them on the Ponte Vecchio, dies as the result of orders issued by a man at least half drunk and executed by a set of tipsy lieutenants. On these two most overtly political occasions, even in a setting notable for its 'sober and frugal people' (409), excessive drinking exacerbates the disorder manifested in Baldassare's challenge in the gardens and Spini's attacks on the bridge.

Romola's Research

By the time Romola returns to Florence, the experience of life in the plague village has helped equip her to face the task of deciphering Savonarola with fresh energy, a task which begins with establishing the authoritative text, considering the opinions of her fellows, depending on her intuition, and analyzing the tone of his confessions. After Savonarola retracts his confession and reclaims the gift of prophecy and, tortured again, retracts his retraction, Romola decides to attend the execution to deduce what she can from Savonarola's demeanor and his possible statements. With the support of Savonarola's biographer, Romola watches for evidence from the monk himself. But, faced only with taunts and scorn from the Florentines, Savonarola's voice passes 'into eternal silence' (671). The daughter of Bardo di Bardi thus needs to call on all her scholarship to draw her final conclusions about Savonarola.[13]

The epilogue to the novel suggests that Romola is, in the end, at peace with her interpretation as she prepares to celebrate the anniversary of Savonarola's death. For her, he has reverted to the status of honored hierophant. But the guests who arrive to share in the preparations make an odd pair: Piero di Cosimo and Nello, the barber. And again, as with the 'Florentine Joke' chapter, the metaphor helps make sense of an otherwise odd choice.

Of the two, Piero is the more likely visitor. He has always shown a partiality for Romola, and he is the single reliable porte parole in the novel. This is not to say that the paintings of Florence always deliver unambiguous meaning. On the contrary, the narrator blames Tessa's misinterpretation of Tito on her exposure to Last

Judgment frescoes.

George Eliot and George Henry Lewes saw a number of Last Judgments during their travels. They did not earn George Henry Lewes's admiration: he disliked the fresco in the Sistine Chapel (11 April 1860) and had only slightly better words for Giotto's in the Arena Chapel. The absolute grouping of people into categories of saved and damned was not the reason for the dislike: on the contrary, he thought Giotto's better because of its 'clearer presentation of the story–you are in no doubt as to *his* saints and his demons–or his blessed and damned' (his italics 129). But in the character of Tessa, George Eliot blames Last Judgments for their misleading depictions of the condemned as ugly and the saved as beautiful. Tessa believes in Tito's goodness because she envisions him, in his beauty, as one of the *eletti*. When Tito asks her why she feels safe with him she replies: 'Because you are so beautiful–like the people going into Paradise: they are all good' (158). Like the other *Pharmaka* in the novels, painting can either deliver truth, as in the case of Piero di Cosimo, or it can delude and mislead as it does Tessa.[14]

Consequently Piero is a *Pharmakeus* who starts out operating from a state of poise (like Tito or Savonarola) to either kill or cure. The historical Piero, like his contemporary compatriots, procured his colors at a pharmacy and belonged to the pharmacists' guild. In addition, many of the colors in use in the era of Piero's Florence had toxic potential. Emerald green contained arsenic, and Flake white and Naples yellow were lead-based, as was Minium red, often used during the Middle Ages in the illumination of manuscripts (Mayer 50, 51, 60, 61).

But despite Piero's associations with poisons, his representations, especially of Tito as a man living in fear, are reliable, even prophetic, especially as he is the single character to question Tito's apparent goodness from the beginning.[15] His contributions to Romola's celebration of Savonarola suggest that the reliable porte parole respects, though he may not share, her estimate of the monk. As a *Pharmakeus* who conveys truth, he delivers a valuable endorsement of Romola's veneration of Savonarola.

Nello's presence calls for a more elaborate explanation. In the beginning of the novel he chooses Tito as his favorite because, unlike Piero and like Tessa, he accepts Tito's smiling, beautiful surface. Indeed he quarrels with Piero's doubts, and even provides lodging for the newcomer at the Apollo and Razor. Because of his similarity to an innkeeper, as well as the traditional barber's relationship to medicine, he too qualifies for the *Pharmakeus* archetype but labors desperately to stay in his state of poise. Not only does Nello's conversion from Tito's side to Romola's endorse the validity of her judgment, but George Eliot's pairing Nello and Piero creates an affiliation generated by the metaphor which again explains an otherwise awkward detail and integrates it with the rest of the novel.

In *Romola* George Eliot's shifts between mimesis and metaphor (at times the words for *alcohol* signify only an intoxicating drink; at other times the intoxicating drink is also a metaphor) continue patterns observable in and among her previous novels, as when Maggie suffers from a figurative addiction but Molly Farren succumbs to a literal one. But in *Romola* they become part of the most important theme she considers: the problem of how to elicit meaning responsibly in a world where significance is problematic and how to restabilize communities in the throes of rapid political change.

The fifteenth-century Florentine locations, the prominence of the *Pharmaka* of paint and dye, and her research on the medicinal roles of gems provide increased justification for their increased importance in the metaphor, and, continuing a process begun in the yards in *Silas Marner*, her volatile settings consisting of spaces or absences grow larger, more frequent, and more important in the form of the numerous Florentine *piazze*. Indeed, in *Romola*, she adds settings, the monasteries and the Apollo and Razor, which perform functions similar to those of the public houses in the English novels. She also abandons her previously conventional associations between intoxication and romantic love in favor of more elaborate applications of metaphors of drugs and disease to the problems involved in disorderly political and biological descent and related difficulties of artistic representation.

In addition, the plethora of *Pharmakeus* characters in this novel, who come to rest on one side or the other of the killing/curing dichotomy, suggest parallels with earlier, less developed *Pharmakoi* from previous novels. Silas, for example, develops a closer relationship with other, similar characters as a result of his participation in the *Pharmakeus* archetype.

Silas unites in himself several elements of the characters involved in the metaphor of the writer as distributer of drugs. Like most weavers around Raveloe, he appears 'disinherited' (51). Raveloe is therefore suspicious of his origins: 'How was a man to be explained unless you at least knew somebody who knew his father or mother?' (51). Because he 'came from distant parts' (51), he also earns the suspicion of his neighbors on the basis of his unnecessary dexterity which they come to see as 'of the nature of conjuring.' Silas is, moreover, believed capable of causing as well as curing disease: not only is he adept with the medicinal herbal knowledge he has inherited from his mother, but the children in Raveloe believe his gaze can cause 'cramp, or rickets, or a wry mouth' (52). As a weaver, he stands for the author/narrator who weaves tales; as a miser, his activity duplicates that of the banker; as an herbalist, he duplicates the physician; finally, as a chronic cataleptic, he is a patient as well as a healer. Thus Silas fits in with other George Eliot characters who are doctors, patients, magicians, publicans, spies, rhetoricians, librarians, and alcoholics with addictions less figurative than his.

He also fits in with what George Eliot was becoming, for as she matured and gained fame, she herself began to fit the archetype more closely. She constructed her writing self as a brewer, distiller, or vintner by referring to her novels-in-progress, especially *Middlemarch*, as fermenting beverages. In a letter to Sara Hennell she begs her friend to refrain from commenting on the novel until it has 'gone thoroughly from the wine-press in to the casks' (*GEL* 5: 214). Lewes, too, applies a wine metaphor to *Middlemarch*. In his correspondence with Blackwood he repeats George Eliot's continuing doubts about the quality of her current work in comparison with *Felix Holt*: 'She felt she "could never write like that again and that what is now in hand is rinsings of the cask"' (*GEL* 5: 237).

The Sundays at the Priory eventually took on an air of Sabbatarian worship: Charles Dickens for one refers to them as attendance at 'service' (454), a description only partly related to the name of the house or the day of the week. Regarded with awestruck reverence by many of her visitors, she assumed the oracular role immortalized in F. W. H. Myers's sibyl-in-the-gloom anecdote (Haight 464-5). On the one hand the sibyl-in-the-gloom is the most tedious of George Eliot anecdotes. On the other, it constructs George Eliot as oracular and therefore likely to be seeking wisdom and inspiration by chewing laurel leaves. However oddly the Theuthian archetype groups George Eliot with a heterogeneous gallery of her own characters, it also creates her as priestess, weaver of plots, and author of books she herself represents as drugs.

Notes

1. See, for example, Lawrence Poston III, Jerome Beaty, and J. B. Bullen.
2. Mary McCarthy argues that fourteenth-century textile workers in Florence, led by Michele di Landro, were 'premonitory of the Lancashire spinners and weavers in the England of the Industrial Revolution' (80). Because I am dealing more with George Eliot's representations of Florence than with establishing historical events there, I depend on McCarthy's *Stones of Florence* as a sort of general, non-specialized source.
3. According to McCarthy, an acute cross-class political sensitivity created in Florence a constant 'threat of direct democracy or piazza

rule' (80), partly dependent on Florentines as a group being 'in fact, too articulate, politically' (80).

4. Scholars have often noticed the increased volatility of language in *Romola*. Bonaparte depends partly on this language to suggest that *Romola* is an epic poem, citing George Eliot's 'repeated use of the word "image" and sometimes "symbol"' (5). George Levine bases his argument that the novel is a fable on its dependence on symbol. Jan Gordon connects the instability of meaning in George Eliot's Florence with its crisis in political succession and its fading manuscript culture.

5. In 'Affiliation as (Dis)semination,' Gordon suggests that absence in George Eliot's Florence, especially 'the missing son or the missing manuscript—is perhaps best symbolized in the loggia, the traditional "amendment" even architecturally, to large family houses' (161). Because the loggia is a family-built structure, it draws attention to the tensions surrounding marriage and succession in Florence. As Gordon points out, many fruitless confrontations between Tito and Romola occur on the loggia of the house on the Via de' Bardi. Similarly, and far more pervasively, the *piazze* draw attention to familial fractures.

6. Andrew Sanders illustrates the negative response to this chapter in his introduction to the Penguin edition, calling it 'ungainly and unnecessary' (19). But Margaret Homans comes closer to my point in finding it, although for different reasons, a source of unity rather than disjunction. She makes a linguistic connection between words and the demonism of the baby monkey, identifying language as demonic and the false mother and child as a perversion of a Madonna image (215). In *George Eliot's Serial Fiction*, Carol Martin also finds unity in the scene. Noticing its substantial length, she finds parallels between the monkey's situation and Tito's and argues that in ridding Florence of the monkey and the quack, 'Nello stages the very action that Tito fears for himself' (161). The joke also, she believes, delivers to Tito a warning regarding Florentine implacability.

7. The Bardi family ceased being bankers in 1339 in a way that again connects Italy and England. The bankruptcy of Edward III resulted in conclusive losses (McCarthy 30).

8. D. A. Miller describes Lydgate as a scapegoat (*Discontents* 119).

9. Bonaparte believes that the similarities between Tito and Savonarola relate to 'the inherent paradox in language . . . for it is language that betrays them both and through which they both betray Florence' (*Triptych* 223).

10. Bonaparte also points out that Bacchus is also the god of the poppy (50). Deirdre David, in *Intellectual Women*, suggests that Tito's representing Romola as Ariadne to his own Bacchus 'reduces her status (literally and psychologically)' (196). Hilary Fraser proposes Titian's *Il Bravo*, a painting with a possibly Bacchic subject, as a source for George Eliot's construction of Tito.

11. The sojourn in the plague village forms yet another problem spot in *Romola*. Poston concludes that 'the introduction of the plague-stricken village seems to be more an evasion than a solution' (365). But Susan Winnett describes this sequence as a shift from patterns of traditional narrative to the logic of the legend in response to a need George Eliot perceived to 'rescue female experience from the margins of narrative' (515). Similarly, David Carroll sees the plague village as a step out of history and Florence and into an a-historical mode which provides a mythic preparation for her evaluation of Savonarola. He concludes that 'it is only after this experience of the hermeneutic of innocence that the heroine is able to return and make a definitive interpretation of Savonarola's martyrdom, overlaid as it is at the complex dialectics of history by the hermeneutic of suspicion' (200).

12. Cottom devotes an entire chapter to the 'culture of the sickroom,' suggesting that George Eliot's rebellion against her father appears in her pattern of sicknesses that reduce need: the sick person cannot rebel against authority. John Reed notes that Victorians found the idea that sickness simplifies in Taylor's *Holy Dying*, a book George Eliot places in the Tulliver household (*Victorian Conventions*).

13. Kristin Brady's double reading of *Romola* as, like the rest of George Eliot's fiction, both a reinforcement and a subversion of patriarchal values focuses on Savonarola as representative of the patriarchy. His 'silence is the speaking voice of patriarchy' (135).

14. This ability of painting to produce delusion somewhat weakens Karen Chase's argument, in 'The Modern Family and the Ancient Image in *Romola*,' that after the plague village episode George Eliot replaces the frantic instability of metaphor in Florence with more reliable pictorial images. Chase believes that George Eliot's 'commitment to fact was too great to allow her to find a solution that was merely metaphoric' (312). However, as I shall argue in the next chapter, this is precisely the hazard to which she succumbs in her novel *Felix Holt* and in her 'Address to Working Men by Felix Holt.'

15. Many scholars have noted Piero's importance, primarily as porte

parole, among them Chase, Alley, Bonaparte, Carpenter, Poston, Witemeyer, and Edward T. Hurley.

Felix Holt fails to recruit students for his school from among the sons of the drinkers at the Sugar Loaf, one of many drinking places in George Eliot's most overtly political novel.

7

Felix Holt's *Muddled Metaphors*

A friend of ours, long a victim to dyspepsia, was earnestly recommended to try a 'digestive powder' which promised to restore any amount of lost 'vigour.' The recommendation came from one who had great confidence in the powder, because he knew that *the advertiser made a very good living out of it.*

G. H. Lewes 1862
'Physicians and Quacks'

Readers usually consider *Felix Holt* one of George Eliot's less successful novels, not so bad as *Romola*, but not nearly so good as *Adam Bede*, *The Mill on the Floss*, *Silas Marner*, or *Middlemarch*. Its elitism, sentimentality, nostalgia, inconsistency, and excessive idealization of the main character usually take the blame for the inferiority. Elsewhere, I have argued that its confusing politics, a mixture of the Wollstonecraftianism of Mrs Transome's plot and the Burkean gradualism of Felix's, help account for the failure. But the conflict between expressed and implied attitudes toward metaphor, as indicated in various aspects of the intoxicant complex, also creates disturbing disjunctions. More obviously than the fiction, the companion 'Address to Working Men by Felix Holt' also loses effectiveness because its persona offers only metaphorical solutions to social problems. Felix the essayist falls into a practice he objects to as the youthful protagonist of the fictional work.

Partly because public houses serve as campaign headquarters, during the election that forms the main action, major disturbances and disruptions occur at the many drinking-place settings throughout this novel. After various minor conflicts result from treating, electioneering, and rabble rousing at the Sugar Loaf, the

Marquis of Granby, the Ram, and the Seven Stars, the climactic riot gains its chaotic force both from events that occur at the inns and ale houses and from the mob's interest in attacking the breweries which account for much of Treby Magna's prosperity. Similarly, legitimate heritage and the printed word both suffer from dangerous manipulations on the night on which Mr Christian buys enough drink for Tommy Trounsem so that he can substitute his own campaign poster handbills, which allude to the open secret of Harold's illegitimacy, for the ones Tommy has engaged to post.

Such interactions among the print and oratory of the election, the people who manage it, and the places where the activities of the campaign go forth guarantee the prominence of the drug metaphors and metonymies in this, the novel in which George Eliot takes her most overtly political stance. In both *Felix Holt* and in the 'Address to Working Men by Felix Holt' she offers her clearly stated remedies for the Condition of England.

The Pharmakon

In addition to being more pervasive than in her previous novels, drugs and drinking are more Platonic in *Felix Holt*. Like many of her contemporaries, as the nineteenth century wore on, George Eliot moved away from an Aristotelian/mimetic aesthetic to find certain elements of Platonism more acceptable. By the sixties and seventies, new translations attracted attention to the single important Greek philosopher ignored in mid-century because Victorians considered his idealism too remote from the concerns of quotidian reality to benefit society. Frank Turner includes Benajmin Jowett, a close friend of the Leweses whose scholarship George Eliot read and commented on favorably, among the most prominent revivalists.

With *Felix Holt*, George Eliot's participation in the late Victorian Platonic revival begins to take distinct shape in her fiction. Whereas in her earlier works she divides representation of the realism/romanticism opposition between alcohol and opium, now her metaphor more closely resembles the Platonic *Pharmakon* as it occurs in the *Phaedrus*: a volatile killer/healer associated primarily (though not exclusively) with written language. She also expresses a Platonic emphasis on the condition of the receiving body, whether the dose is medicine or rhetoric, and the Theuthian agent continues as malevolent and almost as pervasive as in *Romola*.

The Platonic *Pharmakon* metaphor, in which drugs directly represent the written word with its ambiguous power to kill or cure, occurs when Mr Lyon, who, like many George Eliot characters, sees religious texts as remedies, describes himself as 'given to question too curiously concerning the truth–to examine and sift the medicine of the soul rather than apply it' (149). It recurs in Felix's belief that he can disturb his mother's confidence in Divine endorsement of the quack medicines by representing the Bible as toxic. She reports that he tells her, 'I'd better never open my Bible, for it's as bad poison to me as the pills are to half the people as swallow 'em' (136). In a revival of the metaphor from young Mary Ann Evans's 1839 letter, the narrator also describes Mrs Transome's conventional education as composed of 'stupid and drug-like' (105) ideas generated by reading superficial literature. Portrayals of the written word as medicine, poison, and narcotic again demonstrate a tenuous potential for healing (as in Rufus's 'medicine for the soul') in the face of more powerful tendencies toward poisoning.

And the spoken word also has toxic potential in *Felix Holt*. Harold Transome asserts the independence of his thinking to Esther by arguing that 'half those priggish maxims about human nature in the lump are no more to be relied on than universal remedies' (528). The Reverend Augustus Debarry dislikes 'the political sermons of the Independent preacher, which in their way, were as pernicious sources of intoxication as the beer-houses' (127). Felix, too, represents language as poison during his speech to the crowd on nomination day, when he describes one aspect of the power of ignorance as the unrestrained tendency 'to talk poisonous nonsense' (399). Mrs Holt praises her departed husband on the grounds that 'it was as good as a dose of physic to hear him talk' (135). The failure of the debate between Rufus Lyon and the inarticulate Mr Sherlock epitomizes the failure of dialogue in this polarized community which often perceives talk as drug-like.

George Eliot's well-known emphasis on the elaborate web of causality affecting human events appears in her metaphors involving the workings of drugs on the human body. In her fiction many causes located in both the remedy and the patient contribute to the instability of the medicine and the unpredictability of its effects on any single body. For one thing, both social and individual physical bodies are mixtures made up of chemical and spiritual components, and the word *mixture* appeared on the labels of the many patent medicines sold under this name. The resulting need for exact knowledge of the condition of the patient before prescribing is basic to George Eliot's and Plato's applications of the drug metaphor to the word, for both believe effective rhetoric whether spoken or written depends on careful audience analysis.

Like Felix Holt's father and the quacks who dispense drugs indiscriminately, Plato's bad orator neglects the knowledge of 'to whom' he would give his medicines, and 'when' and 'how much' (*Phaedrus* 268C). Summing up the similarities between rhetoric and medicine, Socrates observes, 'Medicine has to define the nature of the body and rhetoric of the soul–if we would proceed, not empirically but scientifically, in the one case to impart health and strength by giving medicine and food, in the other to implant the conviction or virtue which you desire, by the right application of words and training' (*Phaedrus* 270B). Volatile medicines, other drugs already present in the receiving body, and the variousness and individuality of each patient all make prescriptions of both real and metaphorical remedies a touchy business in George Eliot's novels. In *Felix Holt*, as well as in *Middlemarch*, the working people are often drunk, while the reading audience is more metaphorically polluted by the reading of romance or partisan newspapers.

Characters such as Felix and Rufus who hope to solve problems in Treby Magna must therefore deal with the challenge of adjusting their arguments to the understanding and needs of a mixed audience. In George Eliot's setting, change has resulted in 'mixed political conditions . . . acted on by the passing of the Reform Bill'

(129), which thus performs as a chemical catalyst. Mixtures affect the community opinion of Rufus Lyon, the sincere but ridiculed preacher, because 'the good Dissenter sometimes mixed his approval of ministerial gifts with considerable criticism and cheapening of the human vessel which contained those treasures' (158). This mixed attitude leads his parishioners to offer Rufus only the 'weaker tea' and the 'home-made wine' (158). The motto to the chapter relating how Scales's joke on Christian results in the loss of the tell-tale pocketbook describes Scales's humor as a 'mixture of spite and overfed merriment which passes for humor with the vulgar' (232). In this chapter George Eliot also emphasizes the unstable condition of the receiving body by attributing Christian's deep sleep to the fact that 'certain conditions of his system had determined a stronger effect than usual from the opium' (234).

In *Middlemarch*, George Eliot's emphasis on mixtures contributes to her simultaneously acknowledging and making fun of the Victorian (indeed Lewesian) idea that the nature of the individual constitution varies. At Dorothea's engagement party Mrs Cadwallader and Lady Chettam have a long conversation about doctors and medicine during which they express their belief in the variations among constitutions. Mrs Cadwallader points out how potatoes nourished on the same soil often thrive (or don't thrive) in drastically various ways. Lady Chettam voices her faith in her erstwhile subservient medical practitioner: 'He was coarse and butcher-like, but he knew my constitution' (67). Indeed the opening lines of *Middlemarch* describe 'man' as a 'mysterious mixture' whose behavior varies under the 'experiments of Time' (3). The 'Finale' to *Middlemarch* describes Dorothea's unheroic fate as the 'mixed result' of the 'conditions of an imperfect social state' (612). Chemically, politically, linguistically, nothing is uniform in George Eliot's Warwickshire novels.

Another Platonic element of *Felix Holt* occurs in its plethora of Theuthian agent/villains, an increasingly frequent archetype from *Romola* on. George Eliot's characters such as Mr Jermyn, Mr Christian, and John Johnson embody the Platonic, Derridean archetype of the duplicitous tamperer with language, heredity, and poison. The narrator's description of Jermyn is especially Theuthian: he 'came from a distance, knew the dictionary by heart, and was probably an illegitimate son of somebody or other' (125). The narrator emphasizes the medical connection by pointing out that Jermyn has 'very much the air of a lady's physician' (113). His failure with the Treby Magna spa indicates his failure as a civic physician, and because of the irrational loathing between himself and Harold he is possibly the worst father in all of George Eliot's fiction. His crowning insult to Mrs Transome occurs when he asks her to inform Harold about his paternity so as to save himself from the suit their illegitimate son intends to bring against him.

Mr Christian, too, tampers with heredity, written language, and poison. His opium addiction is the clearest case since Molly Farren, and his crimes begin with an act that perverts both writing and heredity. Jermyn charges him with forgery, specifically with writing 'a check on your father's elder brother, who had intended to make you his heir' (311). He substitutes Quorlen's handbills for Tommy Trounsem's as he listens to Tommy's narration of his fruitless pursuit of his heritage. Finally, Christian commits the ultimate sin: he asks for pay for his absence. He offers his information to Harold at a price of £2000 to be paid in return for his vanishing along with his dangerous knowledge of Esther's existence. Characters such as Christian (and, in *Daniel Deronda*, Lush) exemplify the class of which George Eliot disapproved most: the wastrels who have squandered their inheritance. In the 'Address to Working Men,' she argues that eliminating hereditary wealth would destroy the knowledge that is part of that heritage. Consequently, squanderers of this treasure are worse than the working people who succumb to the ignorance which forms their inheritance.

Attar of Roses: the Perfume Pharmakon

Felix's relationship with Esther also demonstrates the drug metaphor, for she exemplifies the characters whose romantic reading, in her case Byron and Chateaubriand, poison the reader.

In Esther, George Eliot introduces the perfume version of the *Pharmakon* by metonymic contiguity. When Felix upsets her workbasket early in the novel, the poetry book and the attar of roses tumble out together. Afterward, Felix several times applies metaphors of poison to Esther's reading. To him, the Byronic hero deliberately sickens himself: Byron's 'notion of a hero was that he should disorder his stomach and despise mankind' (151). The fine-lady romanticism George Eliot represents through the perfume, together with what Esther reads, have made her into a dangerous and volatile substance, as Felix puts it, capable of becoming 'either a blessing or a curse' (211) to the man she marries.

As Esther shuttles between Malthouse Yard and Transome Court, she also shuttles between these two opposite forms of oral language, one the blessing associated with the ecclesiastical environment of the chapel, the other the curse represented by the drugs, sickness, and illegitimacy at Transome Court. By assigning her the volatile potential of the unswallowed drug whose possible toxicity he has already attributed to her reading and attached through contiguity to her perfume, Felix makes Esther herself a *Pharmakon,* indeed one of George Eliot's most persistently ambiguous.

When Esther flees Transome Court, where Mrs Transome has become sicker and sicker, she, like Caterina Sarti, is fleeing an unhealthy atmosphere. Intoxication metonyms pervade both of the country-house settings in *Felix* (Transome Court and Treby Manor), the loci of inherited power and privilege. At Treby Manor the narrator reports 'more wine, spirits, and ale drunk, more waste and more folly, than could be found in some large villages' (183). Mr Scales serves cognac and whiskey, and Mr Christian, the social leader of backstairs society, brews punch for the group and, on his own, takes opium to combat an unnamed pain. At Transome Court, Harold's mother manifests her waning power partly by insisting her tenants defer to her frequent whims 'to change a labourer's medicine fetched from the doctor and substitute a prescription of her own' (106). Although she carries her own drugs about with her and occasionally samples something from her portable pharmacy, she tries to cure herself more by dispensing them to her tenants than by consuming her own, using a drug administered to them as a remedy for her own emotional problem. Her major ailment, discontent, is not physical, but 'the opiate for her discontent' (106) is to dispense drugs as both symbol and manifestation of her remaining power over her decaying estate.

Another drug consumer connected with Transome Court is Mrs Transome's brother, the amiable Parson Jack Lingon, a daily heavy drinker. He decides to abandon his party in favor of his nephew's Radicalism after two bottles of after-dinner port. Mr Lingon changes his politics quickly if somewhat drunkenly; Philip Debarry is forced to stand for election to a seat he would previously have gained through inheritance. The passage of the Reform Bill has de-stabilized the bastions of inherited power.

The unhealthiness of Transome Court increases with Harold's return from Smyrna. Although the narrator does not name the substance he inhales from his hookah, the allusions to an Orientalism well established as drug-connected in the work of DeQuincey and Coleridge earlier in the century, together with the importance of this city in the ongoing drug trade, suggest that Harold enjoys a daily high. The narrator explicitly connects Harold with Byronic Orientalism by identifying him as a giaour.

Unlike *The Mill*, *Felix Holt* contains no lengthy speculation on the effectiveness of metaphor. Indeed, this novel and its companion piece, the 'Address to Working Men by Felix Holt,' reveal that George Eliot can succumb to the same hazard that besets Mr Stelling in the earlier novel. Once call social problems (for example) manifestations of class warfare rather than diseases in a social organism, and one's ingenious conception of improvements as medicines seems to settle nothing. In *Felix*, George Eliot, like her characters, sometimes applies metaphorical remedies to such problems. Indeed, all the forces for good in Treby Magna succumb to the author's, the narrator's, or their own applications of metaphorical remedies to problems that exist in the physical world.[1]

The hero of the novel, Felix, has already achieved sobriety

before the action begins. As he explains to Rufus Lyon, he has experimented with debauchery during his days as an apprentice at Glasgow and come to the conclusion that 'pig wash, even if I could have got plenty of it, was a poor sort of thing' (142). Consequently he rejects his life in search of 'easy pleasure' (143) which has included daily encounters with 'old women breathing gin as they passed me on the stairs' (143). He also rejects the career as an apothecary for which his father's legacy has purchased the apprenticeship, and, as the novel opens, is finally beginning to take steps to end the selling of his parents' quack medicines. Thus he starts out in a position other George Eliot characters, such as Fred Vincy, require the length of the novel to gain: he is clean and sober.

He also appears to have turned his back on lax applications of metaphor. Felix comes closest to addressing the difficulties of metaphor during his argument about the public house treating through which Harold's agents, notably John Johnson, are trying to foment disorder and attacks on rival candidates. When Harold justifies the treating by telling Felix that 'a bridge is a good thing–worth helping to make, though half the men who worked at it were rogues' (275), Felix replies: 'Give me a handful of generalities and analogies, and I'll undertake to justify Burke and Hare, and prove them benefactors of their species' (275). His accusation blames the fluidity of analogy for justifying 'nuisance' (275). According to Felix, the tricks of language are capable of effectively transforming murder, in this case murder performed in connection with medicine and money, into social heroism.

The problem is that, despite his objections to Harold's metaphorical evasions, Felix himself applies drug metaphors. He begins with a reversal, repudiating the drugs on whose profits his parents have nourished and raised him. To keep his mother from continuing their sale, he intends to write a letter to the editor of the local newspaper. He thus hopes to use the written word to eliminate poisonous substances. When he tries to make the miners save their drinking money to start a school for their sons, his attempt repeats the same sequence. So far so good: Felix tries to replace intoxicants, here as in Milby physical remedies which fail to alleviate spiritual/social problems, with the spiritual/social remedy of non-violent civic activism and education. At the conclusion of the novel he persists in offering the written word to replace intoxicants by conceiving the project of setting up a library with the money from Esther's legacy. Because books cost money, the couple will need some of Esther's inheritance to buy the library–an act of exchanging inherited cash for the written word.

However, although Felix rejects the quack medicine business, he continues to think of himself as a doctor. He takes the sick child Job into his care and is bandaging his finger when Esther arrives with her watch which has an 'ailment' (319). After taking care of Job, Felix asks Esther, 'You want me to doctor your watch?' (319). Felix also describes both himself and his mission through alcoholic metaphors. He describes his temper as intoxication: 'There's some reason in me as long as I keep my temper, but my rash humor is drunkenness without wine' (238).[2] He believes his enemies depend on 'law and opodeldoc' (394), a combination of written language and opium ointment.

Then, during the betrothal scene of Esther and Felix, when she tells him she is giving up her money, they both apply the metaphor of attar of roses to manifestations of her inherited rank. Furthermore, Esther assures Felix that giving up the money will save her from illness: poor women, she tells him, are 'healthier' (602) than rich women. But Esther does not choose complete poverty and contradicts her statement about poverty and health by devising an income adequate in case 'sickness came' (602). If money belongs to the mixture of romanticism, drugs, physical sickness, and illegitimacy destroying Transome Court, she nevertheless also realizes it can remedy physical illness by permitting the patient to avoid work and to buy medicine and care.[3] Esther's only partial rejection of her inherited fortune compromises her choice of Felix and poverty. Unlike the poor people whom they hope to benefit, Felix and Esther have a safety net unavailable to their neighbors which prevents their participating fully in the impoverished community they pretend to be choosing. But neither of them notices the contradiction.

This closure, together with the drug metaphors applied to positive characters such as Rufus Lyon, ultimately deconstructs the representations on the mimetic level as well. In this novel, George Eliot's application of metaphorical remedies for the Condition of England only confirms the inadequacy of metaphor, leaving the setting in the same state of unjust and unequal distribution of power as at the start, its people as fuddled as ever. Her removal of most of the main characters from Treby Magna at the end of the novel creates a final representation of the town as an absence, abandoned to drunkenness and political chicanery. The departures of Felix, Esther, Rufus, and even Jermyn suggest that the town's problems are insoluble. Through their metaphorical confusions, most of these characters have already bungled their efforts to meliorize its condition.

Coaches, Drugs, and the Candidate for Guzzletown

The famous 'Introduction' to *Felix Holt*, with its coach ride across the central plain bounded by the Avon and the Trent, presents a range of allusions and metaphors connected with politics, language, and drugs. Twentieth-century Victorian scholars, notably Susan Cohen, have paralleled George Eliot's coach with Thomas DeQuincey's 'English Mail Coach,' and nineteenth-century readers, especially *Blackwood's* readers, were likely to do the same. Consequently a DeQuincey association occurs in the opening paragraphs of *Felix Holt*, partly because of the opium DeQuincey's persona takes just before the climactic near-disastrous accident in 'Mail Coach' and partly because of the permanent association with opium as a result of the *Confessions of an English Opium Eater*. The advertising on the side panels of early Victorian coaches often hawked the nineteenth-century patent medicines composed primarily of alcohol and opium. As they rolled across the countryside, they served as a visual inducement to drug-taking.

The 'Introduction' also initiates the centrality of alcohol and its effects in this novel's plots. Its first sentences describe a coaching inn utterly unlike the humble ale houses which occasion the narrators' manifestoes of realism in George Eliot's earlier works. Rather than being miserable pot houses at whose dinginess a responsible narrator must never flinch, these drinking places are part of the coach roads' 'glory' (75) and serve up their beverages in 'well-polished tankards' (75). Their barmaids are 'pretty' (75); their ostlers, 'jocose' (75). All these details directly contradict George Eliot's earlier references to disreputable barmaids such as Molly Farren and humble drinkers whose vulgar humor degenerates with each quart pot.

However, the narrator's nostalgia for the coaching inn contains its ironies, for it is shared with the driver of the coach, Mr Sampson, whose narratives occupy the entire day-long drive. Like many early nineteenth-century coachmen who mistakenly believed in the warming effects of alcohol, Mr Sampson is drunk: 'well warmed within and without' (81). Although the railroads will affect him in many negative ways, the disaster he laments most vocally is the possibility that 'every inn on the road would be shut up!' (81). His lament and his condition remind us that, for all the charm accorded it in the first sentences of the 'Introduction,' a coaching inn remains a drinking place with much of the volatility and all the linguistic connections elsewhere in George Eliot's fiction. Unlike Byron's drunken 'Don Juan' persona, or Browning's Fra Lippo Lippi, the coachman is not the main narrator of the work. Nevertheless, his drunkenness casts a shadow on the authority of narrators in general, including that of the primary narrator of *Felix Holt*, especially because of the nostalgia for coaching inns this narrator shares with the drunken Mr Sampson.

In addition, Mr Jermyn establishes a mutually unflattering metaphorical connection between the coachman and himself later in the novel. When Harold and Felix approach Jermyn with the latter's objection to the Sproxton treating, Jermyn points out Felix's political inexperience: 'If he had ever held the coachman's ribbons in his hands, as I have in my younger days--a--he would know that stopping is not always easy' (279). Felix brushes aside Jermyn's metaphor: 'I know very little about holding ribbons' (279). But Jermyn has linked himself with the drunken coachman of the Introduction, characters linked in any event as embodiments of the Theuthian archetype.[4] He also has reenforced the connection with DeQuincey. Like the young men on DeQuincey's English mail coach, Mr Jermyn has enjoyed taking a turn as driver during his youth.

With DeQuincey's presence hovering over *Felix Holt* from the beginning of the novel, its hookah-smoking Radical candidate gains another Oriental association. Although Barry Milligan asserts that George Eliot does not Orientalize her opium, he limits his evidence to two characters: Ladislaw and Lydgate. But a grouping of the two *Middlemarch* characters with Molly Farren and Harold Transome reveals that George Eliot does participate in the usual Orientalizing of opium.

Because the narrator describes Molly's addiction as enslavement to 'demon Opium' (164), her condition metaphorically duplicates the bondage in Britain's colonies, especially since slavery did not end there until 1833, some years beyond the time of Molly's death in the novel. The personification of opium as demonic also hints at the Orient by means of its exoticism. George Eliot figures even the addiction of the totally English barmaid as Romantic, distant, diabolic and therefore Oriental.

Lydgate, specifically excluded from Orientalizing associations by Milligan (10), also has subtle Eastern connections, specifically with the expansionism by which Milligan links opium and Orientalism. The narrator applies to Lydgate's ambitions a metaphor of exploration: pathology is 'a fine America for a spirited young adventurer' (109). Later, Mr Farebrother calls him a 'circumnavigator' (131). Although not by any means on his way to the Orient of Kubla Khan, Lydgate thus has a metaphorical connection with expansionism. Rosamond Vincy, inspired by Thomas Moore's 'Lalla Rookh,' which features a character who is a disguised prince, imagines Lydgate as a romantic stranger whose aristocratic connections attract her with a promise to rescue her from the antithesis of the Orient: humdrum Middlemarch.

The other opium user in *Middlemarch*, Ladislaw, too, is seen in terms of expansionist metaphors and allusions. Exotic by birth because of his Polish ancestry, he becomes associated with Robert Bruce and Mungo Park, explorers and authors of exotic traveler's tales, when Mr Brooke inquires about the objects of Will's travels. The Orientalism of these two *Middlemarch* characters clinches the suggestion that Harold Transome, the more emphatically Orientalized hookah-smoker, is not restricting himself to rose leaves or nuts, among the substances smoked in the hookahs in Benjamin Disraeli's *Tancred*, a novel Marian Evans read as a young woman in Coventry.

Although 'Canvassing for Votes,' Plate II of William Hogarth's 1755 'Election' pictorial narrative, differs drastically in mood from *Felix Holt*, its detail duplicates much of that of George Eliot's 1866 political novel. Treating, to which Felix objects as part of Harold Transome's campaign, forms the moral center of the picture in which the 'Candidate for Guzzletown' campaigns. And, as in many of Hogarth's scenes, inn signs carry much meaning. In the midst of the tumult, a new sign, that of 'Punch,' appears hastily tacked over the old Royal Oak sign which signifies the King (and in this picture also the order supposedly imposed by monarchic government). As in some of George Eliot's early novels, the replacement of one sign for another represents non-progressive political replacement.

George Eliot's post-Reform setting, eighty years later than Hogarth's, increases the likelihood of election-day chaos. Indeed when George Eliot returns to a frankly Warwickshire setting for her most overtly political themes, she makes drinking a major difficulty of the 1832 election. The Treby Magna setting includes more public houses than any of George Eliot's previous novels, and the climactic riot results directly from alcoholic excess. By all accounts, political manipulations of working men through alcohol disastrously affected the early post-Reform elections. Indeed, because legislation forbidding candidates to use taverns as campaign headquarters did not pass until late in the century, this problem survived from the period of George Eliot's settings well into the time during which she was writing.

Treby Magna supports at least four drinking places: the Marquis of Granby, the Ram, the Cross Keys, and the Seven Stars. The town's reputation depends primarily on the 'celebrated' (125) Wace and Company Brewery, and, besides the Waces, its prominent citizens include Mr Tiliot, who sells spirits, and Mr and Mrs Muscat, named after a variety of grape. The prosperity Felix's father and mother have gained from the sale of the various Holt remedies indicates the quantities of quack medicines consumed in the area. Stubbornly toxic, Treby cannot convert itself into a remedy: the narrator reports the failure of Jermyn's plan to build a thriving spa around its saline springs in the paragraph which introduces him. Treby Magna's drinking places always retain dangerous tendencies toward political disorder.

The public houses in Treby range from the Marquis of Granby, the top-of-the-line farmers' inn; through the less elite Ram and Seven Stars, 'where there was no fish' (299); to such dismal places as the Cross Keys at Pollard's End and the Sugar Loaf at Sproxton. But despite the rigorous segregation of Treby drinkers according to social class, political volatility arising directly from attempted reforms occurs at all the drinking places. During the climactic riot the mob invades the Seven Stars searching for Spratt, the manager of the colliery. At the ale houses, the agents of the politicians treat the patrons in return for support of their candidates. At the better inns, the candidates set up their campaign headquarters. Again the names of the drinking places describe the characters who frequent them. The Marquis of Granby, with its aristocratic name, serves as headquarters to Philip Debarry, the scion of the local nobility, while the Ram serves the outsider Harold Transome who wants to butt his way into Treby politics.

On down the social scale, the Cross Keys and the Sugar Loaf also serve functions associated with intoxication, heredity, and the voting reform permitted to begin to replace government exclusively by hereditary privilege. The narrator introduces the Cross Keys through a number of metonymies of sickness: 'One way of getting an idea of our fellow-countrymen's miseries is to go and look at their pleasures. The Cross Keys had a fungous-featured landlord and a yellow sickly landlady, with a large white kerchief bound round her cap like a resuscitated Lazarus; it had doctored ale, an odor of bad tobacco, and remarkably strong cheese' (373-4).[5]

At the Cross Keys, Mr Christian seeks out Tommy Trounsem not only to pump him about his hereditary status as a Transome but also to divert the printed word by replacing Tommy's pro-Transome broadsides with broadsides which draw attention to Harold's illegitimacy. A former publican himself, Trounsem aspires to a life in which he can 'live at publics and see the world' (379). He has his single valid insight regarding his heredity at a Red Lion when he realizes that Johnson is acting for Jermyn in warning him not to try to claim his heritage. As the haunt of Trounsem, the Cross Keys provides the setting for serious diversions of hereditary power.

Furthermore, the sign of the Cross Keys itself implies confused descent. St Peter, the Father of the Christian Church, disappeared from this sign, leaving only his keys to the kingdom of heaven, when the Tudor Church changed from Catholic to Anglican. Its remaining keys, with their phallic association, are crossed, suggesting misdirection. The absence of St Peter suggests the disinheriting conclusively accomplished in Trounsem's death.

The Sugar Loaf also has associations with both politics and parenthood. Its two additional names, Chubb's and the New Pits, emphasize volatile possibilities regarding future transformations of its patrons into either responsible fathers or into a mob. To achieve this, Felix targets the money the miners spend on their drink as the money they should spend on educating their sons. In a perhaps unintentionally vivid testicular image, Felix resolves, 'I'll lay hold of them by their fatherhood' (219). Unfortunately, Felix's visit coincides with the appearance of Mr Johnson who has come to buy drinks for the still voteless colliers in exchange for their vocal support on election day. Felix loses his audience to the alcoholic persuasion offered by Johnson, who has already substituted alcohol for the education Felix hopes to extend to the miners' sons before he has a chance to offer his persuasion. Thus he fails to achieve his goal: to divert the ignorance that forms the only inheritance the colliers pass along to their sons.

In the novel with the most inns, the issue of inheritance and responsibility receives its closest scrutiny in the paternal/filial plots. Perhaps the worst character in *Felix* is John Johnson, the author of the broadsides that allude to the open secret of Harold's heredity. As agent for Jermyn who is handling Harold Transome's campaign, Johnson is an agent for an agent who justifies his duplicity with the argument that 'to act with doubleness towards a man whose own conduct was double, was so near an approach to virtue that it deserved to be called by no meaner name than diplomacy' (385).[6] Johnson poisons the populace directly with his treating at the Sugar Loaf and defends it with a claim based on his electioneering expertise: 'A man must know the English voter and the English publican' (283). Johnson's name, with its allusion to the paternal/filial relationship, ironically draws attention to the proper descent Johnson also thwarts. As with David Faux's confections in 'Brother Jacob,' the sweetness in the name of the Sugar Loaf represents the easy pleasures of drinking, especially as they contrast with the slower but ultimately more rewarding efforts involved in education, especially education that will benefit only the subsequent generation.

Johnson himself makes an agent of the publican at the Sugar Loaf, Mr Chubb, a personality so exasperating that the usually austere George Eliot narrator suggests that he drives people to drink. Impervious to the effects of alcohol himself, his manner 'would have compelled you to take a little something by way of dulling your sensibility' (217). More directly politically involved than any of George Eliot's other publicans, Mr Chubb also does the most harm. Although he runs the Sugar Loaf, his name also offers a connection with the Cross Keys, a connection repeated from 'Brother Jacob,' in which David Faux can easily steal his mother's money because of her 'simple key (not in the least like Chubb's patent)' (5). This reference in 'Brother Jacob' to the lock-and-key company begun in 1818 and surviving today as Chubb Security Systems indicates that George Eliot was well aware of associations between the name Chubb and the keys that figure in many of her inn signs.

The public house signs of *Felix Holt* also problematize the construction of Rufus Lyon, a parent whose acts toward Esther diverge both from strict honesty and fidelity to his vocation. Mr Lyon is abstemious and well intentioned and, like Silas Marner's, his responsible child raising earns him the faithful love of a young woman who chooses to be his daughter. He neither drinks alcohol nor abandons parental responsibility. But George Eliot's location of the chapel at Malthouse Yard raises questions regarding the metaphorical construction of the preacher. Literally, a malthouse produces ingredients for intoxicants; figuratively, Malthouse Yard produces what the Debarrys regard as those 'pernicious sources of intoxication' (127), Rufus's sermons.

In addition, as Ina Taylor points out, George Eliot names Rufus himself for a public house, indeed, as her journal passage regarding the travelers' inns indicates, a favorite. According to Taylor, George Eliot has 'contrived to give the teetotal Baptist minister the name of a public house in slightly disguised form' (183). Red Lion public houses occur in nearly all the fiction beginning with Dempster's in 'Janet's Repentance.' A Red Lion is Dunsey Cass's favorite house, and Tommy Trounsem also patronizes a Red Lion. In *Middlemarch* Fred stays at a Red Lion when he buys the drugged horse Diamond in hopes of paying his gambling debts. The Red Lion in Holborn was a meeting place for Lewes and his friends early in the forties and supposedly forms the prototype for the Hand and Banner in *Daniel Deronda*. The plethora of Red Lions in both nineteenth-century England and George Eliot's fiction intensifies the likelihood of Taylor's interpretation of Rufus Lyon's name, an interpretation which, rather than simplifying, complicates the character of the virtuous but silly Evangelical clergyman.

Finally, the White Hart at Loamford forms the setting for Jermyn's melodramatic revelation to Harold of his fatherhood, a revelation that confirms the narrator's favoring merit over heritage. The natural antipathy between Harold and his father and Jermyn's perversion of his paternal role through the theft of his son's estate again connect irresponsibility and biological parenthood. Mrs Transome cannot induce Jermyn to promise to avoid quarreling with Harold, and Harold brings suit in Chancery against his natural father as soon as he can after the election. Having learned Esther's identity, Harold no longer fears Jermyn's knowledge and goes on with the suit, meanwhile refusing to see Jermyn at all. Jermyn's desperate announcement at the White Hart gains him nothing but the scorn of the group and wins for Harold the gentle help of Sir Maximus who has scarcely spoken to the younger man since Harold's declaration of his Radical partisanship. The rightness of Jermyn's fate at the White Hart repeats George Eliot's treatment of the irresponsible father Godfrey Cass in *Silas Marner*.

Medicinal Metaphors of Meliorism

In the 'Address to Working Men by Felix Holt,' George Eliot revives her character from the 1866 novel and also repeats the difficulties with metaphor that create problems in the novel. Just as the drinking in the 'Introduction' associates the narrator of the novel with the drunken Mr Sampson and hence with the vicious Mr Jermyn (consequently undermining the narrator's reliability), the metaphors of the 'Address' indicate that George Eliot failed to work out the implications of her drinking, drug, and illness metaphors completely in the *Blackwood's* essay. For one thing, Felix, who in the novel attacks Harold's and Jermyn's metaphors of bridges and coach ribbons, in the essay himself addresses a supposed audience of newly enfranchised 'working men' through a variety of 'generalities and analogies' (275) such as he criticizes in the novel through his allusion to Burke and Hare.

The essay embodies George Eliot's most direct expression of the organicist metaphor: 'Society stands before us like that wonderful piece of life, the human body, with all its various parts depending on one another, and with a terrible liability to get wrong because of that delicate dependence. We all know how many diseases the human body is apt to suffer from, and how difficult it is even for the doctors to find out exactly where the seat or beginning of the disorder is. This is because the body is made up of so many various parts, all related to each other, or likely all to feel the effect if any one of them goes wrong' (614-5). However, when Felix refers to his audience as a body (611, 614, 618, 620), he is distinguishing the body of the working class from other bodies, specifically on the grounds that 'as a body we are neither very wise nor very virtuous' (610). By distinguishing this body from that of the privileged classes, Felix unintentionally suggests that the social body described above does not represent all of society. Rather, a number of bodies represent the different classes that make up society in general. His organcist metaphors ultimately divide classes rather than uniting them under a mutual concern stemming from a sense that harming the whole inevitably harms the part.

George Eliot further divides the classes through Felix's illustrations of the law of inheritance. He concedes that the 'wealth' (621), specifically the 'treasure of knowledge . . . which is carried on from the minds of one generation to the minds of another' (621), forms the inheritance of the upper classes. At the same time he figures ignorance as disease. To educated people (that is, the wealthy), the opposite of ignorance (that is, learning) can produce a delight that 'lessens bodily pain' (621). But sending poor children to work rather than to school breeds 'a moral pestilence' (624) and exposes them to the 'infection of childish vice' (623). While the people born to privilege inherit leisure and wealth, wealth both in its literal sense and in the sense of opportunities for learning, the poor inherit disease.

Felix's contrasting wealth/disease metonyms for the differing heritages of the rich and the poor lay a heavy obligation upon the poor who must cure themselves. The successful replacements of fathers such as Thias, Godfrey, and Mr Vincy with such non-biological but mutually responsible parental/filial relationships such as those between Bartle Massey/Adam Bede, Silas Marner/Eppie, and Mr Garth/Fred exemplify this heroic divergence from a highly determining force. As in the novel, Felix urges the working classes to change this particular law of inheritance by educating their children. Thus his solution parallels the plots that rearrange heritage by replacing the biological parent with a responsible one.

Felix typifies the nineteenth-century belief in an intimate

relationship between vice and health when he tells the working men: 'I suppose there is hardly anything more to be shuddered at than that part of the history of disease which shows how, when a man injures his constitution by a life of vicious excess, his children and grandchildren inherit diseased bodies and minds, and how the effects of that unhappy inheritance continue to spread beyond our calculation' (613). At the same time, depriving the wealthy class of its inherited responsibilities diminishes the condition of everyone and would 'injure your own inheritance and the inheritance of your children' (622). George Eliot's fiction does not dwell on the intellectual heritage of wealth: she seldom portrays a wealthy character who takes advantage of his opportunities and becomes a brilliant thinker. Rather, (although, as the drug/disease metaphor suggests, possibly a bit desperately) she suggests how demonstrations of responsibility in working class characters for whom circumstance has made such heroism improbable, nevertheless can thwart the coercion of inherited conditions.[7]

At the end of the 'Address,' Felix makes a reference to amputation which inevitably evokes a threat to the social body. But Felix alludes to amputation, not to demonstrate the horror of revolution but rather to call attention to the opposite of revolution, that is, to the dangers of thoughtless adherence to custom. Ever since her review of Riehl in 1856, George Eliot dramatized the surrender of her working class characters to the coercion of tradition. Indeed the paternal replacements alluded to above demonstrate a breaking away from the determinism of a paltry or damaging inheritance, an escape which Felix calls for in the 'Address.'

The reason Felix mentions amputation is to demonstrate the discovery of 'right remedies' (625). He praises the ingenuity of seventeenth-century physician Ambrose Paré who replaced the technique of searing the arteries to stop post-amputation bleeding with the technique of tying the arteries. Felix's recommendation of leaders like Paré returns him to his favorite version of the drug/disease metaphor, the version which links himself with a physician who remedies social ills.

If the Felix who delivers the 'Address' is the same Felix from the novel, he would be around sixty years old before the enfranchisement of the working man could occasion his 'Address.' But Felix has been consistent. He still considers himself a working man, and he still believes in educating the children of the working class so 'as not to go on recklessly breeding a moral pestilence among us' (624). Again in keeping with the Felix from the novel, he ends his 'Address' with a plea for 'a resolution that is mixed with temperance' (627). The last word we will ever get out of Felix Holt thus contains an ambiguity of genus and species. His main ostensible meaning concerns political moderation of all kinds. But its specific nineteenth-century connection with anti-drink movements repeats his methods in Treby. The crusader who as a young man visits the Sugar Loaf at Sproxton to try to get the patrons to spend their money on a school rather than on Sunday ale has modified neither his belief in alcohol as the problem nor the metaphors in which he perceives the solution.

This punning about temperance groups Felix with George Eliot's punsters, some of whom pun deliberately. Mr Stelling favors jokes that confuse meanings. Not only does he have fun taunting Tom at the dinner table about 'declining' roast beef, but his own favorite author is Theodore Hook, author of *The Will and the Widow; or, Puns in Plenty*, and, according to Robert Colby, 'the most widely read author in England' (3). The *Mill* narrator puns about 'public'(-house) opinion and war in the passage discussed in Chapter 4 regarding Mr Poulter's narratives at the Black Swan. This precedent in an earlier novel sets up the pun (surely unintended?) that occurs in Felix's first speech, the one about the power of public opinion he delivers on the nomination day at Duffield in the novel. The narrator of this incident takes care to mention the names of the inns where the candidates headquarter on nomination day (the Crown, the Three Cranes, and the Fox and Hounds), even though they appear but briefly in the narrative. Whether intentionally or not, in a move that emphasizes playful language, George Eliot subverts the thrust of Felix's speech by indicating that 'public' opinion on nominating day at Duffield is also very likely public-house opinion.

Notes

1. Proceeding from a different set of conflicts (ideological versus aesthetic rather than metaphorical versus literal), Terry Eagleton arrives at a similar conclusion. George Eliot's '*metaphorical* closure of ideological conflict' (124) gives way to '*metonymic* resolution' (his italics 124). The inadequacies of closure which proceeds from organicist metaphors subvert this closure and produce 'absences and dislocations' (125). Philip Fisher notes similarly inadequate resolutions in *Silas Marner* and 'Brother Jacob': 'The chain of events that created the danger is historically and psychologically literal, while the deliverance, the redemption of the self as in *Silas Marner* or of society in 'Brother Jacob,' is accurate only symbolically' (25).
2. Joseph Wiesenfarth argues that George Eliot's conception of Felix leads her to emphasize his hypocrisy: 'Drunkenness is condemned by a man who can be drunk without wine' (*Mythmaking* 177).
3. See Gallagher's 'Body' on this monteray/medicinal relationship.
4. The coach reins form another allusion to the *Phaedrus*. Shuttleworth connects the reins as a metaphor for Grandcourt's control of Gwendolen to this dialogue (188), but it occurs with more prominence in *Felix Holt*. See Cohen's article, 'Avoiding the High Prophetic Strain: DeQuincey's Mail Coach and *Felix Holt*,' which compares DeQuincey's and George Eliot's Tally-Hos.
5. Carolyn Lesjack perceives the alehouse scenes as a way to 'mute class conflict . . . the working class is represented in the pub or the home thereby allowing it to be defined in terms of its pleasures rather than its productive activities' (81).
6. Welsh's chapter on *Deronda* notes the importance of this character.
7. Gallagher believes that George Eliot does not tie up her inheritance plots: Felix must deny his personal inheritance in favor of a national inheritance. But the 'Address' clarifies George Eliot's point: the wealthy need to accept their treasure of knowledge; the poor need to reject their heritage of illness, drunkenness, ignorance, and disease. Adam's, Felix's, and Eppie's escapes from drugged parents is thus explained. See Altick's *Common Reader* regarding Victorian hopes for replacing pubs with libraries (229).

During the writing of *Middlemarch*, George Eliot and George Henry Lewes visited Harrogate, a spa which listed remedies for alcoholism among the cures available.

8

Middlemarch: *'Profit Out of Poisonous Pickles'*

And yet he was but esy of dispence.
He kepte that he wan in pestilence,
For gold in phisik is a cordial,
Therefore he loved gold in special (441-4)

Chaucer's *Canterbury Tales*

In *Middlemarch* George Eliot creates a society that suffers many ills she has heretofore associated with drinking and drug-taking: political instability, irresponsible parenthood, class ambition, various addictions, deficient educations, physical and moral sicknesses–all presented concurrently with failed attempts to produce stable effects from such volatile and powerful kinds of language as prayer, romantic poetry, wills, mythography, medical treatises, and gossip.[1] In this novel, George Eliot creates a protagonist (or co-protagonist) whose healing occurs on the mimetic rather than the metaphorical level. Lydgate's ultimate aggravation of the social ills of Middlemarch reiterates George Eliot's close association between the physical and the spiritual health of the community because all Lydgate's medical expertise and care for its physical problems cannot save either himself or the town from the dismal physical *and* moral results of ignoring its social dynamics and spiritual needs, in effect, the state of the entire organism. In the end, his effects on Middlemarch carry the duality of the *Pharmakon*. On the one hand, he has contributed much to Middlemarch medicine, especially the infirmary and the fever hospital; on the other, his departure leaves the health of the town in the hands of its inferior colleagues and its residents stewing in the sensational aftermath of the death of Raffles.

In *Middlemarch*, George Eliot also returns to conspicuous

comments on and dramatizations of the dangers of misinterpreting signs, especially in the plot of Dorothea's mistaken reading of Casaubon, the character represented as a book in a number of ways (Wiesenfarth *Mythmaking* 189).[2] Having herself succumbed to excessive metaphorization in *Felix Holt* and 'Felix Holt,' she places the question at the center of the plot and makes metaphor a major concern of the narrator as well, a concern often dramatized by events that link drinking, drugs, and disease with problematic inheritance, absence, and repetition. The characters who interpret responsibly succeed best in *Middlemarch*.

As in *Silas Marner*, the ability to overcome addictions helps measure success or failure in this novel, specifically through a contrast between two male characters, Lydgate and Fred. Lydgate, who begins with talent, ambition, and a habit of drinking sugar water at parties, cannot overcome his entanglements with drugs and drug figures, even though his miserable fate does not include alcoholism. While Lydgate must relinquish his physician's role in Middlemarch, Dorothea, who leaves metaphorical intoxication behind her, assumes this role on the metaphorical level. Fred Vincy, on the other hand, wins many rewards for abandoning his dangerous habits, even though those habits have not yet reached the addictive stage. Meanwhile, the novel's most negative characters all have either mimetic or metaphorical connections with drinking and drugs.

Casaubon, Rosamond, Featherstone, and Bulstrode

Characters in general drink less in *Middlemarch* than in *Felix Holt*. Two scenes of drunkenness involve circumstances described as rare. Dagley's indulgence at the Blue Bull, which he regards as an 'extravagance' (289), prepares him to speak especially rudely to Mr Brooke who comes to the farm to report Dagley's son's poaching. On the day of the speech that ends in his pelting, Mr Brooke's sherry affects him so strongly precisely because he rarely drinks. Raffles' name associates him with a form of gambling, with general profligacy, and, possibly, with a Singapore inn which was already prominent in the nineteenth century. Only he incessantly creates havoc through his intoxication.

George Eliot's expanded drug paradigm involves all the most negative characters with intoxication and/or addiction. The social status of Mr Casaubon, Rosamond Vincy, and Mr Bulstrode means that none of these characters could possibly frequent a public house, and Mr Featherstone, by the time the novel opens, has become too sick to leave Stone Court. But George Eliot creates metaphorical links between these destructive characters and intoxication. All four are or become physically ill, and all four tamper with heredity in drastic ways. The characters who allow themselves and their actions to become twisted in intoxicant metaphors and the processes they represent are the villains in this novel.

Mr Casaubon's fatty degeneration of the heart, like Captain Wybrow's heart complaint, is both literal and metaphorical. George Eliot attributes his ill health to the life of the scholar and the reading it demands as a cause of his disease. In addition, as W. J. Harvey and Neil Hertz agree, Casaubon's punctuation-mark blood identifies him not only as a reader of books but as a book himself. In this character, self-poisoning occurs as a result of a progressive physical illness that feeds on his own bookishness. His representation as a mummy (preserved in an unctuous gum which can have healing properties) recurs in the exclamations of Sir James and continues in the many tomb settings where George Eliot places him. In *Darwin's Plots*, Gillian Beer points out that myth, the moving force of Casaubon's scholarly life, provides the reassurance of 'recurrence' (174). In his scholarship, therefore, Casaubon searches out repetition: the repetition created by similarities among the myths in various cultures. He relies intellectually on the same process as the addict, and his project aggravates his illness.

Nor does Rosmond Vincy show any signs of overindulgence in alcohol or, with the exception of her financial problems, its metaphorical equivalents. However, she has grown up in a residence that Mrs Vincy, the daughter of an innkeeper and a former barmaid, runs very much like a public house. Her father mixes politics and drink. He prefers to act the role of the genial 'host' (258), boring Lydgate mightily with his inevitable evening drunkenness during the period of the courtship which Lydgate wants to abbreviate. As the novel advances, Rosamond, the innkeeper's granddaughter, becomes increasingly poisonous herself. After her miscarriage, Lydgate becomes 'conscious of new elements in his life as noxious to him as an inlet of mud to a creature that has been used to breathe and bathe and dart after its illuminated prey in the clearest of waters' (427). The mistake of marrying her begins to 'work in him like a recognized chronic disease' (431). The 'Finale' brackets the report of Lydgate's early death with its famous representation of Rosamond as poisonous basil, the 'plant which had flourished wonderfully on a murdered man's brains' (610). With George Eliot's usual creativity in rearranging traditional metaphors, the image reverses the causes and effects of death. Instead of killing the murdered man, the plant benefits from his death.

In Featherstone's plot, a second family home, Stone Court, also becomes an open house. One potential legatee, the auctioneer Borthrup Trumbull, relishes the ham and ale served there and praises Mary Garth for her careful measuring of Featherstone's medicines. In locating similarities between *Middlemarch* and Wilhelmine von Hillern's *Ein Arzt de Seele*, E. A. McCobb describes Hartwich, the Featherstone character in the German work, as 'intemperate' (572). Like Mary Garth, Hartwich's daughter refuses him a deathbed request, not for a piece of writing like Featherstone's will, nor for a box of money, but for schnapps (581). Peter's introduction of Rigg Featherstone into the family works upsets legitimate family members who consider themselves 'brewed' (246) Featherstones. Jonah Featherstone chooses to sit in the kitchen corner at Stone Court because its comforts remind him of 'the bar at the Green Man' (225). The scene involves sickness, legacies, ale, language, and medicines, and Jonah finds in Stone Court a strong resemblance to a public house. When Fred and Mary move in, they transform Stone Court from its state when in possession of Bulstrode and Rigg Featherstone, back into a family home. The banker and the money changer depart.

Like Featherstone, Bulstrode is unwell. The narrator believes he has a 'sickly aspect' (91), and Lydgate verifies this through his 'unfavorable opinion of the banker's constitution' (92). Bulstrode's health deteriorates as his problems worsen. By the end of the novel he has decided on a trip to Cheltenham for its health benefits. Furthermore, his faulty neighbors see his attention to their business as moral wine-tasting: 'If you are not proud of your cellar, there is no thrill of satisfaction in seeing your guest hold up his wine-glass to the light and look judicial' (91).   Despite his abstemiousness, Middlemarch itself applies a drink metaphor to his moral judgments of its residents.

All Bulstrode's businesses are drug-related. The pawnshop business, permanently connected with Gin Lane in Hogarth's popular engraving, gives way to his banking and other enterprises when he moves to Middlemarch. He profits from dyes that destroy the cloth they color, and earns Mrs Dollop's suspicion and loathing by making her an offer for the Tankard, a little-noticed example of Bulstrode's hypocrisy. As the most prominent Evangelical in Middlemarch, he also is subject to George Eliot's characters' continued representations of Evangelicalism as disease, a perception attributed to communities from Milby through Middlemarch.

Bulstrode himself continually mis-applies drug metaphors. Remembering the processes by which he has abandoned his early ideals, he reflects through an alcoholic metaphor that he is not the founder of the pawnshop business: 'Is it not one thing to set up a new gin-palace and another to accept an investment in an old one?' (451). His agricultural view of such businesses 'as implements for tilling Thy garden' (451) exemplifies the 'metaphors and precedents' (451) by which he justifies himself. Lydgate's distaste for his troublesome sponsor reaches a peak during the scene in which Bulstrode selfishly frets about the possibility of cholera. Lydgate feels revulsion toward Bulstode's 'broken metaphor and bad logic' (498).

As each of Bulstrode's businesses replaces its predecessors, the replacements propel him up the ladder of respectability. His wealth proceeds directly from interrupting a line of descent that should have led from Mrs Dunkirk to Will Ladislaw through Will's mother Sarah. When Bulstrode poisons Raffles he obliterates a drunken man after the failure of his repeated attempts to exchange money for Raffles' absence. Similarly, Mr Casaubon sunders all contact with his young cousin, Rosamond helps brings about her own miscarriage, and Featherstone diverts his money to his illegitimate son. All four characters, metaphorically and mimetically associated with drinking, drinking places, and drugs, disrupt descent in some way.

Good Doctor/ Bad Doctor

Because *Middlemarch* includes both the mimetic remedies which occur in Lydgate's plot and metaphorical poisons such as occur in Rosamond's pursuit of a romantic life, scholars have been discussing some aspects of the drug/disease metaphor in *Middlemarch* for decades. Genre critics who define the novel form as anti-romance emphasize Rosamond's representation in the 'Finale' as a devouring basil plant. Her tenacious romanticism contrasts with Dorothea's progress from a state of illusion to a state of mature understanding of   something they call 'reality.' (George Eliot clinches her suggestion that Dorothea's marriage to Casaubon results from a shortsightedness that is both physical and intellectual in the famous 'disease of the retina' [144] image applied to her muddled perceptions of Rome on her honeymoon.)[3] The explicit comments on metaphor have attracted many later scholars who write as deconstructionists (for example, J. Hillis Miller, D. A. Miller, and Jan Gordon), many of whom notice drug-related metaphors in particular. Meanwhile, Anna Kitchel's edition of the 'Quarry for *Middlemarch*' and Jerome Beaty's '*Middlemarch*: From Notebook to Novel' prove the thoroughness with which George Eliot researched (mainly in *The Lancet*) such aspects of Reform-era medicine as the status of Lydgate's profession, his theories on treatments for alcohol poisoning, and his plans for dealing with the cholera epidemic.[4] Because of his profession, such discussions of illness, medicine, money, drugs, and bodies often focus on Lydgate.

Like the drugs represented by Plato's *Pharmakon* metaphor (and like Esther Lyon and Gwendolen Harleth), Lydgate starts out in a state of poise between opposite fates as healer and killer. Perceptions of doctors in Reform-era Britain aggravate his problems with money, drugs, and language, any of which has the ability to move him suddenly in one direction or the other, especially because of the impending cholera (a disease frequently treated with opium-based mixtures [Parssinen 23]). As a physician, Lydgate cannot escape the tendency of the public not only to confuse him with his drugs but also to attribute to him their volatility. When this happens, his reputation in Middlemarch does not so much decline as move precipitously from one side to the other of a traditional dichotomy.

In the beginning and on the mimetic level Lydgate is conscientious about dispensing drugs and about ascertaining the condition of the individual body to which he administers the dose. Even (especially) in the case of Raffles, the narrator leaves no doubt that his diagnosis and prescription are in line with the diseased and alcoholic condition of the body of the patient. But Lydgate fails as a physician partly because he does not heed Plato's advice about considering the individual nature of the receiver of his language (a reader or an auditor) as well as of his medicine. He alienates Mr Mawmsey through literary allusions beyond the grocer's understanding, and goes on to alienate the rest of Middlemarch through similar examples of condescension to their ignorance.

George Eliot draws on a set of long-held cultural representations of physicians, modified by developments in early Victorian medical science, to create the set of problems that helps destroy Lydgate. A variety of physicians and allusions to physicians throng the pages of *Middlemarch*, including some of the earliest practitioners such as Hippocrates, Theophrastus, and Galen, as well as characters modeled on physicians George Eliot knew personally. And, whether from past or present, fiction or history, these physicians are often engaged in conflicts with each other. Having mentioned such physicians at odds as Pilgrim and Pratt in 'Amos' and Paracelsus and Avicenna in *Romola*, she sustains the pattern in *Middlemarch*. James Hill mentions among Lydgate's models during his medical education in Paris two physicians who disagreed, Broussais and Louis. George Eliot's medical practitioners not only exist in mutual hostility over opposing methods of treatment, for example the heroic versus the homeopathic, but the physicians in her literature, as in her life, nearly always fall on one side or another of the good doctor/bad doctor dichotomy.

People as sickly as the Leweses could not help but become acquainted with a number of physicians, and many of these physicians took positions on opposite sides of medical questions, as well as on opposite sides of the good doctor/bad doctor dichotomy. From her earliest days in Nuneaton, Evans was used to hearing of medical controversy. Mr Bucknill, often called in by the Evanses, was one of the harshest critics of his incompetent colleague, Mr Lloyd. Together with Mr Nason, he brought action against Lloyd for libel in 1830 at the Warwick Assizes ('Occurences'). Charles Bray's newspaper, for which Evans wrote during the mid-1840s (and which, I have argued elsewhere, provided a certain amount of the conflict in *Felix Holt* and *Middlemarch*), records many medical arguments and differences. An article in the 'Literature and Science' column in December 1846 (where Evans published her reviews), begins its review of the *British and Foreign Medical Review*, with the question, 'When doctors differ who shall decide?' (2). Her research in *The Lancet* acquainted her with the 'combative' editor Thomas Wakley (Altick *Presence* 553) who himself dichotomised physicians in his attacks on quacks, in particular St John Long.

Most of the physicians in George Eliot's life also fall on one side or the other of the good doctor/bad doctor dichotomy. The many doctors of her acquaintance proposed as models for Lydgate (suggested by Kitchel, Ellman, Haight, and McCarthy) indicate the extent of her knowledge of physicians, and, despite their own doctors' lack of success in enhancing or even maintaining her and Lewes's health, she seems to have been satisfied with them. During her girlhood, Mr Bucknill was among the family's closest friends, as his name appears in Robert Evans's journal at a rate of about once a week over several decades. They frequently had dinner or tea together, and he remained their physician over many periods of illness in all the family members. In 1836 he served as one of the pall bearers at Christiana Evans's funeral.

As an underappreciated young woman, Evans enjoyed the approval of Dr John Bury who treated her father at Griff and praised her nursing highly. When she moved to London her friendship with feminist Barbara Bodichon resulted in expressions of admiration for Dr Elizabeth Blackwell, the first British woman physician. Her writing suggests an admiration for Dr Andrew Combe (*GEL* 2:80), and she and Lewes both placed their health in the care of Andrew Clarke and Sir James Paget for the last, and sickliest, years of their lives.

On the bad doctor side, one might place Dr Robert Brabant who toyed with her affections in 1843 (Haight 49) and whose unsuccessful healing can be measured in his inability to get Samuel Taylor Coleridge, his most famous patient, off the opium. Dr John Chapman, at various times George Eliot's friend, enemy, lover, and editor, was, according to Haight, probably a quack. He earned his medical degree in 1857 from a Scottish diploma mill (Haight 229).

As it happens, these doctors' attitudes toward drugs indicate their good doctor/bad doctor status. Combe, whose articles on homeopathy for the *British and Foreign Medical Review* were reviewed in the same issue of the *Coventry Herald and Observer* in which Evans's first publications appeared, advocated the drug-free course of treatment in which the physician may 'even be the means of saving the patient's life, and yet not give one particle of medicine' (4 December 1846). When tending Evans's father, Dr Bury *pre*scribed only sea air and *pro*scribed wine (Haight 64-65), treatments most likely acceptable to his patient whose diary records a stoical attitude toward sickness and drugs. On 15 July 1832, when prescribed mercury by Mr Bucknill, he notes in his journal his intention to try to 'do without.' When George Eliot read *The Anatomy of Melancholy* she marked Burton's passage on Arnoldus de Villa Nova: 'A wise physician will not give physick, but upon necessity, and first try medicinal dyet, before he proceed to medicinal cure' (345). Brabant, on the other hand, with his unsuccessful record with Coleridge, failed to control the huge and constant opium consumption for which the poet is famous. John Chapman's ambition centered on an attempt 'to startle the world with some marvelous nostrum that would make his fortune' (Haight *George Eliot and John Chapman* 114). Chapman's single publication in medicine is a seven-page pamphlet on *Chloroform and Other Anaesthetics: How They Act, How They Kill, and How They May Be Safely Used*, published in 1858. Lydgate's resolution to avoid selling drugs aligns him, at least in the beginning of the novel, with good doctors who, unlike Chapman and Brabant, are reluctant to rely on dosing their patients.

'Physicians and Quacks,' which Lewes wrote for *Blackwood's* in 1862, distinguishes between the two on the basis of their attitudes toward drugs. According to Lewes, administering a specific as if it were a panacea loses a practitioner his status as physician: 'Let a man employ quinine as a panacea, instead of a specific–that is to say, let him give it as a cure for all, or many diseases, besides ague–and he becomes a quack' (167). Lewes stresses the individual constitution in this article, as well as the ambiguity of the drug: the quack 'has but one arrow in his quiver, and with it he cures or kills' (167). His article also deplores the false testimonials of drug advertisements, thus anticipating an issue George Eliot raises in both *Felix Holt* and *Middlemarch*.

Money is only one substitutional system with which doctors have peculiarly intimate relationships. Famous for hideously poor handwriting, they nevertheless write one of the most directly powerful kinds of language. During the act of purchase, the prescription combines with money to replace the drug at the pharmacy. When the patient consumes the drug another replacement occurs: if the drug is working properly it will replace the disease in the body. This replacement of disease by drug and of drug by a combination of the patient's money and the doctor's writing, despite its medical inaccuracy, embodies nineteenth-century perceptions of a beneficent process of substitution. Nevertheless, at each stage of such replacements among money, writing, and drugs, the power to kill as well as the power to cure might release itself.

In representing his work as writing, both Lydgate and the narrator demonstrate his failures. Lydgate describes his professional ambitions in his favorite lines from the Samuel Daniel sonnet. He wants 'To do worthy the writing, and to write/Worthy the reading and the world's delight' (320).[5] But the narrator points out some threatening aspects of representing medical activities as writing. Describing the reasons for the positive side of Lydgate's reputation, the narrator reveals that his fame as an effective healer depends on misinterpretations, in particular of his success with the servant-girl's cramp. Evoking the advertisements that appeared on the first pages of nineteenth-century provincial newspapers (including the Coventry *Herald*) for such remedies as the Cordial Balm of Syriacum, the Concentrated Detersive Essence, Brodie's antisyphilitics, and Holloway's Pills, the narrator calls such cures 'fortune's testimonials' which 'deserve as much credit as the written or printed kind' (328), that is, none. As Altick notes, 'The venerable quack-medicine trade had been one of the chief early supports of the primitive advertising industry' (549), yet another association between drugs and writing. Because of 'increasing literacy and cheap access to printed means of communication' quackery became 'a road to easy riches' (549). Ads for medicines appearing everywhere, including in the pages of Victorian novels themselves, created yet another reason for applying the Platonic figure of writing as drug.

Because Lydgate's non-writing of prescriptions represents his moral success in achieving cures without drugging his patients, while his unwritten articles represent his failure to fulfill the words of the Daniel sonnet, another kind of absence occurs, and non-action represents something.[6] The drastic ambiguity attached to Lydgate attaches to his treatments, his writing, and his speech as well. None is entirely or essentially pernicious; they all have the potential to either kill or cure, although in the outcome, they are more likely to kill.

Like many of George Eliot's most flawed and befuddled characters, Lydgate persistently applies drug/disease metaphors himself. To clinch his confidence in his mental superiority as a scientist over mediocre artists, he perceives 'indifferent drawing or cheap narration' (122) as reflections of life 'in a diseased dream' (122). Because they result from a 'vulgar and vinous' (122) sort of inspiration, he believes these drawings and stories are entirely dissimilar to the products of his own scientific imagination. He applies the famous Voltairian arsenic/sheep metaphor to his relationship with Bulstrode, imagining that he can separate the 'arsenic-man' (130) from his accompanying incantations.

He and Ladislaw squabble over their relative disinterestedness regarding the concerns of their sponsors, Mr Bulstrode and Mr Brooke, after Lydgate's accusation that 'you political writers' (341) go 'crying up a measure as if it were a universal cure, and crying up men who are a part of the very disease that wants curing' (341). In this conversation Lydgate makes an error he avoids scrupulously when prescribing, but constantly falls into when talking and writing. Speaking 'blind to what Ladislaw might infer' (342), he fails to analyze the mixed mental condition of his friend (the receiving body) who listens to the political attack he couches in medical metaphors.

The approach of cholera in Reform-era England led to the prevalence of a set of metaphors that, according to Frank Mort, attached the conditions of poverty (overcrowding, promiscuity) to its cause and the conditions of the middle-class life (for example, cleanliness) to its cure, especially 'in the industrial parishes of the midlands and the north' where 'cholera was a favourite subject for Sunday sermons when local vicars used lurid metaphors of disease to demonstrate that sickness was God's chastisement for sin' (31).[7] John Phillips Kay, for one, 'mobilized Old Testament language to argue that cholera was a messenger of death, which had been sent to punish the corruption of the people and a flawed system of government' (30). Lydgate's precarious position on the brink of losing all his money and possessions places the threat of causing rather than curing cholera especially close to his experience. The threat of precipitous financial failure that terrified Victorians carried the additional terror of eventual dissection. A complete failure that might place Lydgate among the genuinely impoverished would transform him from dissector to dissected, for by this point the temporal setting has reached the period just after passage of the Anatomy Act, which provided the necessary corpses from among impoverished and unclaimed deaths, rather than from among executed criminals (Richardson).

On the one hand, George Eliot's assumptions regarding the intimacy of the physical and spiritual suggests the interchangeableness of moral and physical causes of both illness and recovery; on the other, her emphasis on sorting out metaphors calls for taking care *not* to confuse the causes and effects of, for example, sin, with the causes and effects of disease. Especially in *Middlemarch*, with its many allusions to the individual constitution and its opening description of 'man' as a 'mysterious mixture' (3), the complexity of the factors affecting health is intimidatingly great. As with her own narrative efforts to trace the multiple complex causes of results both trivial and momentous, the complexity means that the effort at analysis must stop somewhere. The problem with Lydgate's effort is that it stops too soon.

And despite his scrupulosity regarding the sale of drugs, Lydgate's effort to escape the bad-doctor side of the physician's dichotomy ultimately fails. Whereas he sees himself as Vesalius, Middlemarchers identify him with St John Long (333), another believer in the effectiveness of a single medicine, in his case his own caustic liniment (Altick *Presence* 553). Lydgate's medical colleagues, indulging in large quantities of both wine and professional jealousy, see him as ambiguous: he is 'arrogant' (331) and yet full of 'crawling subservience' (331) to Bulstrode. Middlemarchers often demonstrate their dual perceptions of Lydgate, all of which have connections with heredity, language, and politics, at drinking places.

Lydgate's major failure as a physician causes the death of a patient in whom alcohol and disease already mix in a soupy complexity which demands the most careful prescription of remedies.

Whereas in *Felix Holt* George Eliot presents the working class in unruly numbers, in *Middlemarch* she allows only Raffles to emerge conspicuously from the mass of ignorant Britons. Consequently he becomes a synecdochic representative of his class. The crowd that gathers at the public house considers him one of their own, 'the best of company' (530), but like his unenfranchised fellow drinkers, he is polluted by ignorance and alcohol, an embodiment of the popular nineteenth-century notion of the working class as perpetually drunk. Lydgate describes Raffles' physical condition: like working-class Britain, he is a victim of 'long-standing complications' with a 'system' in 'a ticklish state,' but (another pun) the owner of a 'robust constitution to begin with' (512). The condition of the receiving body here is decidedly alcoholic. Like the reading, drinking, gossiping public that gathers at the public, Raffles is already full of poison. In his morally and physically polluted body, the alcohol combines with the opium administered by Bulstrode to act as pure poison. George Eliot's synecdochic portrayal of his class through the body of Raffles resembles her method in the 'Address to Working Men by Felix Holt.' Again she contrives a figure that detaches a lower-class body from a body that would represent society as a whole.

The deficiency in Lydgate's treatment of Raffles that eventually leads to the loss of the patient is that Lydgate fails to supervise the dosing. Distracted by money worries, he puts its administration into hands other than his own, and his agent tampers with it. Bulstrode's loan transforms Lydgate's remedy and therefore the physician himself from healer to killer of Raffles because of the toxic effect of combining money and drugs. In the case of Raffles, Lydgate's accurate estimate of the condition of the receiving body cannot stand against the intrusion of monetary considerations on his treatment.

It is at the Tankard Inn that Lydgate conclusively moves from one side to the other of the good doctor/bad doctor dichotomy when its drinkers associate him with Bulstrode's money, applying the common perception in their culture that a rich doctor is a bad doctor, probably a poisoner. At the Green Dragon, the drinking site for the higher classes, Mr Bambridge, Frank Hawley, and Mr Hopkins combine their information regarding relations between Bulstrode and Raffles to convict Lydgate as well as Bulstrode of murder. The narrator mentions three times that this conversation occurs as the men lounge under the archway of the inn, thus reviving the shape that conducts the party at the Rainbow to their suspect conclusion regarding the nonexistent peddler/thief in *Silas*

Marner. Arches, particularly the arches spanning the entrances to the yards of the drinking places, encourage coercive plots that conceal all or part of the truth in both cases.

The town of Middlemarch, which 'counts on swallowing Lydgate' (114) comfortably, functions like a body, again, as in 'Felix Holt,' a body distinct from that of English society at large. Middlemarch's intention of swallowing Lydgate manifests the town's persistent confusion between the physician and his drugs. But instead of swallowing Lydgate comfortably, Middlemarch expels him, vomits him up and out. Having assigned him the role of poisoner, the town cannot digest him because his composition does not agree with the condition of this receiving body. A subtle indication of Middlemarch's queasy stomach occurs in the name of one of its newspaper editors. In 'Why Did Mr Keck Edit the Trumpet,' D. M. Hill points out that the *OED* assigns the meaning *to vomit* to the word *keck* (713), which also refers to a trumpet-shaped flower. Both poisoner and poison, Lydgate in the end departs for the watering place where the physician fails to heal himself.

The Reform and Education of Fred

In contrast with Lydgate, Fred Vincy reduces his involvement with all the drug or drinking-related distractions that increasingly occupy his brother-in-law. His first predicament, the need for a testimonial from his Uncle Bulstrode to pacify Mr Featherstone, arises because of his bragging at the Green Dragon after some serious wine drinking. He also gambles heavily on billiards, and his academic failure testifies to his shaky relationship with the written word. But as the plot advances, he leaves behind all his potentially addictive occupations and even learns to write legibly as part of his redemption.

Among readers who have questioned Fred's merit, Bruce Martin argues that the young man improves little after the disastrous note costs the Garths their savings: 'But for returning to the university and passing examinations his subsequent behavior contains nothing essentially different' (9). Consequently Fred 'hardly merits the protective cocoon provided him' (9). Martin believes that Fred receives preferential treatment from his creator which undermines, indeed 'unravels,' the morality and ideology of the novel. However, like Silas's, Fred's achievement lies in overcoming incipient and sometimes metaphorical addictions. Martin approaches this interpretation when he concedes that 'Fred does convert from a lazy pursuit of gentlemanly ease to at least some version of the "business" ethic offered by Caleb Garth' (19).   But in the end he underestimates Fred's achievement.

The activities Fred leaves behind bring together gambling, drinking, repetition, and both metaphorical and mimetic disease, while the activities to which he turns his attention include three varieties of responsible dissemination. As he rides off to the horse fair at which he hopes to recoup his losses, the narrator applies an intoxication/disease metaphor/simile: 'Fred was not a gambler: he had not that specific disease in which the suspension of the whole nervous energy on a chance or risk becomes as necessary as the dram to the drunkard' (172). But the society of Horrock and Bambridge consists of Horrock's silence and Bambridge's repetition which 'like the fine old tune, "Drops of Brandy," gave you after a while a sense of returning upon itself in a way that might make weak heads dizzy' (174). The episode at the Red Lion poisons Fred literally. He issues from the public house to inspect Diamond and on his way to the stables picks up a physical sickness that endangers his life. He also acquires a horse that turns out unmanageable, probably because the calming drugs administered by Diamond's sellers have worn off. During this destructive phase of his fortunes, gambling, drinking, repetition, a drugged horse named after a jewel, and his ensuing literal sickness form a conspicuous cluster. Consequently, despite the narrator's disavowal, Fred's activities are incipient addiction.

By the same token, when Fred's fortunes improve, he replaces gambling and drinking with a life devoted to agriculture (dissemination), writing (dissemination), and fatherhood (also dissemination). Indeed the publication which represents his success in the 'Finale,' 'Cultivation of Green Crops and the Economy of Cattle-Feeding,' is metaphorical dissemination (because it is published) which concerns mimetic dissemination. Furthermore, he finds both his substitute father and his vocation following an incident in which he acts to turn some rebellious drinkers away from violent acts.

When Fred helps Caleb Garth subdue the group of laborers rebelling against the building of the railroad he gains a career Dorothea describes as 'healthy' (402). Solomon Featherstone has been agitating the laborers against the building of the railroad, a topic as locally stimulating as 'the imminent horrors of Cholera' (403). The inhabitants of the dismal town of Frick enjoy talking about the railroad more than about political reform because the consequences of the Bill are vague. Unlike the 'definite promise' implied by such non-political reform as 'a publican at the "Weights and Scales" who would brew beer for nothing' (404), the effects of the Reform Bill are distant and unpredictable. The discussion of the ruin that will result from the railroad flourishes at the Weights and Scales public house, and, when the laborers try to run off the railroad surveyors, they are fresh from 'their mid-day beer' (406). As a result of Fred's action in quelling the rebellion of these tipsy laborers, Caleb offers him a career, after which the episode culminates with Caleb's horror at Fred's illegible handwriting. His first task as an agent-in-training is to learn to write clearly.

One difference between Lydgate and Fred at the time of the crucial evening at the Green Dragon is that Fred has already gone through two failed fathers (Featherstone and Mr Vincy) and has found a responsible substitute in Caleb Garth. Lydgate, on the other hand, has no responsible father. Daunted by the refusals of Uncle Godwin and Mr Vincy, he has tried all possibilities for a loan except Bulstrode. He has already lost patients because of Bulstrode's conspicuous sponsorship; indeed, Mrs Taft (while knitting) conceives and then circulates the idea that Lydgate is Bulstrode's natural son. Lydgate's putting the wrong man into the authoritarian role parallels the results of post-Reform elections that empowered the wrong candidates.

George Eliot connects the gambling at the Green Dragon, which tempts both Fred and Lydgate, directly with heredity and disease. Initially, neither wine nor opium tempts Lydgate because he has 'no *hereditary* constitutional craving after such transient escapes' (my italics 489). As for gambling, in Paris he regards it 'as if it had been a disease' (489). But as he deteriorates he begins to see gambling not as a disease but a cure, a cure the narrator specifically links with his opium use: 'Just as he had tried opium, so his thought now began to turn upon gambling' (490). Most importantly, the narrator's indirect discourse suggests a substitutional relationship between his science and drugs: in the beginning his work is 'better than any opiate to quiet and sustain him' (489). But this substitutional relationship between the science and the drug prepares him to reverse their roles when his spending impels him to stop his research, smoke some opium, and go to the Green Dragon.

On the same occasion, Fred flees his writing lessons to get drunk. The narrator specifically brackets the pleasures of drinking, gambling, and talking in the report of Fred's effort to assure himself and his friends that 'if he abstains from making himself ill, or beggaring himself, or talking with the utmost looseness which the narrow limits of human capacity will allow, it is not because he is a spooney' (492). Rejecting these addiction-connected activities gains him more moral weight than he has traditionally been allowed.

Turning Wine to Water

Like Fred, although on a much smaller scale, Dorothea moves from potentially addictive behavior to an ability to resist the seduction of dangerous metaphors and compelling or compulsive narratives and in doing so demonstrates her resistance to the addictiveness of narrative in the particular form of Middlemarch gossip. The Middlemarch gossipers lean on the arches of repetition and predictability; Dorothea refuses to let such coercive plots form her explanations. Mrs Cadwallader's stories regarding Ladislaw and Rosamond only provoke her to an indignant defense. But as she passes 'under the archway of the lodge-gate at the Grange' (461) her fears about Rosamond and Will create a 'sickening certainty' (464). Her reward for her staunch resistance comes almost immediately as she encounters Will and learns he loves her.

After the 'sanitary' meeting at which Lydgate's assistance to Bulstrode links the two conclusively in the minds of Middlemarchers as murderers of Raffles, Dorothea responds to the story about Lydgate with efforts to salvage his reputation. When Mr Farebrother points out that character 'may becomes diseased as our bodies do' (538), she turns his metaphor around: 'Then it may be rescued and healed' (538). In Ladislaw's case, Dorothea's interruption of his scene with Rosamond leads to an angry attack that makes Rosamond sick, and again Dorothea helps.[8] Indeed Sally Shuttleworth writes of Dorothea: 'It is she, not Lydgate, who is the novel's true physician' (170). Without ever calling her own actions cures or herself a physician (as does, for example, Felix Holt), Dorothea improves conditions in Middlemarch.

During the often-discussed scene in the first chapter in which Dorothea and Celia divide their mother's jewels, Dorothea tries to endow them with meaning that will transform them from baubles of vanity into religious symbols. First she sees them as intoxicants: 'If I were to put on such a necklace as that, I should feel as if I had been pirouetting. The world would go round with me' (10). Then, under a new 'current of feeling' she adds a symbolic function, turning them into 'spiritual emblems,' and, in highly sexual language, compares them to perfume: 'How deeply the colours seem to penetrate one, like scent' (10). Dorothea pays dearly for the inability she here demonstrates to sort out symbolic meanings, but by the end of the novel, she can discern the various terms of metaphor and resist the coercion of pre-made plots, and she turns these abilities to productive ends.

George Eliot's famous association between Dorothea and St Theresa of Avila, established in the 'Prelude' and taken up again in the 'Finale,' adds a punning allusion to Dorothea's role as healer, as well as another evocation of the good doctor/bad doctor dichotomy. Dorothea mistakenly compares Casaubon to St Augustine, 'who united the glories of doctor and saint' (18); the narrator associates Dorothea with the female doctor of the church, St Theresa. Hence Casaubon is one metaphorical doctor; she, another. But whereas he dies of jealousy and books, she dispenses life and health. The good doctor/bad doctor dichotomy describes their marriage as well as Lydgate's reputation.

In the 'Finale' to *Middlemarch*, poisons surround the fate only of Lydgate who ends his life a wealthy but failed healer at a watering place. (Spas such as Harrogate, where the Leweses visited in 1864 and again in 1870, specify alcoholism among the conditions treatable there.) Fred and Mary and Dorothea and Will, on the other hand, succeed in establishing families that carry on legitimate descent. *Middlemarch*, in which George Eliot gets less entangled in her own metaphors than in *Felix Holt*, ends with the return of the Ladislaws to the community, rather than with a total abandonment like that at Treby Magna.

Will, too, like his wife, contrasts with the characters who muddle metaphor and divert heritage. He early demonstrates sensitivity on matters of inheritance and, like Fred, leaves behind mildly dangerous drug-connected behavior. Recognizing his deserts as a family member, he accepts Casaubon's financial support without falsely humble gratitude and refuses Bulstrode's tardy efforts to assuage his guilt by making ill-gotten gains available to the rightful heir. Early in the novel, the narrator refers to Will's experiments with opium, and dramatizes his wagering a bottle of champagne in a bet with Naumann about the origins of a bust in the Vatican Museums. Mr Frank Hawley, albeit mistakenly, anticipates his arrival to edit the *Pioneer* by supposing he is a drinker: 'some loose fish from London' (262). But George Eliot places Will in the position of fearing and resisting the effects of drugs rather than in the role of consumer. After he learns of Casaubon's codicil, he repeatedly dreads the possibility that Dorothea's friends are 'poisoning her mind with their suspicions of him' (395). Will's engagement to Dorothea occurs simultaneously with the Lords' throwing out of the Reform Bill, both only temporary setbacks, the one to increased democracy guaranteed by a written law, the other to non-pernicious inheritance. The Bill passes, Will becomes an

M.P., and the family reunites. The son of Dorothea and Will will inherit Mr Brooke's estate, while Will illustrates George Eliot's idea of exactly the kind of man who should gain power as a result of electoral politics.

The happy family reunion of the 'Finale' results from the legitimate birth of a son but also from writing and sickness. Mr Brooke's runaway pen issues an invitation to the young Ladislaws the same morning Celia receives Dorothea's letter with its news of sickness in childbirth. Writing, even Mr Brooke's irresponsible writing, works to reunite the family but only together with Dorothea's sickness, which culminates in legitimate birth, and, like much sickness in George Eliot's novels, has a positive effect. The 'Finale' thus contains hope for healing the Condition of England through measures that do not depend on disturbing inheritance and through writing, a return on the metaphorical level to the conventional hope that education will restore order in England without disturbing orderly descent among the upper classes. These conclusions echo the 'Address to Working Men.'

The metaphors in the final paragraph of the novel further invigorate the hope through a replacement of wine with water.[9] The narrator represents the political and marital success of the day-to-day love which produces a successful Member of Parliament and a restored legacy in a metaphor of water (the many-channeled river of Dorothea's diffuse influence), rather than wine. In *Adam Bede*, the love of Dinah and Adam contrasts with Arthur's love for Hetty which has been represented as poison: 'the slight words, the timid looks, the tremulous touches, by which two human souls approach each other gradually, like two quivering rainstreams' (411). Dorothea and Will's engagement occurs against a background of a rainstorm, and Will's effect as a husband is to turn the intoxication that has represented romantic love elsewhere in George Eliot's fiction into this life-sustaining water that represents Dorothea's wifehood. The narrator concludes that both the inmate of the unvisited tomb and the influence represented by water diminish the general 'ill' (613) of the world at large.

Notes

1. Carroll writes that all George Eliot's characters grapple with the 'problem of interpretation' (3).

2. A number of scholars have dwelt on gossip in *Middlemarch*. Timothy Morris' 'The Dialogic Universe of *Middlemarch*' describes in Bakhtinian terms George Eliot's position on the side of heteroglossia as opposed to 'monologic purifiers of language' (295). Morris notes that 'Middlemarch is a town of gossip' (286) in which Lydgate's act of writing a prescription for Fred Vincy leads to rumors that both attack and approve of his doctoring. This sequence concludes with Mrs Taft's confused notions of Lydgate's paternity. Patricia Spacks also connects money and gossip in *Middlemarch*, as does J. Hillis Miller in his contribution to *Approaches to Teaching Eliot's* Middlemarch. Beer includes gossip among the systems of circulation which help structure the novel.

3. Of many discussions of this passage, Hardy's in *Particularities* is most thorough.

4. More recently, Beer describes the many circulatory systems that organize *Middlemarch* (money, gossip, blood, the penny post, drains, and railroads), systems often joined in the novel and in nineteenth-century experience by metaphorical slippage. Beer's paradigm connects money (debt, gambling), gossip and other narrative, circulation (both of language and of blood), and Lydgate (a physician). But she stops short of observing George Eliot's particular contribution to the common nineteenth-century figuring of society as a human body, a step which would result in adding intoxicating substances, writing, heredity, and absence to her paradigm. Daniel Cottom also recognizes the metaphorical resonance of the penny post as a system of circulation but believes that circulatory metaphors replaced other Victorian metaphors: specifically 'of blood, breeding or inheritance' (18). In George Eliot's fiction, however, as Beer proves, metaphors of money, blood, and inheritance coexist with other circulatory metaphors, especially in *Middlemarch*..

5. Wiesenfarth chooses this quotation as the motto for *A Writer's Notebook*.

6. As Alan Mintz points out, his trivial treatise on gout accurately measures his failure on both professional and human levels (80).

7. Gertrude Himmelfarb contests this assumption, arguing that members

of the working classes shared important values with their betters but lacked the resources that might enable them to practice such habits as cleanliness and industriousness.

8. Correspondingly, Beer points out that Lydgate fails to work out narrative. As scientist and physician, she argues, his task parallels the narrator's in that he looks for causal relationships (*Darwin* 165). His fate indicates that his imaginative failure is essentially narrative. Carroll also describes *Middlemarch*'s narrator as a doctor (8).

9. At the 1996 'Culture and Addiction' conference at Claremont Graduate Center in California, Helena Michie's paper on 'The Rise of the Water Drinker' noted that Victorians perceived an opposition between alcohol and water that implied that consuming water precluded dependence on alcohol.

In *Daniel Deronda*, George Eliot models Sir Hugo Mallinger's Topping on Lacock Abbey, where pioneering photographer William Henry Fox Talbot lived during the nineteenth century.

9

Daniel Deronda: *After the Opium Wars*

Ground away, moisten and mash up thy paste,
Pound at thy powder–I am not in haste!
Better sit thus and observe thy strange things
Than go where men wait me and dance at the King's.

Robert Browning
'The Laboratory' 1844

Though *Middlemarch* ends with some hope for England's recovery from its Condition, *Daniel Deronda* abandons this hope, not only for Britain but also as it concerns most of Europe. In line with this abandonment, intoxicants and illnesses pervade the sections of the novel usually called the English half or the Gwendolen side, whose characters also travel to settings on the Continent. Illness and intoxication also affect Jewish characters who repudiate their heritage: the terminally ill Princess Halm-Eberstein and the compulsive gambler, Lapidoth.

Indeed, maintaining the traditional Leavisite division of the novel into its Gwendolen and Mordecai parts reveals that the Jewish world, in contrast with the English, finds health and life and, simultaneously and without effort, becomes a sort of teetotal culture in which no one gets intoxicated. The Mordecai side of the novel also divorces language, especially written language, from all forms of intoxication. It even divorces its intoxicants from intoxication. It has a rational public house, a saintly invalid, and a version of the written word entirely free of poisonous potential. Biological heritage is reestablished, valorized, and reconnected with political order, indeed with political salvation, and many of the events which engender hope for order occur at the most benign drinking place in George Eliot's fiction, the Hand and Banner.

Sir Hugo's World: Poisoned Arrows

The increased quantities of poisons in George Eliot's last novel contribute substantially to her creation of the sick society of Sir Hugo's world. Poison appears rarely as a weapon in George Eliot's fiction. Early in their acquaintance, when John Blackwood tried to interest the Leweses in the Madeline Smith case, they both responded with ennui. George Eliot wrote back, 'I think Madeline Smith one of the least interesting of murderesses' (*GEL* 2:362). Only in her least typical (and most romantic) story, 'The Lifted Veil,' does a character even consider murder by poison. Only in 'Janet's Repentance' does even a minor character, Mr Tryan's abandoned mistress, presumably a suicide, die by poison.

Nevertheless, the allusions in *Deronda* link women, poison, and sexual competition to create a firmer connection than in any of the previous fiction. Throughout the nineteenth century, as elsewhere in literature, writers have associated women and poison. A number of the forms of powerful female demons Nina Auerbach finds everywhere in Victorian culture include the lamia, the serpent, and the spider woman, all of which produce fatal substances. Margaret Hallissy notes many literary connections between women and poisons over a long period, a number of which appear in George Eliot's novels. According to Hallissy, John Lydgate's *Examples Against Women* attributes the first of many attempts to poison men to Eve in the garden (16). George Eliot's constructions of both Rosamond and Gwendolen exploit how the lamia 'preys on other women's children and also on young men, whom she lures to her lair and eats' (90).

During the 1870s, the decade of the publication of *Deronda*, a number of political changes, including the growth of feminism, increased the cultural links between women and poisons. The politically conservative literature of the late-Victorian science fiction craze produced texts such as Percy Greg's *Across the Zodiac*, Edward Abbott Abbott's *Flatland*, and Edward Bulwer-Lytton's *The Coming*

Race, all of which connect women's speech with some sort of mysterious source of energy, a demonic fluid, or a poison.

But Hermione DeAlmeida emphasizes that even the Lamia retains a healing, positive potential. Despite Lamias that include Rappaccini's Beatrice and other poisonous girls deliberately infected so as to deliver disease to an enemy, Lamias can also include 'the virginal poison girls or boys of the eighteenth and early nineteenth century in Europe, who were employed for therapeutic purposes during epidemics of venereal disease either as a cure for syphilis or as protection against its infection. As poison girl, Lamia could be both the source of deadly infection and a pure innocent possessed and made victim of the intricate and infecting sophistic designs of Lycius and Apollonius' (193). When Grandcourt returns from his travels in a jaded state to find a pure young woman to marry he follows a pattern in which bridegrooms who contracted diseases and addictions during their Grand Tours sought out fresh young virgins to act as restoratives, young virgins who then often became infected themselves.

Gwendolen's evasion of Grandcourt's first attempted proposal at Diplow emphasizes a Lamia/*Pharmakon*-like poise between benefit and poison partly through her suggested comparison between women and flowers, not for their shared beauty, but for a shared ennui. She believes that stationary flowers get 'poisonous' (171) out of boredom. Another floral/drug metaphor describes Grandcourt's stillness during his abortive proposal: both he and Gwendolen seem possessed by 'a sort of lotus eater's stupor' (172). Gwendolen's floral poisons differ from the narcotic poison that proceeds from Mrs Glasher because the effects of lotus flowers and poppies can be euphoric as well as sickening. The younger woman still precariously retains her potential to become either a remedy or a poison; her predecessor illustrates the unmixedly toxic consequences of succumbing to poisoned love.

In addition to emphasizing the healing potential of the women she portrays as *Pharmaka*, George Eliot diverges from patriarchal portrayals of venomous women by distinguishing among her three poisonous-women characters. According to Hallissy, women who are venomous are less evil than women who administer poisons because the venom is part of their nature, whereas poisoning someone requires making a moral choice. In *Deronda*, poisons connected with sex appear more conspicuously than in any of George Eliot's other fiction, but the venom assigned to Gwendolen, Lydia, and the Alcharisi sometimes reduces their responsibility. More victims than villains, they suffer rather than consciously inflicting suffering. George Eliot's assignment of venom rather than poison to these women characters suggests a feminist acknowledgment of the power of the many determining factors limiting women's choices.

However, George Eliot's often noticed incorporation of the *Medea* in the Grandcourt/Gwendolen/Lydia plot (Wiesenfarth) assigns more guilt to Lydia, despite her victimization by Grandcourt, for Medea's poison is external to her essence, and close analysis of degrees of choice takes the moral center of this novel. George Eliot, like the 1870s science fiction writers, often associates women's venom with speech. Lydia's outbursts result from her having bottled up the words she fears to address to Grandcourt (387, 388, 394). For her, his news of his engagement to Gwendolen has 'chill sickness in it' (392), and he leaves Gadsmere only after asserting 'You have made me feel uncommonly ill with your folly' (399). Although most often described as venomous, Lydia takes the next step toward toxicity when she metaphorically poisons and literally sickens her rival Gwendolen by means of a combination of the words of her letter and the package of diamonds delivered on the Grandcourts' wedding night. Lydia's deliberate acts thus make both Grandcourt and Gwendolen sick.

Like the Jason/Medea allusions, the often noticed *As You Like It* material in the English half of *Deronda* also carries poisonous associations. One of Goerge Eliot's favorite reference works, Anna Jameson's *Sacred and Legendary Art*, emphasizes that 'arrows have been from all antiquity the emblem of pestilence' (414). The Archery Club events form the occasion for the *As You Like It* motif, and the concluding speech of Shakespeare's play includes the admonition that 'good wine needs no bush.' Tradition attaches this statement to the symbolism of the ale stake: good liquor maintains its quality regardless of the signs meant to prove its goodness. Mrs Arrowpoint writes about Tasso who himself writes about poisons in Canto IV of *Jerusalem Delivered* in which characters trade accusations concerning poisonings. Yet another allusion, which also occurs at the Arrowpoints' party, associates Gwendolen with a drinking place. When she disparages her singing in Goethe's words from *Faust*, '*die Kraft ist schwach, allein die Lust ist gross*' (75), she repeats lines spoken in the Auerbach's Cellar scene. Thus the scenes in the English world of *Deronda* are shot through with drink, drinking places, poisons, illness, and wounds even though the characters seldom drink much.

Typhoid Gwendolen

As time goes on, Gwendolen, too, makes people sick, first among them Rex Gascoigne in whose love plot George Eliot portrays romantic love as both literal and figurative wounds and sickness. She introduces a Rex with a 'healthy nature' (86) and begins the chapter narrating his futile attraction to Gwendolen with a quotation from Charles Lamb which refers to young love as 'the kindliest symptom' (97). George Eliot surrounds Rex's first attempt to express his feelings on the day of the local fox hunt with associations among drinking, wounds, and class mobility. No women other than a former kitchen maid participate in the hunt, and Mr Gascoigne specifically warns Gwendolen against the loss of class dignity that might result from her putting herself on a level with Mrs Gadsby. The hunt meets at the Three Barns, another example of an inn setting that involves potential class mobility. Rex's ensuing sickness results from both these events and Gwendolen's rejection. As in the childhood incident in which she refuses to reach her mother the needed medicine, Gwendolen precipitates and aggravates both spiritual and physical illness.

Lydia's arrival further toxifies the English world. George Eliot is careful to specify that she stops at the Golden Keys. The first part of the name as usual suggests the materialism of the conflict, while the second indicates the function her information will perform in the narrative of Grandcourt's past. The phallic symbol of the key emphasizes that both Grandcourt and Lydia consistently see the question in terms of the inheritance of their son. The epigraph for the chapter in which Lydia meets Gwendolen at the Whispering Stones refers to gems stolen by one woman from another's dead arm, thereby introducing the pharmaceutical sign of Grandcourt's love which will accompany the note of vengeance on Gwendolen's wedding night. This message brings such potent poison to Gwendolen partly because the receiving body is already in a volatile state. Gwendolen's appearances as a lamia and a narcotic flower allow her potentially poisonous essence to combine with the words of Lydia's letter and the diamonds to sicken her. When she hears Lydia's story she gets a 'fit of diseased numbness' (187). She accounts to the party for Grandcourt's absence by suggesting he has suffered an 'apoplectic fit' (191). As she departs for Leubrunn with the von Langens, the narrator blames her unrealistic reading for her illusions. Without emotional distance, the 'cancerous vices' (193) in the novels she reads resemble a 'rheumatism' (193). Seeking cure at the spa, she gambles, pawns her jewelry, and finally plummets in social status.

After Gwendolen returns from Leubronn to find herself and her family poverty-stricken, her metaphorical health becomes increasingly fragile. As she arrives at the train station, her view of the Railroad Inn prepares her for the dreary manifestations of loss of social status she will encounter at home. Klesmer's opinion of her chances for success as an actress turns her self-confidence into a 'bleeding wound' (305), and the idea of subjecting her talent to critical judgment is 'poisoned' (305). This truth comes to her 'like a lacerating thong' (307), and consciousness of her situation creates 'bruises' (310). Possessed by a 'sick motivelessness' (318), she fears she has lost her 'magic' (335), and when her mother asks her to guess who has written the letter from Grandcourt she feels 'as if a bruise were being pressed' (336). Sickness, injuries, and poisons combine to represent her experience during her temporary poverty.

When Grandcourt's proposal promises to rescue Gwendolen and her family she does not entirely recover her metaphorical health. Instead, metaphors of intoxication replace those of sickness and injury.[1] When Grandcourt offers to care for her mother, his words convey 'the effect of a draught of wine, which suddenly makes all things easier, desirable things not so wrong, and people in general less disagreeable' (347). She postpones setting a wedding date until after the 'gallop over the downs' for which she is 'thirsty' (360). The next day, she looks forward to having 'her blood stirred once more with the intoxication of youth' (359). Like the period dominated by the floral metaphors, this stage of Gwendolen's intoxication retains a euphoric side. Indeed, she offers Grandcourt an attractive 'tricksiness' (365), George Eliot's repetition of the term Lewes applied to alcohol (the 'tricksy spirit') in *The Physiology of Common Life*.

On the actual wedding day the drug signifiers continue to proliferate. The narrator begins the description of her nuptial state with similes of gambling and sickness, together with a metaphor of poison: 'She had wrought herself up to much the same condition as that in which she stood at the gambling-table when Deronda was looking at her, and she began to lose. There was enjoyment in it: whatever uneasiness a growing conscience had created, was disregarded as an ailment might have been, amidst the gratification of that ambitious vanity and desire for luxury within her which it would take a great deal of slow poisoning to kill' (401).[2] Despite this condition, she thinks she can control things better now because of a return of an 'intoxication of youthful egoism' (402), despite her suspicion 'that she was a little intoxicated' (402). After she burns the letter she enters a kind of trance, 'knowing little more than that she was feeling ill, and that those written words kept repeating themselves in her. Truly here were poisoned gems' (407).

The narrator continues to include the metaphor in all the subsequent passages of analysis of the Grandcourts' marriage. Naive about Theuthian machinations, Gwendolen fails to deduce 'Lush's agency' (616) in engineering the encounter at the Whispering Stones because her fear hinders her 'from imagining plans and channels by which news had been conveyed to the woman who had the poisoning skill of a sorceress' (616). She goes to parties dressed in 'pale green velvet and poisoned diamonds' (617), and when Grandcourt implies to her that Deronda and Mirah are sexually involved, she compares her misery to how she felt 'moments after reading the poisonous letter' (649). When Lydia contrives to confront the couple during their ride in Rotten Row, the discarded mistress is finding a bit of relief 'in an outlet of venom, though it were as futile as that of a viper already thrown to the other side of the hedge' (668), and again the venom reaches and harms Gwendolen. Meanwhile, Gwendolen continues to respond to marriage with Grandcourt with real, metaphorical, and feigned sickness. She suffers a 'hidden wound' (625); she succumbs to a 'sick dream' (650); she is 'sickened of life' (666); she fears the 'infection from her husband's way of thinking' (671); and she often excuses herself from his company by pleading illness.

Grand-Court

In Gwendolen's husband, George Eliot creates her most complete villain out of absences which, together with his lizardliness, not only sicken his compatriots but disturb the conditions through which responsible heirs might gain property. As Hugh Witemeyer observes, his description rests on negatives: he has no smile, no hair, no self-consciousness, a faded complexion, and eyes which express 'nothing' (145). He comes late to the archery meeting so that Lord Brackenshaw must account for his 'non-appearance' (140). His occupations are non-actions: he does not drink or read or write, and, rather than frowning, he enjoys withholding his smiles. Gwendolen considers accepting his proposal solely out of appreciation for his negations, and her fear of empty spaces culminates in her husband's death, an obliteration of a man made up of vacancy, therefore a double obliteration.[3] As Gillian Beer points out, Gwendolen's triumph is her barrenness, yet another

Grandcourt-(non)generated absence.

Because part of Grandcourt's repulsiveness results from his refusal to use language, George Eliot constructs his first conversation with Gwendolen largely out of pauses, inserting eleven of them in parentheses between the lines of their dialogue. Grandcourt is 'not a wordy thinker' (169). His 'brief' speeches 'give signs of a suppressed and formidable ability to say more' (168). He enjoys 'abstaining from literature' (366). A fit of perversity postpones his proposal to Gwendolen, and the dual meaning of *speak*, both to articulate and to propose marriage, accounts for his balking. When he makes out his will he insists that Lush communicate its content to Gwendolen because writing is unthinkable to him.[4]

Meaningless himself, Grandcourt gains respect and a wife because his society assigns him significance: 'Suitors must often be judged as words are, by the standing and the figure they make in polite society: it is difficult to know much else of them' (358). Both Sir Hugo and his wife see him primarily as a 'sign' (196, 323). For this couple, Grandcourt's vacancy is doubly negative because not only do the Mallingers contribute the meaning, the meaning they contribute concerns what they lack: an heir.

Indeed, George Eliot often associates Grandcourt with physical vacancies. One of his own favorite metaphors describes various settings as absences: his word for the gambling spas at Leubronn and Baden, as well as for the train station at Gadsmere, is 'hole' (322). In her letter to Gwendolen, Lydia applies and develops the metaphor of holes created by Grandcourt by telling Gwendolen: 'I am the grave in which your chance of happiness is buried as well as mine' (406). Indeed, Grandcourt's name refers to an absence and evokes the setting for political/linguistic volatility introduced in *Romola*: like a piazza, a court is an enclosed emptiness, and the first syllable of the name adds emphasis.[5] Indeed, from her childhood George Eliot was used to associating courts with disease. The 1849 Nuneaton Board of Health report mentions the town's 287 pigsties, 346 cesspools, and 15 slaughter houses and blames the common architectural arrangement of numbers of houses around a single 'filthy' court for the many health dangers afflicting the town (Bates, *Midland Daily Tribune*, March 1952). During the Middle Ages, 'so-called merchants' courts' were 'early forms of the tavern' (Schivelsbusch 189).

George Eliot repeats the association between architecturally created empty spaces and the absent father when Daniel first confronts the possibility of his illegitimacy. According to Haight, George Eliot bases Topping Abbey, where Daniel makes his discovery, on Lacock Abbey, a Wiltshire property owned in the nineteenth century by William Henry Fox Talbot, producer of the first photographic *negative*. Like Topping Abbey, Lacock combines architecture from the twelfth century with the work of every subsequent century, and George Eliot reproduces in Topping a number of details from Lacock including the cloister, the space that supplies the setting for Daniel's speculations about his ancestry. When Daniel reads about the pope's nephews and makes his momentous inquiry of his tutor, he is surrounded by the pointed arches that enclose the grassy space in which he lies.

Only a few feet from the cloister at Lacock is a room characteristically present in monasteries, the infirmary. This would make a fortunate placement in Topping as well, since metaphors of wounds now enter the story. Daniel first confronts his possible illegitimacy 'as a maimed boy feels the crushed limb which for others is merely reckoned in an average of accidents' (209). The narrator compares his sadness with 'Byron's susceptibility about his deformed foot' (213). The Byron connection is attached specifically to illegitimacy as something unavoidably thrust on him: 'an entailed disadvantage–the deformed foot doubtfully hidden by the shoe' (215). Seeing it as an 'injury' (675), Daniel continues to describe Sir Hugo's concealment of his heritage with this metaphor throughout the novel.

The metaphors of emptiness applied to Grandcourt combine with weaving metaphors to emphasize Deronda's illegitimacy, as usual developed simultaneously with health metaphors. Deronda applies both to the man he assumes is replacing him as heir to

Topping: 'His notion of Grandcourt as a "remnant" was founded on no particular knowledge, but simply on the impression which ordinary polite intercourse had given him that Grandcourt had worn out all his natural healthy interest in things' (456). Mr Vandernoodt agrees when he describes the new husband as a 'washed-out piece of cambric' (486). Deronda connects the construction of the story of Grandcourt's past and his marriage to Gwendolen with his speculations about his own illegitimacy through another fabric metaphor: his attempts to evoke his own origins make him 'active in weaving probabilities' (488). George Eliot thus draws on metaphors of weaving and absence to suggest illegitimacy: Grandcourt is an absent father, an empty sign, a piece of fabric, as well as metaphorically unhealthy.

Among the other sick or addicted characters of the British half, Grandcourt's agent, Mr Lush, who closely resembles Christian in *Felix Holt*, is George Eliot's last and most devastating version of Theuth. The 'toad-eater least liable to nausea' (327), Mr Lush's arguments with Grandcourt about Gwendolen are metaphorical gambles (329), and even after his defeats he retains his 'latent venom' (331). He is a double agent, working for both Grandcourt and Sir Hugo, and the *OED* confirms that the nineteenth century did apply the word *lush* to drinkers.

Sir Hugo, the most socially powerful figure in the British half, suffers from a 'small chronic complaint of facetiousness' (462). He goes to Leubronn because of his gout, but is so confused about how to retrieve or maintain health that he agrees 'with the Archbishop at Naples who had a St. Januarius procession against the plague' (434). This confusion between legitimately medicinal remedies and remedies whose effect proceeds only from symbolism characterizes the corrupt and hopeless English side of *Deronda*. Like Mirah's father and the Princess Halm-Eberstein, Sir Hugo participates in thwarting legitimate descent.[6]

Hans Meyrick, who enters Sir Hugo's world at the end of the novel by going down to Diplow in preparation for doing portraits of Sir Hugo's daughters, increases his remedies as his sickness intensifies. When Hans brags to Daniel about his sprouting genius, Daniel calls this 'only a fungoid growth, I daresay–a crowing disease in the lungs' (512). Hans in turn indulges himself with opium binges and resolves to give up wine, with the addition that this sacrifice should permit him to 'get a little drunk on hope and vanity' (520), that is, the hope and vanity manifested in his love for Mirah. Cynthia Chase's location of great instability in Hans's letter to Deronda in her seminal proto-deconstructionist essay, 'The De-Composition of the Elephants,' acknowledges the volatility of this character.[7] Just as Deronda flees the intoxicated British world, his opium-taking, metaphorically drunk and sick painter friend replaces him there.

Detoxifications

In the Jewish part of *Daniel Deronda*, key chapters take place at a public house which lacks all the dangers of the drinking places in George Eliot's earlier fiction and all the health threats of the English locations in *Deronda*. No riots begin at the Hand and Banner. Instead, a group of reflective working men drink moderately and engage in restrained discussion about national heritage. And, although its name is highly metaphorical, the metaphors do not involve intoxication, but rather foreshadow Daniel's mission in Palestine: the establishment of a Jewish state that will require a new national ensign.

In addition to detoxifying many usual sources of poisons, the Jewish world detoxifies the written word as well. During Mirah's stay in New York, she gains her only knowledge of Judaism from reading her landlady's Bible and prayer book and spends her money on books which she believes bring her into 'companionship' (254) with her distant mother. Mordecai attempts to cultivate Jacob's racial memory by repeating to the child a Hebrew poem of his own; he sees the repetition as 'a way of printing' (533). When Daniel finds his inheritance in a chest of manuscripts, the written word connects him to his family. Free of poisons, the box of manuscripts allows Daniel to restore his own and his people's heritage, in obedience to his father, grandfather, and substitute father Joseph Kalonymos. Giving Deronda the chest, Kalonymos makes a little ceremony of concern that Daniel might lose its 'curious key' (725), the phallic key that combines with the chest to constitute and represent Daniel's inheritance from his grandfather. The written word in this case heals and does not kill.

Like Dorothea Brooke, and in opposition to Gwendolen, Grandcourt, and Mirah's father, Daniel cures people not only in the role many scholars have assigned him as pseudo-psychologist to Gwendolen, but physically as well. His unselfish care for Hans Meyrick, unable to study because of an injured eye, results in his own mediocre performance at Cambridge. He also self-prescribes. He looks toward Judaism as a treatment for the creeping boredom of English society: 'an effectual remedy for *ennui*, which unhappily cannot be secured on a physician's prescription' (411). When tempted by Gwendolen, he offers himself 'a self-administered dose of caution' (466).

Daniel becomes an effective healer to Mordecai despite Mordecai's ultimate death. When Daniel arrives at the Cohens', Mordecai 'was in a state of expectation as sickening as that of a prisoner listening for the delayed deliverance' (577). As they go out, Daniel warns him to 'cover your mouth with the woollen scarf' (579). Mordecai finds in Daniel's voice 'a cordial' (557). When Daniel moves his chair closer to Mordecai, the sick man 'felt the action as a patient feels the gentleness that eases his pillow' (596). Mordecai dies happily in the presence of the healer who has completed his life partly by assuming his mission and partly by continuing his heritage through marriage to Mirah. In this way Daniel succeeds at the job that challenges physicians most severely. Despite Mordecai's physical illness, his moral health and the attendance of Dr Deronda result in an inevitable but happy death.

But with Gwendolen's moral illnesses, Daniel's metaphorical remedies succeed less well. When she complains of ennui he says, 'I think what we call the dulness of things is a disease in ourselves'

(464). He recognizes a 'poor soul within her sitting in sick distaste of all things' (466). He advises, 'All reckless lives are injurious, pestilential' (501) and that she should submit to unalterable wrong 'as men submit to maiming or a lifelong incurable disease' (506). And there is complete sincerity in Gwendolen's response: 'I am tired and sick of it' (507). Her narrative of Grandcourt's death, which Judith Wilt describes as 'half narcotized' ('He Would' 313), does not cure her. When Daniel tells her of his identity she feels her veins flow with a 'confusing potion' (873). Having helped kill Grandcourt, she remains permanently in the English world, the permanently sick society.

Lapidoth, too, a turncoat Jew, causes illness: in his wife, in Mirah, and in Mordecai, all of whom fall sick as a result of the father's kidnaping of Mirah. Indeed Mordecai's tuberculosis develops specifically out of this event: the grief following Mirah's disappearance, his abandonment of his ambitions, and his poverty all contribute to his illness. Mordecai himself detests Jews like Lapidoth who make fun of their own people for the amusement of Gentiles and who 'All the while feel breathing on them the breath of contempt because they are Jews, and they will breathe it back poisonously' (587). His poem adds a metaphor of wine to this idea: 'The oil and wine from presses of the Goyim,/ Poisoned with scorn' (534). Although both Mordecai's tuberculosis and these images of poisons occur in the Jewish half of the novel, the poison emanates from the non-Jewish world. Mordecai's world must constantly repel the toxicity and disease which threaten its heritage.

Lapidoth's gambling is an illness: Daniel believes gambling 'is a besotting kind of taste, likely to turn into a disease' (383). Mirah's troublesome parent saves his child the ultimate burden: that of rejecting him despite her devotion to the value of filial piety. Hopelessly addicted to gambling, he scoops up Daniel's ring, and, loaded down with his addiction and the gem that represents both this addiction and his paternal irresponsibility, just goes away. The other irresponsible Jewish parent, the Princess, who has made a lifetime project of thwarting legitimate descent, also ends up in the non-Jewish world. Morally and physically sick, she limps back to her second family to die.

Lapidoth's theft of Daniel's jewel to replenish his gambling resources and his disappearance from the Jewish world result in the betrothal of Mirah and Daniel. The simultaneous absence of both the ring and the father/jewel thief/addict promotes the continuation of the line. At the wedding of Daniel and Mirah, the 'sacramental wine' (881) seals the marriage and does not intoxicate anyone. The marriage is described in terms of its promise. The guests' might 'wisely wish offspring' (881) for this couple. Gwendolen's generous wedding note reverses the toxicity of Mrs Glasher's: to Daniel it is 'more precious than gold and gems' (815). The conclusion to the Jewish half of the novel detoxifies all the signifiers so poisonous in the earlier novels (and the English half of this novel): the drinking places, the wine, the problems of heredity, the wedding note from the other woman, and the gems connected with it. But in the conclusion to the English half, the drug/disease/intoxication metaphor only exacerbates the sense of illness, for George Eliot's society had begun by this time to share her perception of alcoholism and other addictions as diseases.

Daniel, on the other hand, departs for Palestine free from any baggage of imperialism. His mission distinguishes him from both military and merchant imperialists: instead of searching for loot, as did the Crusaders and their successors, he goes laden with a collection of his own, the portable library-in-a-trunk bequeathed him by his father and delivered by Joseph Kalonymos. His journey reverses the direction of Harold Transome, who returns from Smyrna with his hookah and a lot of money. His path also reverses the route traveled by opium on its way to England. Consequently he reverses the route of both the drug courier and the imperialist.

In *Deronda*, events occur on a worldwide stage that suggests a geographical spread of infection, at least throughout the European environment of its irretrievably English characters. The novel opens in the 'gas-poisoned' atmosphere of a gambling spa peopled with 'very distinct varieties of European type: Livonian and Spanish, Graeco-Italian and miscellaneous German, English aristocratic and

English plebian' (36). All these people possess a 'uniform negativeness of expression . . . as if they had all eaten of some root that for the time compelled the brains of each to the same narrow monotony of action' (37). Major scenes occur at Leubronn, and when Daniel goes to meet his mother in Genoa one of his first reactions is to remember the story of the landing of the plague-stricken Jews that also forms part of *Romola*. Gwendolen's 'world nausea' and her barrenness occur in this wider setting; England no longer contains its toxicity. Her poisonous essence has spread its effect as far as Genoa, the 'gem of the sea' (824), where, as predicted in the motto which begins the novel, 'Vengeance . . . O'er the fairest troop of captured joys/ Breathes pallid pestilence' (32). At the conclusion of George Eliot's last novel, the Condition of England has only spread its infection far beyond national boundaries and begun to toxify the entire continent just as a general perception is taking shape that the whole world is sick. Together with the other drug material in *Deronda*, this spread implies that, as the century went on, George Eliot had little reason to become more optimistic about the Condition of England. Far from yielding to the many remedies applied, the Condition had become *Weltschmerz*.

As the twentieth century began, a number of factors helped limit the role of the public house and its product in daily life. Although the roadside taverns whose loss Mr Sampson laments in *Felix Holt* enjoyed a revival when motoring became a recreation in the early twentieth century, the variety of the drinking place's functions decreased. Other buildings took over most of roles that supplemented the provision of drink and lodging for the traveler. Together with the growing power of the teetotal societies evident on both sides of the Atlantic in the early part of the century, the Defense of the Realm Act of World War I contributed to these limits by setting up the pub-closing hours finally abandoned only recently.

At the same time, turn-of-the century decadence helped broaden the recreational appeal of drugs, while medicine continued to seek new remedies and anesthesias in narcotics. The 1868

Pharmacy Act helped decrease sales of opium, although, with the increased use of morphine, it no longer served as medicine or anesthesia. Nor had two opium wars discouraged the English sea captains who continued to act as drug dealers to the other side of the world, defiantly continuing to run opium from India to China as honest merchants. By the 1920s a cocaine subculture had appeared in London.

Meanwhile, the relationship between drugs and creativity continued to intensify, as modernists sought both surcease from the despair of living in a chaotic and meaningless universe and artistic stimulation in the escape provided by mind-altering substances. The alcoholic author became common in both British and American literature. The creative relationship between drugs and art culminated in the sixties in such admissions as Ken Kesey's that he devised his narrator for *One Flew Over the Cuckoo's Nest* while acting as a subject for the testing of LSD at a university hospital.

Now, at the turn of the century, 'the age of recovery,' artists who have survived dependencies have been obliged to replace the stimulus of drugs with new creative strategies. The literary drunkalogue has become its own subgenre. John Cheever and Pete Hamill, for example, have narrated how their recovery from alcoholism altered their approaches to writing, and Ringo Starr has pointed out that recording without simultaneously consuming alcohol and drugs requires an entirely new approach to his music. George Eliot's suggestion in *Deronda* that recovery from the Condition necessitates recovery from the various misapplied remedies used to address it anticipates both the modernist refuge in altered states and the post-modernist adoption of many of the same strategies for recovery she outlines in 'Janet's Repentance.' Because of this continued relevance, George Eliot's intoxication themes and metaphors assert once again her wise vision about the ongoing difficulties of the human, and not just the English, Condition.

Notes

1. Mary Carpenter's Lacanian reading, 'A Bit of Her Flesh,' exemplifies the delight this narrative takes in pain through the scene of Rex's hunting injury. She also connects wounds with love. Judith Wilt believes that Gwendolen's intoxication takes the form of a 'stupor' she finds attractive as a reaction against 'the phantasm of freedom of choice that had humiliated her with Klesmer' ('He Would' 217). She associates Gwendolen with Tennyson's poisoned queen, Guinevere.

2. Philip Weinstein applies the poison metaphor to Gwendolen's effort to accept Deronda's prescriptions: 'The moral regime enforced upon the heroine is an inimical physic, opposed to the central "irridescence" of her personality. She is overcome, not cured by it . . . Not just the vanity, but her entire psychic economy has been subjected to "a great deal of slow poisoning"' (102-3).

3. Daniel, on the other hand, bridges gaps. Bonnie McMullen believes his wedding, with its diverse guest list, 'signifies a tentative marriage, between the English and the Jewish worlds of the novel' (131). She accounts for   Daniel's name partly through its association with the name of the bridge at Ronda in Spain. Of course the Blackfriars Bridge scene where Mordecai sees Deronda also supports her points. Elizabeth Ermath connects 'gaps' (43) with breakdowns in communication, and Susan Weisser finds 'a double gap in the narrative of *Daniel Deronda*: the evasion of adultery and the representation of the female sexual will as a seeming absence' (11). Evelyne Ender takes manifestations of Gwendolen's sickness, which, like many psychoanalytic scholars, she identifies as hysteria, as 'failures in the process of signification; moments of textual absence or semantic voice' (239). Because Ender points out that the narrator represents hysteria in visual images rather than through narration, her interpretation connects Gwendolen's sickness and the absences that jeopardize meaning.

4. Sally Shuttleworth assigns to Grandcourt a 'naive theory of signification' (192) which seeks a one-to-one correspondence between 'sign and sign' (192).

5. Derek Miller's interpretation of the name, 'a big sway over a tiny constitution' (19) differs from mine but does not conflict. Andrew Dowling explains Grandcourt's name in terms of Gwendolen's reluctance to consider divorcing him: it 'evokes images of a sovereign

power, but it also suggests a grand court in the legal sense, one that will subject the "spoiled child" to the severest of trials' (332).

6. Most critics find *Deronda* the text in which descent plays its most important role. Gillian Beer believes descent is one of the novel's 'ordering principles' (*Darwin* 182) which are also its 'unsolvable problems' (182). Because of the temporal proximity of the 1865 setting, Beer believes that 'descent is no longer implied in that primary reader/text relationship, as it had been in *Middlemarch*. We are granted no privileged vantage point in history' (186). The weakness in this argument proceeds from George Eliot's earlier questionings of descent in the plots of Godfrey Cass and Rufus Lyon and in the necessity of descent as the main 'ordering principle' of Deronda's enterprise in Palestine. Dianne Sadoff concludes that Daniel's story 'subdues . . . fatherhood into brotherhood' (102). Her argument about brothers gains support from the *Middlemarch* incident in which, Lydgate's fathers having failed him, his friend Fare*brother* and his brother-in-law rescue him at the Green Dragon.

7. Nancy Pell also believes Meyrick is a key character: his dissoluteness contrasts with his sisters' positive qualities.

8. Scholars have taken both sides of the imperialism question in *Daniel Deronda*–including Edward Said, Deirdre David, Patrick Brantlinger, Julian Wolfreys, Susan Meyer, Katherine Bailey Lineham, and Sophia Andres. The opposing arguments made by Meyer and Lineham draw on some of the same passages from the novel to take positions on opposite sides of the question, with Meyer arguing that the novel's nationalism and anti-feminisim are of a piece with an imperialist proto-Zionism, while Lineham finds political inconsistency in the novel's conflicts among these ISMS. Wolfreys believes even more strongly that Daniel's mission is imperialist because 'it is . . . Englishness that is ultimately valorized' (16).

Epilogue:

A Biographical Speculation

While the prominence of drinking and drugs in George Eliot's fiction reflects their importance in nineteenth-century culture, it also proves a personal expertise on these topics about which I and other scholars have speculated. In support of his point that 'George Eliot would make a damn good doctor' (64), J. W. Bennett cites the detailed accuracy of her portrayals of alcoholics in 'Janet's Repentance': 'We learn more about delirium tremens from George Eliot than from *DMS-III-R /Diagnostic and Statistical Manual*' (61). In 'Pink Toads in *Lord Jim*,' Christopher Ricks also notes the accuracy of George Eliot's knowledge of delirium tremens (143).

In 'George Eliot and the Female Alcoholic,' Sheila Shaw agrees, remarking on the accuracy of the portrayal of the stages of Janet Dempster's struggle to recover. When Dempster locks his wife out of their house, Janet finds shelter and rest at Mrs Pettifer's, but in the middle of the night wakes up in terror from a bad dream. According to Shaw, this incident 'happens to be an accurate description of what Janet's physical condition would be after six or eight hours without a drink' (176). Janet's subsequent feelings of elation occur at a time when recovering alcoholics enter a period of well-being and optimism 'when the tremors, and for some, hallucinations, have ended' (176). Indeed, Shaw believes that mid-nineteenth-century physicians knew less than George Eliot about alcoholism and that she gained her knowledge from experience. Shaw suggests Nancy Wallington Buchanan and Maria Lewis as likely women alcoholics whose experience imparted painful knowledge to the young girl.

Certainly Mary Ann Evans had intimate knowledge of Nancy Wallington Buchanan's condition. In addition to observing the tea in October 1831, the tea at which she probably saw both the Buchanans drinking at Griff House, the girl had attended the

Nuneaton school where she had daily experience not only of Mrs Buchanan's difficulties but also of the 'Drinker's Paradise' where they occurred. Evans often mentions sharing the good works of her Evangelical period with Mrs Buchanan. On their deaths, she uses the same term to describe both Mrs Buchanan and her notoriously alcoholic husband. When Nancy Wallington Buchanan died at Margate, her young friend described the departed as 'the almost desolate sufferer' (May 1840). When Buchanan himself died in his gig accident two months later, she applied the same term: Buchanan was a 'poor sufferer' (58). And the Buchanans appear as often in the father's diary as in the daughter's fiction.

But Shaw believes Evans had experience with yet another woman alcoholic in addition to Mrs Buchanan and consequently, although tentatively, suggests Maria Lewis. Less evidence supports this suggestion. The letters Maria Lewis exchanged with Mary Ann and the journals of Robert Evans contain no traces of alcoholic difficulties, and Maria Lewis is rarely if ever identified as a model for a character in the fiction, certainly not for a drinking character. Rather than drinking with Mrs Buchanan, she cared for her friend during her periods of intoxication.

While tending to Mrs Buchanan at Margate, Lewis confided the difficulties of the situation by letter to Evans. Her pupil responded with sympathy for Miss Lewis's having been 'despoiled of your only season of refreshment' (*GEL* 1:54), an offer of the 'tranquillity' (52) Miss Lewis might find at Griff, and commiseration for the 'tumult' (53) her governess is experiencing with Mrs Buchanan. Sympathy for the households of alcoholics recurs in Evans's response to the Gaskell biography of Charlotte Brontë.

Indeed, George Eliot's mother, famous for her sickliness, supplies a far more probable candidate than Maria Lewis for a second alcoholic in her life.

Although exceptions abound, the parents in George Eliot's fiction often fall into two categories: a group of parents associated with drinking and drugs who, though not necessarily saintly, are either ideal or have some ecclesiastical connection. The first group includes Thias Bede, Mr Tulliver, Mrs Holt, Mrs Transome, and Mr Lapidoth. The second includes Milly Barton, Mrs Raynor, Rufus Lyon, and Bardo de Bardi. The riskiness of deducing biography from fiction applies with double strength to Mrs Evans and the parents in the fiction; however, the size of the drinking group does indicate a pattern.

Christiana Pearson Evans, as both Ruby Redinger and Gordon Haight have remarked, sent her daughters to boarding school as soon as she possibly could. Becoming sick or sickly after the birth and death of twin sons in 1821, her invalidism began with her younger daughter's early childhood. As an invalid, whether for medicine or recreation, she had an excuse to resort to such remedies as her early nineteenth-century environment supplied her, remedies whose ingredients consisted almost entirely of alcohol and opium. In this case, Mrs Pullet rather than Mrs Tulliver would supply the *Mill* character based on George Eliot's mother. The ubiquity of drink in Nuneaton and the substantial supplies indicated in the Griff House bills from Mr Whitam's suggest that Mrs Evans had access to alcohol. Such opportunities as a shopping trip to Coventry Robert Evans mentions in 1832 would increase the possibilities. On this occasion, while Mr Evans attended the market, his wife whiled away the afternoon at 'Mr Jeffrey's Hotel (12 October 1832). Not with any regularity but certainly more frequently than her husband, Mrs Evans stayed home from Church on Sundays pleading illness.

Redinger find George Eliot's silence on the topic of her mother especially troubling. She emphasizes the ambiguity of her 1858 observation that 'we can have but one mother' (39). Diana Postlethwaite goes further: She observes metaphorically that George Eliot 'kills' her mother twice, once by means of the long silence and again by assuming a pen name. Mary Wilson Carpenter also speculates about George Eliot's silence and makes it part of her argument about circumcision and pain in *Daniel Deronda*. Knoepflmacher accuses the mother of 'indifference' ('Gender and Genre' 108) toward both Mary Ann and Chrissy and concludes that 'by attributing Mrs Evans's neglect to invalidism and by blaming herself as its cause, the child could deflect from the more painful inference that her mother did not really much care for either of her two daughters' (108). Kathleen Adams, whose knowledge of Nuneaton perhaps exceeds any other biographer's, also treads carefully around the subject. Speculating about Christiana Pearson Evans's remoteness, she suggests that the mother 'may have felt unwell . . . perhaps she needed more rest and quiet than was possible in a household of energetic children' (9). But the nearly complete silence about her mother in over forty years of diaries, journals, and letters conforms to the usual responses of children of alcoholics. Although the silence on its own proves nothing, it is behavior typical of young people who try to deny a parent's addiction.

With more material on Mr Evans available, George Eliot's biographers, notably Bodenheimer, have concentrated on her conflict with her father in Coventry as her major confrontation with a parent. But the novelist's silence suggests a more profound and persistent trouble involving the mother.

Neither Robert nor Marian Evans ever complains about Christiana. Both the father's and the daughter's expressions of grief over her death in 1836 are conventional. Robert Evans writes, 'This is a Great Loss to me as to her Dear Children' (3 February 1836). The daughter, however, does state explicitly that she is more concerned about her father's sickness: 'Since we saw you at Griff, my dear Mother has suffered a great increase of pain, and though she has for the last few days been much relieved, we dare not hope that there will be a permanent improvement. Our anxieties on her account though so great have been since Thursday almost lost sight of in the more sudden and consequently more severe trial we have been called to endure in the alarming illness of my dear Father' (*GEL* 1:3). At the end, Robert Evans confides to his journal that it was a relief 'to see her go off' (3 February 1836). And, lest the grief Evans reports may perhaps seem too sincere for the widower of a troublesome addict, we might compare Gertrude Himmelfarb's report of a wife murderer who used similar language of bereavement regarding his victim: 'Died here at 1 a.m. Mary Jane, my own beloved wife, age 38 years–no torment surrounded her bedside' (23).

The profound unease on the topic of motherhood, which appears occasionally in George Eliot's journals and letters and, less reliably but more frequently, in the fiction, may relate to a sense of relief at her mother's death.

If Mary Ann Evans confided her family troubles to anyone she confided them to Sara Hennell and Cara Bray. In 1845 Cara Bray reports her friend's impulsive effort to go forward and take the pledge in response to Thomas Spencer's preaching, another event suggesting strong reactions concerning drinking. During and after the 'Holy War' with her father about her new agnosticism, Evans's unhappiness with her family resulted in outbursts which, however, did not necessarily apply to her father. After a tea in 1847, Cara Bray produced the following: 'I drank tea with Mary Ann but her father was there. She said our family was the only one she knew in the world who had never done anything mean or to be ashamed of' (August 1824). These allusions to shame and misery in the family circle suggest that the happy family portrait Isaac Evans tried to perpetuate after her death was far from the truth.

A peculiar letter in 1848 to Sara Hennell alludes to parental alcoholism in a fable similar to the Professor Büchenworm letter written a year earlier. In this letter Evans tells the tale of a drunken Mother Nature who irresponsibly approves the creation of a misshapen creature such as Mary Ann by a novice deputy sprite: 'The Old Mother had been rollicking all the autumn in the vintage and wanted no less than a winter's sleep to sober her' (*GEL* 1: 273). Both this letter and the Büchenworm letter offered Evans a strategy for dealing with her homeliness through humor, but this one also attributes drunkenness to a mother.

In the letters written during her religious period, the young girl often applies typically Evangelical alcoholic figures. Regarding emotional relationships, she concludes, 'I find, as Dr Johnson said respecting his wine, total abstinence much easier than moderation' (*GEL* 1:271). Again writing to another Evangelical, she refers to 'intemperance, which I have heard justified on the pleas that since Providence has sent luxuries we are contemning them by

abstinence' (1:10). She describes the flattery of yet another religious
mentor, her Aunt Samuel Evans, as a 'noxious draught, which is too
apt to intoxicate me' (1:20). Like her characters in
Milby/Shepperton and St Ogg's, she has a habit of intoxicant
metaphors.

In her fiction, George Eliot's portrayals of addicted parents and
her many plots in which a responsible parent replaces a wastrel all
suggest her keen sensitivity to the problem of addicted parents, and,
perhaps, a wish for a parental replacement for herself. A number of
odd details in the fiction bolster this suggestion. In *Adam Bede* the
narrator ponders the pain of family likeness in the context of
Adam's impatience with his parents: 'Nature . . . ties us by our
heartstrings to the beings that jar us at every movement' (84). Karen
Chase describes the burden of Savonarola's reprimand to Romola
as a reminder that you can't choose your parents (310). In the
'Introduction' to *Felix Holt*, the narrator specifies that 'Many an
inherited (my italics) sorrow that has marred a life has been breathed
into no human ear' (84). Later in the novel, the narrator comments,
again in the first-person plural, 'Many of us know how, even in our
childhood, some blank discontented face on the background of our
home has marred our summer mornings' (585). In *Daniel Deronda*,
the motto to Chapter 18 introduces the charming, rational (if
somewhat anti-Semitic) Meyrick mother by contrast with a
personification of life as a mother who 'dwells Grim-clad up
darksome alleys, breathes hot gin,/And screams in pauper riot'
(236). In an Appendix to the second edition of Cross's *Life*, Mary
Cash repeats a telling remark. She reports George Eliot's belief that
whereas nothing wipes out a parent's obligations to a child, some
kinds of conduct do exonerate children from filial duty. Would a
parent's daily intoxication supply sufficiently objectionable
exonerating conduct? And does not George Eliot's fiction
repeatedly dramatize such a situation?

Around 1865 George Eliot began to focus her creative
imagination more directly on the great world than on the
Warwickshire town where she grew up. Beginning with her
Saccharissa essays for the *Pall Mall Gazette* in 1865, she turned to

London as a setting in *Daniel Deronda* and parts of *Theophrastus Such*. Nevertheless, even these late works look back to Nuneaton. The gambling spas of *Deronda* are successful versions of the spa that Jermyn plans in *Felix Holt*. The gouty Sir Hugo Mallinger lives in a Gothicized country house that resembles the neo-Gothic home of the asthmatic Sir Christopher Cheverel which in turn resembles, detail by detail, Sir Roger Newdigate's Arbury Hall. Janet Dempster's compulsiveness recurs in the disgusting but no more or less addicted Lapidoth. The bright twelve-year-old who walked the streets of Nuneaton at the time of the First Reform missed nothing that went on in this community, neither the rowdy public houses, nor the marital violence, nor the dealings of unscrupulous lawyers at the Newdigate Arms, and she drew on this material all her life.

The irony of suggesting alcoholism in Christiana Pearson Evans arises from its starting point: George Eliot's silence about her mother. At the same time that this silence conforms to usual behavior of children of alcoholics, it precludes the possibility of assembling more certain evidence. The prominence of drugs and alcohol in the parents in her novels may yet arise only from the keen observation of a precocious teenage girl growing up in 'A Drinker's Paradise.'

Bibliography

*Note: This bibliography includes all works cited, background materials, and, in addition, seminal or particularly relevant works even if not cited directly in the text.

Abse, Dannie, comp. *Doctors and Patients*. Oxford: Oxford UP, 1984.

Adams, Kathleen. *Those of Us Who Loved Her: The Men in George Eliot's Life*. Coventry: George Eliot Fellowship, 1980.

Alley, Henry. '*Romola* and the Preservation of Household Goods.' *Cithara* 23 (1984): 25-35.

—. 'Silas Marner and the Balance of Male and Female.' *Victorians Institute Journal* 16 (1988): 65-73.

Altick, Richard. 'Anachronisms in *Middlemarch*: A Note.' *Nineteenth-Century Fiction* 33 (1978): 366-72.

—. *The English Common Reader: A Social History of the Mass Reading Public, 1800-1900*. Chicago: U of Chicago P, 1957.

—. *The Presence of the Present: Topics of the Day in the Victorian Novel*. Columbus: Ohio State UP, 1991.

Anderson, Roland F. 'George Eliot Provoked: John Blackwood and Chapter Seventeen of *Adam Bede*.' *Modern Philology* 71 (1973): 39-47.

Anderson, William. *Green Man: The Archetype of Our Oneness with the Earth*. New York: Harper 1990.

Andres, Sophia. 'Fortune's Wheel in *Daniel Deronda*: Sociopolitical Turns of the British Empire.' *VIJ* 24 (1996): 87-111.

Ashby, Kevin. 'The Centre and the Margins in "The Lifted Veil" and *Blackwood's Edinburgh Magazine*.' *George Eliot-George Henry Lewes Studies*, 24-25 (1993): 132-44.

Ashmore, Mary. *Bulkington Memories*. Bedworth: Civic Arts Society, n.d.

Ashton, Rosemary. *George Eliot: A Life*. London: Hamish Hamilton, 1996.

—. *George Henry Lewes: A Life*. Oxford: Clarendon UP 1991.

Astly, John. 'Memorandum Book of Occurences at Nuneaton 1810-1845.' Manuscript in the Nuneaton Public Library.

Auerbach, Nina. *Communities of Woman: An Idea in Fiction*.

Cambridge: Harvard UP, 1978.

—. 'The Power of Hunger: Demonism and Maggie Tulliver.' *NCF* 30 (1975): 150-71.

—. *Woman and the Demon: The Life of a Victorian Myth*. Cambridge: Harvard UP, 1982.

Auster, Henry. *Local Habitations: Regionalism in the Early Novels of George Eliot*. Cambridge: Harvard UP, 1970.

Baker, William. *The George Eliot-George Henry Lewes Library: An Annotated Catalogues of Their Books at Dr Williams's Library London*. New York: Garland Publishing Inc., 1977.

—. 'George Eliot's Napoleonic War Novel: A Fragment.' In Smith.

—. 'George Eliot's Reading in Nineteenth-Century Jewish Historians: A Note on the Background of *Daniel Deronda*.' *Victorian Studies* 15 (1972): 463-73.

—. *The Libraries of George Eliot and George Henry Lewes*. Victoria, British Columbia: U of Victoria P, 1981.

Bamber, Linda. 'Self-Defeating Politics in George Eliot's Felix Holt.' *VS* 18 (1975): 419-35.

Barker, Juliet. *The Brontës*. New York: St Martin's Press, 1994.

Barrat, Alain.'The Picture and the Message in George Eliot's *Scenes of Clerical Life*: The Thematic Function of the Rural Setting.' *GE-GHL Studies* 30-31 (September 1996): 48-62.

Barrell, John. *The Infection of Thomas DeQuincey*. New Haven: Yale UP, 1991.

Barrett, Dorothea. *Vocation and Desire: George Eliot's Heroines*. New York: Routledge, 1989.

Bates, J. *Nineteenth-Century Nuneaton*. Series in the *Midland Daily Tribune*. March and April, 1952.

Bates, Richard. 'The Italian with White Mice in *Middlemarch*.' *Notes and Queries* 31 (1984): 497.

Beaty, Jerome. 'History by Indirection: The Era of Reform in *Middlemarch*.' *VS* (1957): 173-9.

—. '*Middlemarch* from Notebook to Novel: A Study of George Eliot's Creative Method.' Urbana: U of Illinois P, 1960.

Beer, Gillian.'Beyond Determinism: George Eliot and Virginia Woolf.' *Arguing with the Past: Essays in Narrative from Woolf to Sidney*. London: Routledge, 1989.

—. *Darwin's Plots: Evolutionary Narrative in Darwin, George Eliot and Nineteenth-Century Fiction*. London: Routledge, 1983.

—. *George Eliot: Key Women Writers.* Ed. Sue Roe. Bloomington: Indiana UP, 1986.

Bellringer, Alan. *Modern Novelists: George Eliot.* New York: St Martin's Press, 1993.

Bennett, J. W. 'The Apprenticeship of George Eliot: Characterization as Case Study in "Janet's Repentance."' *Literature and Medicine* 9 (1990): 50-68.

Berridge, Virginia and Griffith Edwards. *Opium and the People: Opiate Use in Nineteenth-Century England.* New York: St Martin's Press, 1981.

Bickerstaff, Arnold. *A History of Education in the Nuneaton Area with particular reference to the Eighteenth Nineteenth and Twentieth Centuries.* Thesis. University of Nottingham, 1964.

Blackwood's Edinburgh Magazine. 1850-1857, 1862.

Blake, Kathleen. *Love and the Woman Question in Victorian Literature: The Art of Self-Postponement.* Totowa, New Jersey: Barnes and Noble, 1983.

—, ed. *Approaches to Teaching* Middlemarch. New York: MLA, 1990.

Blind, Mathilde. *George Eliot.* Boston, 1883.

Bode, Rita. 'Power and Submission in *Felix Holt, the Radical.*' *Studies in English Literature, 1500-1900,* 35 (1995): 769-88.

Bodenheimer, Rosemarie. 'Mary Ann Evans's Holy War: An Essay in Letter Reading.' *Nineteenth-Century Literature* 44 (1989): 335-63.

—. *The Politics of Story in Victorian Social Fiction.* Ithaca: Cornell UP, 1988.

—. *The Real Life of Mary Ann Evans: George Eliot, Her Letters and Fiction.* Ithaca: Cornell UP 1994.

Bonaparte, Felicia. 'Carrying the Word of the Lord to the Gentiles: *Silas Marner* and the Transformation of Scripture into a Secular Text.' *Religion and Literature* 23 (1991): 39-60.

—. *The Triptych and the Cross: The Central Myths of George Eliot's Poetic Imagination.* New York: NYUP, 1979.

—. *Will and Destiny: Morality and Tragedy in George Eliot's Novels.* New York: NYUP, 1975.

Booth, Alison. *Greatness Engendered: George Eliot and Virginia Woolf.* Ithaca: Cornell UP, 1992.

Brady, Kristin. *George Eliot.* London: Macmillan, 1992.

Brander, Michael. *The Life and Sport of the Inn.* New York: St Martin's Press, 1973.

Brantlinger, Patrick. *The Spirit of Reform: British Literature and Politics, 1832-1867.* Cambridge: Harvard UP, 1977

Bray, Charles. *Phases of Opinion and Experience During a Long Life: An Autobiography.* London, 1884.

Brody, Howard. *Stories of Sickness.* New Haven: Yale UP, 1987.

Brown, Monika.'Dutch Painters and British Novel-Readers: *Adam Bede* in the Context of Victorian Cultural Literacy.' *VIJ* 18 (1990): 113-33.

Browning, Oscar. *Life of George Eliot.* London, 1890.

Buchen, Irving. 'Arthur Donnithorne and *Zeluco*: Characterization via Literary Allusion in *Adam Bede.*' *VN* 23 (1959): 18-19.

Buckrose, J. E. *Silhouette of Mary Ann: A Novel about George Eliot.* London: Hodder, n.d.

Bullett, Gerald. *George Eliot: Her Life and Her Books.* London: Collins, 1947.

Burke, Thomas.*The English Inn.* London: Longmans, Green & Company, 1931.

Burton, Robert. *The Anatomy of Melancholy, What It Is, with All the Kinds, Causes, Symptoms, Prognostics, and Several Cures of It.* London, 1813.

Butwin, Joseph. 'The Pacification of the Crowd: From "Janet's Repentance" to *Felix Holt.*' *NCF* 35 (1980): 349-71.

Carpenter, Mary Wilson. '"A Bit of Her Flesh": Circumcision and "The Signification of the Phallus" in *Daniel Deronda.*' *Genders* 1 (1988): 1-23.

—. *George Eliot and the Landscape of Time: Narrative Form and Protestant Apocalyptic History.* Chapel Hill: University of North Carolina P, 1986.

Carpenter, William Benjamin. 'The Physiology of Temperance and Total Abstinence.' London, 1853.

Carroll, Alicia. 'Tried by Earthly Fires: Hetty Wesley, Hetty Sorrel, and *Adam Bede.*' *NCL* 44 (1989): 218-24.

Carroll, David. *George Eliot and the Conflict of Interpretations: A Reading of the Novels.* Cambridge: UP, 1994.

—. '"Janet's Repentance" and the Myth of the Organic.' *NCF* 35 (1980): 332-48.

Cervetti, Nancy. 'Mr Dagley's Midnight Darkness: Uncovering the German Connection in George Eliot's Fiction.' In *George Eliot and Europe.* Ed. John Rignall. Aldershot: Scolar P, 1997.

Chapman-Huston, Desmond. *Clematis: A Play*. Unpublished play. Warwickshire: Nuneaton Public Library, n.d.

Chase, Cynthia. 'The Decomposition of the Elephants: Double-Reading *Daniel Deronda*.' *PMLA* 93 (March 1978): 215-27.

Chase, Karen. *Eros and Psyche: The Representations of Personality in Charlotte Brontë, Charles Dickens, and George Eliot*. New York: Methuen, 1984.

—. 'The Modern Family and the Ancient Image in *Romola*,' *Dickens Studies Annual* 14 (1985): 303-26.

Clare, Maurice. *A Day with George Eliot*. New York: Hodder, n.d.

Cohen, Susan R. 'Avoiding the High Prophetic Strain: DeQuincey's Mail Coach and *Felix Holt*.' *VN* 63 (1983): 19-20.

Cohen, William A. *Sex Scandal: The Private Parts of Victorian Fiction*. Durham: Duke UP, 1996.

Colby, Robert A. *Fiction With a Purpose: major and minor Nineteenth-Century Novels*. Bloomington: Indiana UP, 1967.

Cottom, Daniel. *Social Figures: George Eliot, Social History, and Literary Representation*. Minneapolis: U of Minnesota P, 1987.

The Coventry Herald and Observer. June 1846-April 1847.

Cranmore, Walter and Joseph Best. *The Kindled Flame*. London: Muller, 1943.

Crehan, Stewart. 'Scandalous Topicality: *Silas Marner* and the Political Unconscious.' *VN* 92 (1997): 1-5

Crompton, Margaret. *George Eliot: The Woman*. London: Cassell, 1960.

Cross, John Walter. *George Eliot's Life as Related in Her Letters and Journals*. New York, 1885.

Cruse, Amy. *The Englishman and His Books in the Early Nineteenth Century*. New York: Benjamin Bloom, 1968.

Cunningham, Valentine. *Everywhere Spoken Against: Dissent in the Victorian Novel*. London: Oxford UP, 1975.

Currie, Richard A. 'Lewes's General Mind and the Judgment of St Ogg's: *The Mill on the Floss* as Scientific Text.' *VN* 92 (1997): 25-7.

Dale, Peter Allan. 'George Eliot's "Brother Jacob": Fables and the Physiology of Common Life.' *Philological Quarterly* 64 (1985): 17-35.

David, Deirdre. *Fictions of Resolution in Three Victorian Novels*. New York: Cornell UP, 1981.

—. *Intellectual Women and Victorian Patriarchy: Harriet Martineau,*

Elizabeth Barrett Browning, George Eliot. Ithaca: Cornell UP, 1987.

Deakin, Mary. *The Early Life of George Eliot.* Manchester: Manchester UP, 1913.

DeAlmeida, Hermione. *Romantic Medicine and John Keats.* NY: Oxford UP, 1991.

deJong, Mary. 'Tito: A Portrait of Fear.' *George Eliot Fellowship Review* 14 (1983): 18-21.

Delderfield, Eric R. *British Inn Signs and Their Stories.* Newton Abbott: David and Charles, 1965.

Demaria, Joanne. 'The Wondrous Marriages of *Daniel Deronda*: Gender, Work, and Love.' *Studies in the Novel* 22 (1990): 403-17.

Derrida, Jacques. *Dissemination.* Tr. with introduction and notes by Barbara Johnson. Chicago: CUP, 1981.

Dewes, Simon. *Marian: The Life of George Eliot.* London: Rich & Cowan, 1939.

Diedrick, James. 'George Eliot's Experiments in Fiction: "Brother Jacob" and the German *Novelle*.' *Studies in Short Fiction* 4 (1985): 461-8.

Dodd, Valerie. *George Eliot: An Intellectual Life.* New York: St Martin's Press, 1990.

Dowling, Andrew. '"The Other Side of Silence": Matrimonial Conflict and the Divorce Court in George Eliot's Fiction.' *NCL* 50 (1995): 322-36.

Edwards, Lee R. 'Women, Energy, and *Middlemarch*.' In Middlemarch: *An Authoritative Text, Backgrounds, Reviews, and Criticism.* Ed. Bert G. Hornback. New York: W. W. Norton and Company, 1977.

Ellman, Richard. 'Dorothea's Husbands.' In Hornback.

Emery, Laura Comer. *George Eliot's Creative Conflict: The Other Side of Silence.* Berkeley: U of California P, 1976.

Ender, Evelyne. *Sexing the Mind: Nineteenth-Century Fictions of Hysteria.* Ithaca and London: Cornell UP, 1995.

Ermath, Elizabeth. *George Eliot.* Boston: Twayne, 1985.

—. 'George Eliot and the World as Language.' In Rignall.

Evans, Marian (George Eliot). *Adam Bede.* New York: Riverside, 1980.

— 'Brother Jacob.' London: Virago Classics, 1989.

—. *Daniel Deronda.* New York: Penguin Books, 1967.

—. Diary. Autograph Ms. Diary. June 1861-December 1879. New York Public Library.

—. *Felix Holt.* New York: Penguin Books, 1968.

—. *The Essays of George Eliot.* Ed. Thomas Pinney. New York: Columbia UP, 1963.

—. *The George Eliot Letters.* 9 vols. Ed. Gordon S. Haight. New Haven: Yale UP, vols. 1-7, 1954; 8-9, 1979.

—. *George Eliot: Selected Essays, Poems and Other Writings.* Eds. A. S. Byatt and Nicholas Warren. London: Penguin Books 1990.

—. *George Eliot's* Middlemarch *Notebooks: A Transcription.* Eds. John Clark Pratt and Victor A. Neufeldt. Berkeley: U of California P, 1979.

—. *Impressions of Theophrastus Such.* Ed. Nancy Henry. Iowa City: U of Iowa P, 1994.

---. *The Journals of George Eliot.* Eds. Margaret Harris and Judith Johnston. Cambridge: CUP, 1998.

—. 'The Lifted Veil.' London: Virago Classics, 1985.

—. *Middlemarch.* Boston: Houghton Mifflin Company, 1956.

—. *The Mill on the Floss.* Boston: Houghton Mifflin Company, 1961.

—. Notebooks of the Carl and Lily Pforzheimer Foundation, New York, mss. 707, 710, 711.

—. *Quarry for* Middlemarch. Ed. Anna Kitchel. Berkeley: U of California P, 1950.

—. *Romola.* New York: Penguin Books, 1980.

—. *Scenes of Clerical Life.* New York: Penguin, 1972 .

—. *Silas Marner.* New York: Penguin Books, 1968.

—. *A Writer's Notebook, 1853-1879 and Uncollected Writings.* Ed. Joseph Wiesenfarth. Charlottesville: UVaP, 1981.

Evans, Robert. Unpublished diaries. The Nuneaton Public Library and Robin Evans, Tiverton.

Fenves, Peter. 'Exiling the Encyclopedia: The Individual in "Janet's Repentance."' *NCL* 41 (1987): 419-44.

Fleischman, Avrom. *The English Historical Novel: Walter Scott to Virginia Woolf.* Baltimore: Johns Hopkins UP, 1971.

Fraser, Hilary. 'St Theresa, St Dorothea, and Miss Brooke in *Middlemarch.*' *NCF* 40 (March 1986): 400-11.

—.'Titian's *Il Bravo* and George Eliot's Tito: A Painted Record.' *NCL* 50 (1995): 210-17.

Freeman, Sarah. *Mutton and Oysters: The Victorians and Their Food.* London: Victor Gollancz, 1989.

Fremantle, Anne. *George Eliot.* London: Duckworth, 1933.

Gallagher, Catherine. 'The Failure of Realism: *Felix Holt.*' *NCF* 35

(1980): 372-84.

—. George Eliot and *Daniel Deronda*: The Prostitute and the Jewish Question.' *Sex, Politics and Science in the Nineteenth-Century British Novel*. Baltimore: Johns Hopkins UP, 1986.

—. *The Industrial Reformation of English Fiction: Social Discourse and Narrative Form, 1832-1867*. Chicago: CUP, 1985.

Gardner, G. *Notes on the History of Nuneaton*. Nuneaton: the Nuneaton Public Library, 1958.

Garrett, Peter K. *The Victorian Multiplot Novel: Studies in Dialogical Form*. New Haven: Yale UP, 1980.

Gezari, Janet. 'The Metaphorical Imagination of George Eliot.' *English Literary History* 45 (Spring 1978): 93-106.

—. '*Romola* and the Myth of Apocalypse.' In Smith.

Gilbert, Sandra M. 'Life's Empty Pack: Notes toward a Literary Daughteronomy.' *Critical Inquiry* (1985): 355-84.

Gilbert, Sandra M. and Susan Gubar. *The Madwoman in the Attic: The Woman Writer and the Nineteenth-Century Literary Imagination*. London: Oxford UP, 1979.

Giovannini, Sandra and Gabriella Mancini. *The Pharmacy of Santa Maria Novella*. Florence: '*Lo Studiolo*,' *Amici dei Musei di Firenze*, 1987.

Girouard, Mark. *The Victorian Pub*. New Haven: Yale UP, 1984.

Goldberg, Hannah.'George Henry Lewes and *Daniel Deronda*.' *Notes and Queries* (NS) 4 (1957): 356-8.

Goldfarb, Russell M. 'Rosamond Vincy of *Middlemarch*.' *CLA Journal* 30 (1986): 83-99.

Goody, Jack and Ian Watt. 'The Consequences of Literacy.' In *Literacy in Traditional Societies*. Ed. Jack Goody. Cambridge: UP, 1968.

Gordon, Jan. 'Affiliation as (Dis)semination: Gossip and Family in George Eliot's European Novel.' *Journal of European Studies* 15 (1985): 155-89.

—. 'Origins, *Middlemarch*, Endings: George Eliot's Crisis of the Antecedent.' In Smith.

Graff, Harvey J. *The Literacy Myth: Literary and Social Structure in the Nineteenth-Century City*. New York: Academic Press, 1979.

Greenberg, Robert A. 'Plexuses and Ganglia: Scientific Allusion in *Middlemarch*.' *NCF* 30 (1975): 33-52.

Gray, Beryl, 'Afterword,' 'Brother Jacob.' London: The Virago Press, 1989.

—. 'Afterword,' 'The Lifted Veil.' London: The Virago Press, 1985.

Haight, Gordon S. *George Eliot: A Biography*. New York: Oxford UP, 1968.

—. 'George Eliot's Bastards.' In *George Eliot: A Centenary Tribute*. Eds. Gordon S. Haight and Rosemary T. Van Arsdel. Totowa: Barnes and Nobel, 1970.

—. 'George Eliot's "eminent failure," Will Ladislaw.' *This Particular Web: Essays on* Middlemarch. Ed. Ian Adam. Toronto: U of Toronto P, 1975.

—. *George Eliot and John Chapman, with Chapman's Diaries*. New Haven: Yale UP, 1940.

Haley, Bruce. *The Healthy Body and Victorian Culture*. Cambridge: Harvard UP, 1978.

Hallissy, Margaret. *Venomous Woman: Fear of the Female in Literature*. New York: Greenwood P, 1987.

Handley, Graham. *George Eliot's Midlands: Passion in Exile*. London: Alison and Busby, 1991.

—. *George Eliot: State of the Art: A Guide through the Critical Maze*. Bristol: The Bristol P, 1990.

Hands, Timothy. *A George Eliot Chronology*. Boston: G. K. Hall, 1989.

Hanson, Lawrence and Elisabeth. *Marian Evans and George Eliot*. London: Oxford UP, 1952.

Hardy, Barbara, '*Middlemarch* and the Passions.' In *This Particular Web*. Ed. Ian Adam. Toronto: Toronto UP, 1975.

—. '*Middlemarch*, Chapter 84: Three Commentaries.' *NCF* 35 (1980): 432-53.

—, ed. Middlemarch: *Critical Approaches to the Novel*. New York: Oxford UP, 1967.

—. '*The Mill on the Floss*.' In *Critical Essays on George Eliot*. Ed. Barbara Hardy. New York: Barnes and Noble, 1970.

—. *The Novels of George Eliot: A Study in Form*. London: Athlone Press, 1959; reprinted with corrections in 1963.

—. *Particularities: Readings in George Eliot*. Athens: Ohio UP 1982.

—. 'The Talkative Woman.' In *Problems for Feminist Criticism*. Ed. Sally Minogue. New York: Routledge, 1990.

Harris, Margaret. 'What George Eliot Saw in Europe: The Evidence of her Journals.' In Rignall.

Harrison, Brian Howard. *Drink and the Victorians: The Temperance*

Question in England 1815-1872. Pittsburgh: U of PP, 1971.

—. *Peaceable Kingdom: Stability and Change in Modern Britain.* Oxford: Clarendon P 1982.

—. 'Pubs.' In *The Victorian City: Images and Realities.* Eds. H. J. Dyos and Michael Wolff. London: Routledge and Kegan Paul, 1989.

Harvey, W. J. *The Art of George Eliot.* New York: Oxford UP, 1962.

Hayter, Alethea. '"The Laudanum Bottle Loomed Large": Opium in the English Literary World in the Nineteenth Century.' *Ariel: A Review of International English Literature* 2 (1980): 37-51.

—. *Opium and the Romantic Imagination.* London: Faber, 1968.

Heilbrun, Carolyn. *Reinventing Womanhood.* New York: Norton, 1979.

Henry, Nancy. 'George Eliot, George Henry Lewes, and Comparative Anatomy.' In Rignall.

Hertz, Neil. 'Recognizing Casaubon.' *The End of the Line.* New York, 1985.

Hewett, Edward and W. F. Axton. *Convivial Dickens: The Drinks of Dickens and His Times.* Athens: Ohio UP, 1983.

Higdon, David Leon. 'George Eliot and the Art of the Epigraph.' *NCF* 25 (1970): 127-51.

—. '*Sortes Biblicae* in *Adam Bede.*' *Papers on Language and Literature* 9 (1973): 396-405.

—. 'Sortilege in George Eliot's *Silas Marner.*' *PLL* 10 (1974): 51-7.

Hill, D. M. 'Why Did Mr Keck Edit "The Trumpet."' *Neuphilologische Mitteilungen* 74 (1975): 714-15.

Hill, J. Spencer. *The Indo-Chinese Opium Trade: Considered in Relation to Its History, Morality, and Expediency, and Its Influence on Christian Missions. London: Frowde, 1884.*

Himmelfarb, Gertrude. *The De-Moralization of Society: From Victorian Virtues to Modern Values.* NY: Vintage Books, 1996.

Homans, Margaret. *Bearing the Word: Language and Female Experience in Nineteenth-Century Women's Writing.* Chicago: U of CP, 1986.

Horn, Pamela. *Education in Rural England, 1800-1914.* New York: St Martin's Press, 1978.

Horowitz, Lenore Wisney. 'George Eliot's Vision of Society in *Felix Holt.*' *Tennessee Studies in Language and Literature* 17 (1975): 175-91.

Houghton, Walter. *The Victorian Frame of Mind 1830-1870.* New Haven: Yale UP, 1957.

Houston, Natalie. 'George Eliot's Material History: Clothing and

Realist Narration.' *Studies in the Literary Imagination* 29 (1996): 23-33.

Howitt, William. *The Rural Life of England*. Shannon: Irish UP rpt. of 3rd ed. London 1844.

Hulme, Hilda M. 'The Language of the Novel.' *Middlemarch*. Ed. Bert G. Hornback. New York: W. W. Norton and Company 1977.

Hurley, Edward T. 'Piero di Cosimo: An Alternate Analogy for George Eliot's Realism.' *VN* 31 (1966-67): 54-56.

Jackson, Michael. *The English Pub*. New York: Harper and Row, 1976.

Jameson, Anna Brownell. *Sacred and Legendary Art*. London 1858.

Jonestone, Peggy Fitzhugh. *The Transformation of Rage: Mourning and Creativity in George Eliot's Fiction*. New York: NYUP, 1994.

Joseph, Gerhard. 'The *Antigone* as Cultural Touchstone: Matthew Arnold, Hegel, George Eliot, Virginia Woolf, and Margaret Drabble.' *PMLA* 96 (1981): 22-36.

—. 'Hegel, Derrida, George Eliot, and the Novel.'*Literary Interpretation Theory* 1 (1989): 59-68.

Karl, Frederick. *George Eliot: Voice of a Century*. New York: W. W. Norton, 1995.

Keily, Robert. 'The Limits of Dialogue in *Middlemarch*.' *The Worlds of Victorian Fiction*. Ed. Jerome H. Buckley. London: Harvard UP, 1975.

Keith, W. J. *Regions of the Imagination: The Development of British Rural Fiction*. Toronto: U of Toronto P, 1988.

Kennard, Jean. *Victims of Convention*. Hamden, Connecticut: Archon Books, 1978.

Kenyon, Frank William. *The Consuming Flame: The Story of George Eliot*. London: Hutchinson, 1970.

Kidd, Millie. 'In Defense of Latimer: A Study of Narrative Technique in George Eliot's "The Lifted Veil."' *VN* 79 (1991): 37-41.

Kingsley, Rose E. 'George Eliot's Country.' *Century* (1885): 30, 3: 338-52.

Knoepflmacher, U. C. 'Fusing Fact and Myth: The New Reality of *Middlemarch*.' In *This Particular Web*. Ed. Ian Adam. Toronto: UP, 1975.

—. 'Genre and the Integration of Gender: From Wordsworth to George Eliot to Virginia Woolf.' *Victorian Literature and Society: Essays Presented to Richard D. Altick*. Eds. James R. Kincaid and Albert J. Kuhn. Columbus: Ohio State UP, 1984.

—. *Laughter and Despair: Readings in Ten Novels of the Victorian Era.* Berkeley: UCP, 1971.

—. 'George Eliot's Anti-Romance Romance: "Mr. Gilfil's Love Story."' *VN* 31 (1967): 11-15.

—. *George Eliot's Early Novels: The Limits of Realism.* Berkeley: U of California P, 1968.

—. '*Middlemarch*: An Avuncular View.' *NCF* 30 (1975): 43-72.

— 'Mr. Haight's George Eliot: "*Wahrheit und Dichtung*."' *Victorian Studies* 12 (1969): 422-30.

—. 'Of Time, Rivers, and Tragedy: George Eliot and Matthew Arnold.' *VN* 33 (1969): 1-5.

—. 'On Exile and Fiction: The Leweses and the Shelleys.' *Mothering the Mind: Twelve Studies of Writers and Their Silent Partners.* New York: Holmes and Meier, 1984.

—. *Religious Humanism and the Victorian Novel: George Eliot, Walter Pater, and Samuel Butler.* Princeton: PUP, 1965.

Kroeber, Karl. *Styles in Fictional Structure: The Art of Jane Austen, Charlotte Brontë, George Eliot.* Princeton: PUP, 1971.

LaCapra, Dominick. *History and Politics in the Novel.* Ithaca: Cornell UP, 1987.

Larwood, Jacob and John Camden Hotten. The History of Signboards, From the Earliest Times to the Present Day. London: John Camden Hotten, 1866.

Laski, Marganita. *George Eliot and Her World.* London: Thames, & Hudson, 1973.

Lee, Peter. 'Old Nuneaton.' Series of articles in the *Nuneaton Chronicle*, 1983-84.

Leonard, Linda. *Witness to the Fire: Creativity and the Veil of Addiction.* Boston: Shambhala 1989.

Lesjak, Carolyn. 'A Modern Odyssey: Realism, the Masses and Nationalism in George Eliot's *Felix Holt. Novel* 30 (1996): 78-88.

Levin, Amy. 'Silence, Gesture, and Meaning in *Middlemarch*.' *GE-GHL Studies* 30-31 (1996): 20-31.

Levine, George. 'George Eliot's Hypothesis of Reality.' *NCF* 35 (1980): 1-28.

Levine Herbert. 'The Marriage of Allegory and Realism in *Daniel Deronda*.' *Genre* 15 (1982): 421-45.

Lewes, George Henry. *Biographical History of Philosophy.* London, 1845-6

—. Journals X, XI, XII and Diaries 1-8. Beinecke, Yale Unversity.

—. *The Letters of George Henry Lewes.* 2 vols. Ed. William Baker. Victoria: U of VP, 1995.

—. 'Physicians and Quacks.' *Blackwood's Edinburgh Magazine* 91 (February 1862): 165-78.

—. 'The Physiological Errors of Teetotalism.' *Westminster Review* 64 (1855): 94-124.

—. *The Physiology of Common Life.* London, 1857.

—. *Ranthorpe.* London, 1847.

Lineham, Katherine Bailey. 'Mixed Politics: The Critique of Imperialism in *Daniel Deronda.*' *TSLL* 34 (1992): 323-46.

Logan, Peter. 'Conceiving the Body: Realism and Medicine in *Middlemarch.*' *History of the Human Sciences* 4 (1991): 197-222.

Longmate, Norman. *The Waterdrinkers: A History of Temperance.* London: Hamish-Hamilton, 1968.

Lynn, Andrew B. 'Bondages, Acquiescence, and Blessedness: Spinoza's Three Kind of Knowledge and *Scenes of Clerical Life.*' *GE-GHLStudies* 30-31 (1996): 32-47.

Mann, Karen. *The Language That Makes George Eliot's Fiction.* Baltimore: The Johns Hopkins UP, 1983.

Marcus, Steven. 'Literature and Social Theory: Starting in with George Eliot.' *Representations: Essays in Literature and Society.* New York: Random House, 1975.

Martin, Bruce K. 'Fred Vincy and the Unravelling of *Middlemarch.*' *PLL* 30 (1994): 3-24.

Martin, Carol. *George Eliot's Serial Fiction.* Columbus: Ohio State UP, 1995.

Mason, Michael York. '*Middlemarch* and History.' *NCF* 25 (1971): 417-31.

Matus, Jill. 'Proxy and Proximity: Metonymic Signing.' *U of Toronto Quarterly* 58 (1988-89): 305-20.

Mayer, Ralph. *The Artist's Handbook: Of Materials and Techniques.* 4th ed. New York: Viking Press, Inc., 1970.

McCann, J. Clinton Jr. 'Disease and Cure in "Janet's Repentance": George Eliot's Change of Mind.' *Literature and Medicine* 9 (1990): 69-78.

McCarthy, Mary. *The Stones of Florence.* New York: Harcourt Brace Jovanovich, 1963.

McCarthy, Patrick. 'Lydgate, "The New Young Surgeon" of

Middlemarch.' SEL 10 (1970): 805-15.

McCobb, E. A. '*Daniel Deronda* as Will and Representation: George Eliot and Schopenahuer.' *Modern Language Review* 80 (1985): 533-49.

—. 'Of Women and Doctors: *Middlemarch* and Wilhelmine von Hillern's *Ein Artz de Seele.' Neophilologus* 68 (1984): 571-80.

McCormack, Kathleen. 'George Eliot and the Pharmakon: Dangerous Drugs for the Condition of England.'*VIJ* 14 (1986): 33-51.

—. 'George Eliot's Earliest Prose: The Coventry *Herald* and the Coventry Fiction.' *Victorian Periodicals Review* 29 (1986): 57-62. .

—. 'George Eliot: Wollstonecraft's "Judicious Person with Some Turn for Humour."' *English Language Notes* 29 (1981): 44-6.

—. 'George Eliot's Wollstonecraftian Feminism.' *Dalhousie Review* (Winter 1983-84): 602-15.

—. 'George Eliot's First Fiction: Targeting *Blackwood's.' The Bibliotheck* 21 (1996): 69-80.

McGowan, John. 'The Turn of George Eliot's Realism.' *NCF* 35 (1980): 171-92.

McMaster, Juliet. '"A Microscope on a Water-Drop": Focusing on the Text, Expanding the Context.' In *Approaches to Teaching* Middlemarch.

Meikle, Susan. 'Fruit and Seed: The Finale to Middlemarch.' In Smith.

Meyer, Susan. '"Safely to Their Own Borders": Proto-Zionism, Feminism, and Nationalism in *Daniel Deronda.' ELH* 60 (1993): 733-58.

Middleton, Victoria. *Elektra in Exile: Women Writers and Political Fiction.* New York: Garland, 1988.

Miller, D. A. *Narrative and its Discontents: Problems of Closure in the Traditional Novel.* Princeton: Princeton UP, 1981.

Miller, J. Hillis. *The Ethics of Reading: Kant, de Man, Eliot, Trollope, and Benjamin.* New York: Columbia UP, 1987

—. *Fiction and Repetition.* Cambridge: Harvard UP, 1982.

—. 'Narrative and History.' *ELH* 41 (1974): 455-73.

—. 'Optic and Semiotic in *Middlemarch.'* In *The Worlds of Victorian Fiction.* Ed. Jerome H. Buckley. Cambridge: Harvard UP, 1975.

—. 'Teaching Middlemarch: Close Reading and Theory.' In *Approaches to Teaching* Middlemarch.

—. 'The Two Rhetorics: George Eliot's Bestiary.' In *Writing and Reading Differently: Deconstruction and the Teaching of Composition and Literature.* Eds. G. Douglas Atkins and Michael Johnson. Lawrence: UP of Kansas, 1985.

Miller, Nancy K. 'Emphasis Added: Plots and Plausibilities in Women's Fiction.' *PMLA* 96, 1 (1981): 36-48.

Milligan, Barry. *Pleasures and Pains: Opium and the Orient in Century British Culture.* Charlottesville: UVaP, 1995.

Mintz, Alan. *George Eliot and the Novel of Vocation.* Cambridge: Harvard UP, 1978.

Moers, Ellen. *Literary Women.* New York: Doubleday, 1976.

Molesworth, William N. *The History of the Reform Bill of 1832.* 2 nd ed. London 1866.

Morgan, Susan. *Sisters in Time: Imagining Gender in Nineteenth-Century British Fiction.* New York: Oxford UP, 1989.

Morris, Timothy. 'The Dialogic Universe of *Middlemarch*.' *SNTT* 22, 3 (1990): 282-93.

Mort, Frank. *Dangerous Sexualities: Medico-Moral Politics in England since 1830.* New York: Routledge & Kegan Paul, 1987.

Mottram, William. *The True Story of George Eliot. In Relation to 'Adam Bede,' giving the real life history of the more prominent characters.* London: Francis Griffiths, 1905.

Mugglestone, Lynda. '"Grammatical Fair Ones:" Women, Men, and Attitudes to Language in the Novels of George Eliot.' *Review of English Studies* 41 (1995): 11-25.

Murfin, Ross. 'Novel Representations: Politics and Victorian Fiction.' In *Victorian Connections.* Ed. Jerome McGann. Charlottesville: UVaP, 1988.

Myers, William. *The Teaching of George Eliot.* Leicester: UP, 1984.

Nason, Edward. 'The Story of Nuneaton.' Series of articles in the *Nuneaton Chronicle,* 1983-84.

Nestor, Pauline. *Female Friendships and Communities: Charlotte Brontë, George Eliot, Elizabeth Gaskell.* Oxford: Clarendon P, 1985.

Newton, K. M. *George Eliot: Romantic Humanist: A Study of the Philosophical Structure of Her Novels.* Totowa, NJ: Barnes and Noble, 1981.

---. 'The Role of the Narrator in George Eliot's Novels.' *The Journal of Narrative Technique* 3 (1973): 97-107.

Nicholes, Joseph. 'Vertical Context in Middlemarch.' *NCF* 45, 2 (1990): 144-175.

Nunokawa, Jeff. 'The Miser's Two Bodies: *Silas Marner* and the Sexual

Possibilities of the Community.' *VS* 36, 3 (1993): 273-92.

Olcott, Charles S. *George Eliot: Scenes and People in Her Novels.* London: Cassell, 1911.

Paris Bernard. *Experiments in Life: George Eliot's Quest for Values.* Detroit: Wayne State UP, 1965.

Parssinen, Terry M. *Secret Passions, Secret Remedies: Narcotic Drugs in British Society 1820-1930.* Philadelphia: Institute for the Study of Human Issues, Inc., 1983.

Paterson, Arthur. *George Eliot's Family Life and Letters.* London: Selwyn, 1928.

Patrick, Anne E. 'Rosamond Rescued: George Eliot's Critique of Sexism in *Middlemarch*.' *Journal of Religion* 67, 2 (1987): 220-38.

Paxton, Nancy L. 'George Eliot and the City: The Imprisonment of Culture.' In *Women Writers and the City: Essays in Feminist Literary Criticism*. Knoxville: University of Tennessee Press, 1984.

—.*George Eliot and Herbert Spencer: Feminism, Evolutionism, and the Reconstruction of Gender.* Princeton: Princeton UP 1991.

Pell, Nancy. 'The Fathers' Daughters in *Daniel Deronda*.' *NCF* 36 (1982): 424-51.

Pemble, John. *The Mediterranean Passion: Victorians and Edwardians in the South.* Oxford: Oxford UP, 1987.

Perlis, Alan D. *A Return to the Primal Self: Identity in the Fiction of George Eliot.* New York: Peter Lang, 1989.

Pettigrew, Thomas. *On Superstitions Connected with the History and Practice of Medicine and Surgery.* London, 1844.

Plato. *Phaedrus.* Ed. R. Hackworth. New York: The Bobbs-Merrill Company Inc.

Poston III, Lawrence S. 'Setting and Theme in *Romola*.' *NCF* 20 (1966): 355-66.

Praz, Mario. *The Hero in Eclipse in Victorian Fiction.* London: Oxford UP, 1956.

Prentis, Barbara. *The Brontë Sisters and George Eliot: A Unity of Difference.* Basingstoke: Macmillan, 1988.

Putzell-Korab, Sara M. and Martine Watson Brownley. 'Dorothea and Her Husbands: Some Autobiographical Sources for Speculation.' *VN* 68 (1985): 15-19.

Pykett, Lyn. 'Typology and the End(s) of History in *Daniel Deronda*'. *Literature and History* 9 (1983): 62-72.

Ragussis, Michael. *Acts of Naming: The Family Plot in Fiction.* Athens:

Ohio UP, 1987.

Romieu, Emile and Georges. *The Life of George Eliot*. London: Cape, 1932.

Redinger, Ruby. *George Eliot: The Emergent Self*. New York: Knopf, 1975.

Reed, John and Jerry Herron. 'George Eliot's Illegitimate Children.' *NCF* 40 (1985): 175-86.

Reed, John.'Victorians In Bed.' *Nineteenth-Century Studies* 4 (1990): 61-91.

Richardson, Ruth. *Death, Dissection and the Destitute*. New York: Routledge & Kegan Paul, 1987.

Richter, Donald C. *Riotous Victorians*. Athens: Ohio UP, 1981.

Ricks, Christopher. 'Pink Toads in *Lord Jim*.' *Essays in Criticism* 31 (April 1981): 142-4.

Robertson, Linda. 'The Role of Popular Medicine in *The Mill on the Floss*.' *GEFR* 13 (1982): 33-37.

Rochelson, Meri-Jane.'The Weaver of Raveloe: Metaphor as Narrative Persuasion in *Silas Marner*.' *Studies in the Novel* 15 (1983): 35-43.

Ronald, Ann. 'George Eliot's Florentine Museum.' *PLL* 13 (1977): 260-9.

Ronell, Avital. *Crack Wars: Literature, Addiction, Mania*. Lincoln: U of Nebraska P 1992.

Rose, Phyllis. *Parallel Lives: Five Victorian Marriages*. New York: Knopf, 1983.

Sadoff, Dianne. *Monsters of Affection: Dickens, Eliot and Brontë on Fatherhood*. Baltimore: Johns Hopkins UP, 1982.

---. 'Nature's Language: Metaphor in the Text of *Adam Bede*.' *Genre* 11 (1978): 411-26

Said, Edward. *Culture and Imperialism*. NY: Knopf, 1993.

Sanderson, Michael. 'Literacy and Social Mobility in the Industrial Revolution in England.' *Past and Present* 56 (1972): 75-104.

Schivelsbusch, Wolfgang. *Tastes of Paradise: A Social History of Spices, Stimulants, and Intoxicants*. Tr.David Jacobson. New York: Pantheon Books, 1992.

Schofield, Robert. 'Dimensions In Illiteracy, 1750-1850.' *Explorations in Economic History* 10 (1973): 437-54.

Sedgwick, Eve Kosofsky. *Tendencies*. Durham, North Carolina: Duke UP, 1993.

Shaffer Elinor. '*Kubla Khan*' and   The Fall of Jerusalem: *The*

Mythological School in Biblical Criticism and Sacred Literature, 1770-1880. Cambridge: Cambridge UP, 1975.

Shaw, Sheila. 'The Female Alcoholic in Victorian Fiction: George Eliot's Unpoetic Heroine.' In *Nineteenth-Century Women Writers of the English-Speaking World.* Ed. Rhoda Nathan. Westport, Connecticut: Greenwood, 1986.

Shiman, Lilian Lewis. *Crusade Against Drink in Victorian England.* New York: St Martin's Press, 1988.

Showalter, Elaine. 'The Greening of Sister George.' *NCF* (1980): 292-311.

---. *The Female Malady: Women, Madness, and English Culture.* Pantheon, 1986.

---. *A Literature of Their Own: British Novelists from Brontë to Lessing.* Princeton: PUP, 1977.

Shuttleworth, Sally. *George Eliot and Nineteenth-Century Science: The Make-Believe of a Beginning.* Cambridge: CUP, 1984.

Sontag, Susan. *AIDS and Its Metaphors.* New York: Farrar, Straus and Giroux, 1988.

---. *Illness as Metaphor.* New York: Farrar, Straus, and Giroux, 1978.

Sorensen, Katherine. 'Conventions of Realism and the Absence of Color in George Eliot's "The Sad Fortunes of the Reverend Amos Barton."' VIJ 22 (1994): 15-31.

Spacks, Patricia Meyer. *Gossip.* New York: Knopf, 1985.

Stange, G. Robert. 'The Voices of the Essayist.' *NCF* 35 (1980): 312-30.

Stephen, Leslie. *English Men of Letters: George Eliot.* London: Macmillan, 1902.

Stevick Philip. *The Theory of the Novel.* New York: The Free Press, 1967.

Stewart, Garrett. '"Beckoning Death": *Daniel Deronda* and the Plotting of a Reading.' In *Sex and Death in Victorian Literature.* Ed. Regina Barreca. Bloomington: Indiana UP, 1990.

Stone, Donald. *The Romantic Impulse in Victorian Fiction.* Cambridge: Harvard UP, 1980.

Stone, Lawrence. 'Literacy and Education in England 1640-1900.' *Past and Present* 42 (1969): 61-139.

Stump, Reva. *Movement and Vision in George Eliot's Novels.* Seattle: U of Washington P, 1959.

Sutherland, John. *Victorian Novelists and Publishers.* London: Athlone 1976.

Swann, Brian. '"Silas Marner" and the New Mythus.' *Criticism* 18 (1976): 101-121.

Swertka, Eve Marie. 'The Web of Utterance: *Middlemarch.*' TSLL 19 (1977): 179-87.

Swindells, Julia. *Victorian Writing and Working Women: The Other Side of Silence.* Minneapolis: UMP, 1985.

Szirotny, J. S.'Maggie Tulliver's Sad Sacrifice: Confusing but not Confused.' *Studies in the Novel* 28, 2 (1996): 178-99.

---. 'Two Confectioners the Reverse of Sweet: the Role of Metaphor in Determining George Eliot's Use of Experience.'*Studies in Short Fiction* 21 (1984): 1-27.

Taylor, Ina. *A Woman of Contradictions: The Life of George Eliot.* New York: Morrow, 1990.

Thomas, Henry and Dana Lee. *Living Biographies of Famous Women.* Garden City: Doubleday, 1942.

Thomas, Jeanie. *Reading* Middlemarch: *Reclaiming the Middle Distance.* Ann Arbor: UMI Research P, 1987.

Thomson, Fred C. 'The Genesis of *Felix Holt.*' *PMLA* 74 (1959): 576-84.

Torgovnick, Mariana. *Closure in the Novel.* Princeton: PUP, 1981.

Turner, Frank M. *The Greek Heritage in Victorian Britain.* New Haven: Yale UP, 1981.

Uglow, Jennifer. *George Eliot.* New York: Pantheon, 1987.

Vargish, Thomas. *The Providential Aesthetic in Victorian Fiction.* Charlottesville: UVaP, 1985.

Veasey, E. A. *Nuneaton in the Making.* Part 3: Social Change. Coventry: Jones-Sands Publishing 1984.

Viera, Carroll. '"The Lifted Veil" and George Eliot's Early Aesthetic.' *SEL* 24 (1984): 749-767.

Vipont, Elfrida. *Towards a High Attic: The Early Life of George Eliot.* London: Hamilton 1970.

Vogeler, Martha. 'George Eliot as Literary Widow.' *Huntingdon Library Quarterly* 51 (1988): 72-87.

Vrettos, Athena. 'From Neurosis to Narrative: The Private Life of the Nerves, in *Villette* and *Daniel Deronda.*' *VS* 33, 4 (Summer 1990): 551-579.

Walker, Richard. 'Infected Ecstasy: Addiction and the Strange Case of the Antipodean Vampire.' Paper read at The Second International Gothic Association Conference, U of Stirling, 1995.

Webb, Robert K. 'Working Class Readers in Early Victorian England.'

England Historical Review 65 (1950): 333-351.

Weinstein, Philip M. *The Semantics of Desire: Changing Models of Identity From Dickens to Joyce.* Princeton: Princeton UP, 1984.

Welsh, Alexander. *George Eliot and Blackmail.* Cambridge: Harvard UP, 1985.

Wheeler, Michael. *The Art of Allusion in Victorian Fiction.* New York: Barnes and Noble, 1979.

Wiesenfarth, Joseph. *George Eliot's Mythmaking.* Heidelberg, Carl Winter, 1977.

---. *Gothic Manners and the Classic English Novel.* Madison: U of Wisconsin P, 1988.

---. ' *Middlemarch*: The Language of Art.' *PMLA* 97, 3 (May 1982): 363-77.

Williams, Blanche Colton. *George Eliot.* New York: Macmillan, 1936.

Williams, David. *Mr. George Eliot: A Biography of George Henry Lewes.* London: Hodder & Stoughton 1983.

Wilt, Judith. '"He would come back": The Fathers of Daughters in *Daniel Deronda*.' *NCL* 42 (1987): 313-38

---. 'Felix Holt, the Killer: A Reconstruction.' *VS* (Autumn 1991): 51-69.

---. *Ghosts of the Gothic: Austen, Eliot and Lawrence.* Princeton: PUP, 1980.

Winnett, Susan.'Coming Unstrung: Women, Men, Narrative, and Principles of Pleasure.' *PMLA* 105 (1990): 505-18.

Witemeyer, Hugh. *George Eliot and the Visual Arts.* New Haven: Yale UP, 1979.

Wolff, Michael. 'Adam Bede's Families: At Home in Hayslope and Nuneaton.' Paper read at the Midwest Victorian Studies Association, April 1985.

---. 'George Eliot, Other-Wise Marian Evans.' *Browning Institute Studies.* CUNY: The Browning Institute Inc., 1985.

Wolfreys, Julian. 'The Ideology of Englishness: The Paradoxes of Tory-Liberal Culture and National identity in *Daniel Deronda*.' *GE-GHL Studies* 26-27 (September 1994): 15-33.

Wormald, Mark. 'Microscopy and Semiotic in *Middlemarch*.' *NCL* 50 (March 1996): 501-24.

Wright, T. R. *George Eliot's* Middlemarch. Hemel Hempstead: Harvester Wheatsheaf, 1991.

Zimmerman, Bonnie. 'Gwendolen Harleth and "The Girl of the Period." *Centenary Essays and an Unpublished Fragment.* Ed. Anne

Smith. Totowa: Barnes and Noble, 1980.

---. '"Radiant as a Diamond" George Eliot, Jewelry and the Female Role.' *Criticism* 19, 3 (Summer 1977): 212-22.

Index